Into the Blue

Black & Blue #2

Into the Blue (Black & Blue #2)
By
Melyssa Winchester

For the Ambrose to my Renee, the Seven Foot Edge to my Carmella, the heel king to my queen, this one's for you. Bada boom, best damn lunatic in the room. How you doin? ;)

"The two most important days in your life are the day you are born, and the day you find out why." – Mark Twain

Prologue

Brady

"Brady...Fuck. Call me when you get this."

Forty-eight hours since everything collapsed and the only call I've gotten is from Merrick.

I landed in Mississippi a little over twenty-four hours ago. The very last place anyone would expect me, but the one place that before my entire world shifted two weeks ago, was the only home I had.

After snowing the lady behind the ticket counter at the airport and making her believe my dumbass story about screwing up my flight info, I'd gotten it changed and well, here I sit.

If everyone wants me back in Florida pretending to be something I'm not, they'll get their wish, but not before I head back to where this shit storm began.

First on the docket though, returning Jax's call.

"Alright, you got me. What's with the cryptic message?"

Releasing what sounds like a half sigh, half groan, he makes my spider senses tingle.

"Where are you, Brady?"

"Mississippi. Why?"

"Fuck."

"Normally I'm cool with you cursing me considering how much shit I cause in order to make it happen, but since I know I didn't screw with you this time; you wanna explain what it's about?"

"You don't know."

"How perceptive of you, man."

"Why aren't you with Emery?"

Tired of the questions and the stabbing sensation I experience at the mere mention of the girl I left behind, I attempt to steer him off and get to the bottom of what the call is about.

"What the fuck is going on, Jax?"

"Emery...Avery...their mom..." he pauses and just like that, all of the air is stripped from my lungs at the pain I hear in his voice.

"What about her?"

"She's gone, man. She passed away yesterday."

Damnit. Even knowing it would eventually come, I still wasn't ready for it to be this soon.

"How?"

"Not sure. Avery..." he pauses again and I just know he's about to drop another bomb.

"Avery what, man! Use your words."

"Where the fuck was that advice a couple of days ago?" he shoots back and that seals it. Something went down between him and Avery the same way it did with me and Emery.

"In Delaware where it should still be. Now just answer my question before I lose what's left of my shit here."

"Avery didn't say. All I know is Emery got a call while she was working but didn't get the message until she was done and by the time she got home Rebecca was gone."

She came home to find her mother gone.

The only thing I pull from all of that besides the fact that Emery's mom passed away, is that she had to deal with it alone. Something she wouldn't have been if I just stayed put.

Stayed where I want to be.

My choice between my livelihood and the woman I love coming around and biting me in the ass.

This entire situation sucks.

"How's Avery holding up?" I ask, imagining a reaction even worse than Emery's considering what I know of the situation.

"I don't honestly know."

Well, I wasn't expecting that.

"What do you mean you don't know? Aren't you with her?"

"I'm in Delaware, yes. But I'm not with her."

"Wait, what?" I question once I realize what him being there means. "What do you mean you're in Delaware?"

Being in Delaware now, twenty-four hours after we were due to be back and affectively missing the show we signed our lives away for, meant he was no longer employed.

"You didn't go to Vegas?"

"No." He answers quickly, with not even the slightest slip in his voice. "I made a choice."

Jax chose Avery.

I might not know what went down between them and why he's in the same town but nowhere near her, but I don't need to. Even knowing that things must have exploded between them during their time together, he still made a choice that I couldn't.

Making Jackson Merrick a better man than I am.

"You gave it all up for her." I say in a state of utter disbelief. "You walked away."

"Yeah, Brady, I did. And even if it doesn't mean shit and I've lost her forever, I'd do it again. I couldn't let her go through this alone. She's done that long enough."

I've spent a lot of time laying into Jax about how serious he was getting with this girl after the short amount of time they'd actually known each other. In fact, it was downright hilarious the rise it would get out of him. Seeing him this way though, so sure of himself and willing to make the same choice again if presented with it, has me eating every damn joke I ever made at his expense.

For all of his intensity and drive when it comes to the business, he was always meant for something more.

I saw it when he was with Melinda and had the point slammed into me again when he met Avery. At first I'd blown it off, assuming it was just the passionate side of him coming through. The same way he was about our matches, appearing in his relationships too.

I was wrong.

Wrestling; as much as I'm sure he wanted to believe otherwise isn't Jax's endgame.

Love is.

A love that for whatever reason he was going to have to fight for the same way that I was. Well, the way I would be once I was done dealing with my shit here and what was waiting back in Florida.

"Have you talked or seen Emery since you got there?" I ask, delving straight into what I really want to know.

"Yeah. I talked to her after Avery boarded the flight home."

"How is she?"

"She's keeping it together a lot more than I thought she would, but Brady, I'm pretty sure it's just for show. She lost her mom. I have to figure she's as destroyed as Avery was when she got the call."

Emery is destroyed.

My girl is broken and I'm not with her.

And that's it, isn't it? She's my girl and instead of fighting for what I saw happening between us, how different she was making things in my short time with her, I turned my back and fled.

Way to go, buddy. You did a real bang up job with this one.

No. It's not going down like that. I screwed up, but it's not over. I can make this right.

I *will* make this right.

"Where are you right now, man?" I pull away from my thoughts and ask. Praying he's where I think and can get me what I'm after.

"About a block down from the house. Why?"

"Get the address and text it to me."

"Again...why?"

"Because you're not the only one that's gotta make a choice. I just hope that even though I screwed up the first time it was presented to me, I'm not too late to fix it."

"And you call me cryptic."

"It'll all make sense soon enough, but until then, can you do me another favor?"

"Name it."

"Watch over my girl? It's gonna take some time before I can and if I can't do it, there's no one else I trust more than you."

"You got a deal, but Brady? You owe me."

"Would expect nothing less."

What Jax doesn't get is that with the way things are playing out in my head now, what I know I have to do and the way I see it all playing out once I do it, he'll be getting paid back in full in no time at all.

I've got a plan and this time, no one is going to stop me.

"Emery..." I whisper once I end the call with Jax. "I swear to God I'll make this right. I'll fix it and prove to you that when it comes to us, there is no choice."

Reaching over into the passenger seat, determined to make good on my whispered promise, I pull the pad out from the side and grabbing a pen down from the visor, start writing.

Committing not only the promise to paper, but my heart too.

No matter what I have to do, how long it takes, who I have to go through and what I stand to lose, nothing is going to sway me.

I've been living my life for someone and something else long enough. It's time to start living for me. I will make it home again.

Home to Emery.

Right where I belong.

Jax

Life is a series of choices.

Some big, some small, but all of them irrevocably changing you once you've made them.

The decision of what direction to go in when you hit the proverbial fork in the road is yours alone to make, but one that once you take the leap and make it, you must be secure in because you're the one that's going to have to live with it when it happens.

Live with it the way I'm having to live with the consequences of mine now.

To tell or hold back. To walk away or stay. To stand and fight or lay down and accept defeat.

Three choices that over the span of the last week I've made, and apart from wishing I could go back and change the choice I made in not telling, all choices that if I had to go back and do them again, I would without hesitation.

I would do it all again...for her.

For Avery.

"Emery, please." I plead, hearing how pathetic I sound but no longer caring. "Just tell me where you're holding the service."

This is not the first time I've asked. Over the course of the last week since I dropped Avery at the airport and caught my own to the same destination—making the second of three choices—I must have asked her this same question at least a dozen times. Always with the same result.

One that I hope changes now, given that it's the day they're laying her to rest.

"Jax," she sighs. "As much as I think you should be there, it doesn't change the fact that she doesn't want you there. I'm sorry. I can't tell you. I can't do that to her. Especially now."

God damnit.

I should have known it was going to be another no. After what happened between me and her sister, that's the only response she should have. Emery has no loyalty to me. Especially after what went down with her and Brady.

"Has she talked to you about what happened with us?"

"No, and something tells me she won't. Avery isn't like us, Jax. She didn't grow up with a full family. All she had was a dad that based on everything I know about him, didn't give two shits about her. At least not enough to bother telling her the truth. She's used to dealing with things on her own."

"You need to get her to talk, Em. I'm not asking for me. She's going through a lot and it's not going to do her any favors keeping it bottled."

After what feels like an eternity of silence, Emery finally speaks again. Dropping what has to be the last thing I ever expected to hear on me when she does.

"Silverbrook."

"Say what?"

"She's being buried at Silverbrook Cemetery in Wilmington."

"Okay, I'm lost." I admit, thankful for the info but not having the slightest clue what changed in order for me to get it. "Why are you telling me this?"

"Honestly," she sighs again. "I'm telling you because even knowing she wants nothing to do with you, you're what she needs. And well, because it's what my mom would want me to do. But Jax?"

"Yeah?"

"Don't make me regret it."

I've made a lot of stupid mistakes in my life, a lot of them recently, but making her regret telling me where they're burying their mother wasn't going to be one of them.

"I won't. She won't even know I'm there. But since you told me where, do you think you can tell me when?"

"Two o'clock. Service is at one and then we're going straight over from there."

"Thank you."

"Don't thank me, Jax. Like I said, this is what my mom would have wanted me to do."

That's where she's wrong. I do need to thank her, because without her, I wouldn't know half of what I do now and the choice I made—what I gave up in order to attempt to make things right—would have been for nothing.

"Whether you're doing it for your mom or for Avery, you're still doing it and I'm thankful. So thank you, Emery. Again. Can you do me one last favor?"

"Name it and we'll see."

"Take care of her. Until I can make things right and do it the way I should be, just take care of her." I tell her, repeating Brady's own request from a week ago back.

Again a heavy silence falls over the line, but before I give up and end the call, I hear a deep inhale and exhale of breath.

"Consider it done, but you've got to do something for me in return."

"Anything."

"Fix what you broke."

Little does she realize that's exactly what I plan on doing. Even if it takes me forever.

I'm not giving up. Not on Avery *or* what we have.

Standing and fighting it is.

"Deal."

Chapter One

Brady

The one thing I didn't expect with the old man's urgency for me to get back to Florida, was for him to be sitting on the sofa when I walked through their front door, paper in hand, like it was any other day of the week.

What I also didn't expect was to find my mother across from him, her eyes expressing what her words once she takes me in, can't.

Sadness.

I just can't be sure it's sadness for what she knows is about to happen or for herself with what she's about to lose when we're done here.

Home is where the heart is.

I think at least once in every person's life, they've had some poor idiot thinking they're all knowledgeable and shit, tell them that. And like me, they didn't pay as much attention to it as they should have.

But with the way the last week has played out—what I've put on the line—that saying has never meant more.

If you'd asked me a year ago where my heart was, I would have said Florida with Kelly, even with things falling apart the way they had already started to at that point.

Fast forward into the here and now, or rather, a week ago even, the answer would be so very different.

As it stands now, my heart and home are separated, and even though I probably don't stand a snowballs chance in hell of fixing what I destroyed when I did what was asked of me and walked away, I am determined to find a way to bring the two of them together again.

The two of us together again.

My heart you see, it's not in Florida where it used to be. It's not even out on the road with CPW.

It's with Emery right where I left it when I stupidly walked away without telling her the truth. Without telling her what I know wouldn't have changed things, but what I also know beyond a shadow of a doubt would have been the most honest words ever uttered.

I wasn't just falling for her. I'd fallen hard and I didn't want to get back up.

I didn't tell her that I love her.

Standing here in my parent's family room though, this is the first step on the road to doing that. The only way I can think of to prove my love being to distance myself from all of the things and people threatening to destroy it.

Taint it and turn it into something it's not.

Placing the paper down onto the table, my father leans forward, his arms coming to rest across his legs. Both of us frozen like two cowboys at high noon.

Ready to do battle.

But unlike the westerns, we're not battling with guns. No, for him, it will be insults and berating. For me, words that pour from my heart. The truth as I know it.

Truth that once armed, not even my father will stand a chance against.

"You're here."

"And it appears as though you're just as stupid as I imagined when I made the call because you're not where you need to be."

Shot one fired. Direct hit.

"I came here first because I wanted to see Mom." I admit, no shame in revealing that knowing the way this would all play out in the end, I was still attempting to keep some form of relationship with the woman that birthed me. The woman that for twenty-eight years, even when it was damn near impossible under his strict rule, loved me no matter what my accomplishments were.

"Your mother stands with me, Brady. She is of the same belief system when it comes to your antics and is as ready as I am to wash her hands of it."

"Is that true?" I turn and ask her. The answer I'm waiting for betraying the words that eventually do fall out of her mouth when she speaks.

"Yes, son. What your father says is right."

What she doesn't seem to get is that I can see through her. I've always been able to. For as long as I can remember, my mom and I, we've had this ability to talk to each other without a single word being uttered. She's doing this now strictly for her husband's benefit. I know the truth.

"I'm gonna need you to explain something to me." I say, turning my attention back to my dad.

"I don't owe you any explanations, son. Your actions over the last couple of months speak for themselves."

Last couple of months my ass.

He means everything since the time Kelly made a public display of leaving me over nothing. An event that at the time he'd given me his support on, instead of his usual way of pissing on me every damn chance he got.

"You mean the last two months I've spent on the road getting my head kicked in, my ass beat on, and my shoulder damn near ripped from its socket, because someone taught me that the show must always go on? Is that what you're referring to?"

The scowl that presents proves I've got him.

"I've done nothing but follow every damn thing you spent years laying into me about. Putting my entire focus into the business, even at the fucking expense of my marriage. A marriage that until two days ago, you still thought was the stupidest thing I'd ever done. Something you were pleased to find out had run its course. So please, Dad. Tell me exactly what antics over the last couple of months you're referring to because I'm at a loss."

"Bill..." the gentle softness of my mother's voice cuts in.

"Diane, stay out of it. This is between Brady and me."

"That's the first thing you've said since I got here that I actually agree with." I interject and the way my mom flinches isn't lost on me. She knows I'm not here to bow and give in like I have in the past and is reacting.

"I've spoken to Smith at length over the past few days, Brady. He's told me that you seem distracted when you're in a match, along with taking unnecessary risks, and then there's this last screw up. Asking for time off to go and wet your dick in Delaware. It's the last straw."

"What did I say about that?" I seethe through gritted teeth. There's a lot of shit I'm willing to take knowing what I'm about to do, but making light of what I had with Emery is something I won't tolerate. No fucking way. I'm gonna shut that shit down.

"As I recall, you went on the offensive for the same reason nine years ago. When just like now, I called you out on what was happening. You're nothing more than a pubescent boy, Brady. You may believe what you did during those days in Delaware amounts to genuine feeling, but I know better. I've always known."

Bullshit.

Just because he landed himself a subservient woman that won't question or push him to be more doesn't mean he knows a god damned thing about me and what I have with Emery.

"If that's all I was, don't you think I would spend my time on the road doing what a lot of the other guys do? Don't you think I'd take full advantage of the ring rats that practically throw themselves at me every night?"

"No you wouldn't because I raised you better than that. You've got more respect for yourself."

Not I've got more respect for women. He doesn't give a rat's ass about that. He's making it about me when the reality is, it's both. I have respect all the way around. The women choosing to throw themselves at men that in the end will just use them for what they're worth and discard them deserving a hell of a lot better, and me not wanting to be just another name on a long list of assholes.

"I've got respect for everyone, Dad. Don't make this about me. I'm not you. The world doesn't revolve around me."

Standing from his chair, he takes a few steps toward me and where in the past I would have tripped over myself in order to create distance, I do the opposite this time. Locking eyes with him and standing my ground.

I'm not a little kid anymore and it's about damn time he realized it.

"If you're not here to rectify the current situation, why are you here?"

"You're wrong. I *am* here to rectify the situation, just not the one you think." I admit, thankful when the words fall that they do so clearly. My father as intimidating as always despite my every attempt not to let him be. "You want to strip me of the money you feed my account every couple of weeks or disown me because I'm choosing to live my life my way, do it."

Pausing as his jaw twitches, the need to go off on me and give me another dose of his reality strong, I don't give him the chance.

"You want to use your respected name in this business to ruin the very real thing I've got going with Smith and CPW, go ahead. Play your hand, Dad. I no longer care. I've spent the last twenty years doing everything your way and look what it's gotten me. I'm alone all the god damned time. I'm empty. I've got nothing left. What I loved about what I do, I now hate. The end of every show the happiest time of the night because it means I can finally fuck off for a few hours and be Brady instead of a Raines."

"Did you shoot your brains off in the piece of ass when you fucked her? You must have given the level of nonsense coming out of your mouth."

Blood rushes to my head and before I can get a grip on what's happening, I'm moving toward him and my tightly knit fist is connecting with his jaw, the sting of the contact not even hitting me as I swing my other hand forward and do it again to the other side, pummeling him to the ground.

There's a lot I'm willing to take, but referring to Emery as a piece of ass, no way.

Filled with a rage I've never known before—different from the shades of it I experience with opponents in the ring—I advance on him until the roles between us are reversed and he's the one stumbling back in fear.

The cries of my mother falling on deaf ears as I crouch down and into his personal space, my fist wound and prepared for another round.

"Don't you *ever* talk about the woman I love that way! You hear me, old man? Mom may take your shit, but I won't. Not anymore. Do it again and I won't hesitate to end you."

"Brady, please! You don't have to do this!"

My mother again trying to keep the peace like always. Too bad she's about twenty years too damn late. There's no saving this. We've reached the point of no return and I make sure that my next words reflect it.

I'm done.

He can take the name, the money and everything that comes along with it and shove it straight up his ass. I don't want anything to do with it anymore.

"You can take your demands and shove them, Dad." I seethe. "As for disowning me, don't bother. I'm doing what I should have done nine years ago. I'm disowning you."

Giving my mother what she wants, I pull back and head toward the door, a flood of satisfaction and pride running through me with every step I take. Pausing before heading around the corner to where the door is waiting for me, I deliver the final nail in the Raines family coffin.

"We're done."

One down. Two to go.

Emery

Some days are great. Easy. I can get through them without feeling the aching pain of loss. A loss that even though I'd been prepared, I'm still struggling to live with.

Other days are decidedly harder. They're also the ones I hate the most.

Today is one of those days.

Which is why today, I'm going to do what has almost become routine with as often as I've done it over the last few weeks. I'm going to be with my mother.

Before you call the people with the white coats, hear me out. I'm not suicidal and I'm not planning on closing my eyes and joining my mother at the big party in the sky.

Being with her for me is something far less dramatic, but meaningful all the same.

I'm going to read her last words. What she'd painstakingly written in her final days and what has only been for my eyes only since she passed.

A letter, just like the one she'd written Avery, but that even though I'd known every line from hers, I haven't felt right about sharing when it comes to mine.

Words that just like they have every day since she left them for me to find, have gotten me through the hard days. The days where going through the motions and running on autopilot drives me so insane that suicide actually seems like a viable option.

A letter that has the power to block out the one I received exactly one week later. One that try as I might, I still can't seem to move past. My heart and head still at war a month later over what to make of it. Of him.

What emotion I'm allowed to feel in response.

Sadness. Loss. Hope and Faith. Disappointment. Regret.

All things I've experienced in the time since I got it, but none of them what has stuck with me in the days since.

That honor goes to love.

Brady's letter. His promise. It makes me feel love most of all.

Which considering how quickly he abided by my request and dived out of here like a bat out of hell the day before my mother passed, is really the last thing I should feel.

Even now, sitting here with my mom's folded words beside me on the bed, it's his words on repeat in my head and not hers, no matter how badly I wish it were the other way around.

Brady's letter the reason for the tremble in my hands and what causes my pause at reaching over to the paper containing the ones I really need to see and hear.

Emery,

If you're reading this...if you're listening, you were right. I screwed up. And I swear to you, the next time we see each other, things will be better.

I'll be better.

I'll be the man you deserve.

I swear it.

Please don't give up on me.

He'd gotten his wish.

I can't give up on him.

The same way my mother couldn't give up on Richard, I can't seem to give up on Brady. The best I've been able to manage being the way I keep him on the outskirts of my mind, only allowing him entrance when I'm alone where no one else can see.

Where I don't have to put on the show of being okay. Pretending that him choosing his family, the money, and everything that goes along with being a Raines over me didn't completely shatter my heart.

Which, if you're keeping up, makes me the most delusional woman on the planet.

"Why can't I let go of you?" I whisper into the empty room, speaking to the universe that despite never answering before, I still hope chooses to do so now.

Hope that based on results, is misplaced.

Finally picking up the letter off the bed and running my fingers over the crinkles that are imbedded into the paper based on the tears I've spent the last few weeks shedding onto it, I unfold it. Letting the woman that raised me do what she's best at.

Show me the way.

Remind me of what it is I'm really fighting for.

My Darling Emery,

One of the first memories I have of you was about a week after we brought you and your sister home from the hospital.

Right from the very first day, you had such bright, inquisitive eyes. Almost as though you were attempting even then, to see beyond the surface of things. To read things in a way that even as we all grow older, not many people take the time to actually do.

But this day, I'd gone into the nursery and while your sister slept peacefully, you were wide awake. Eyes focused on something high up in the ceiling. Even as I came closer, you never looked away. Never lost your focus on whatever it was that held you there.

Looking back now, as I sit here preparing for the inevitable, I think I finally know what it was that caught your attention.

It was something far bigger than you and I, or the lives we led. A knowledge greater than the one we actually use as we grow older. You were remembering where you came from. What you had given up in order to give me the honor of being your mother.

You saw the wonder and beauty then, that as you sit and read this, I am seeing now. The wonder and beauty that even though you were far too young at the time to realize, was preparing you for this moment. Readying you for this day. This moment of true heartbreak.

Readying you for the goodbye.

But when is a goodbye ever really a goodbye? When does the story of our lives truly end?

The answer to those questions is as simple as the wide eyed starry expression on your face that day.

It never ends.

Our stories remain long after our bodies begin to fail because it's not driven by cause and effect, action and reaction. It continues on, never ending, because true love never dies.

Love always wins.

So if you take nothing else with you from our time together, take that.

Close your eyes and breathe it in until it transforms you. Completes you. The same way that loving you and Avery for the last twenty-five years has done for me.

Make that truth your own. Don't shy away from it or excuse it because of the way things have turned out for me. My choices, my mistakes...they were my own. Don't take them on as your own, or I fear we'll both end up living lives filled with regret.

Which brings me to what's most important.

The boy that right now has both captured and broken your heart.

As hard as it may be, don't do what I believe everyone that has come before you has done in regards to him.

Don't give up.

There's beauty there, even in the midst of his tragedy.

Be the one that takes the risk so that what you've done for me, you can one day do for each other.

It isn't often that a man buys flowers for a woman he doesn't even know after all.

He's a keeper.

The same way I knew from the moment I laid eyes on you, you were as well.

It's up to you to carry on. To become to the rest of the world the woman I have always known you to be. The incredibly strong and resilient Emery Davis. The woman who lives vibrantly, but loves even more powerfully.

Take care of your sister. Surround her with the love I know you have buried so deeply inside you. Something tells me she's going to need it now more than ever.

Most of all, Emery, take those words I spoke to you in the quiet darkness and bring them out into the light.

Make her see that the love she so desperately needs and wants is already hers for the taking. She just has to open her heart and trust. The same way you both did all of those years ago when you put your trust in me to be your mother.

The colors may change, but it's there. Just waiting for you both in the blue.

I love you, Emery.

Yesterday, today, tomorrow, and for always.

Mom.

Chapter Two

Avery

"I practiced what I wanted to say so many times that you think the second I hear the beep, it would all come pouring out. Now that it has, though, it's like I dreamed the rehearsals."

Click.

Five messages, this being the first. All from Jax. Each one wearing me down more than the last. All of them filled with confessions, admissions and feelings. Each one different, but with one similarity.

Every word he utters is real. He feels every one. There's not an ounce of insincerity in them, and trust me, I've looked. Well, I suppose in this case, I've listened.

Repeatedly.

The first message sent the week after Emery and I laid our mother to rest. The others, just like the emails and texts that he's sent, appearing like clockwork every few days, or more accurately, one of each every week since.

The last one, the one that will play after I'm done listening—or rather torturing myself—with the sound of his voice in all of the others, marking week five of us being apart. One that he sent two days ago where after leaving the office, I'd looked up and across the street to the parking garage like I do almost every day and caught him staring back at me.

"Avery, I know this is probably the last thing you need to hear, but since I don't know how else to tell you the truth about the day before Emery called, this is how it has to go. The message you read, what you saw and let your mind believe, it's not what you think. I know a lot of people say that, but the difference between them and me is, I mean it. Every word. It really isn't what you think. Please...if you get this message call me. Text me. God, send a smoke signal or something. I'll get it, I swear. Just reach out."

Click.

Reminders of the message I caught on his phone, the one from his ex-girlfriend Melinda, I don't need them. Despite my mind being occupied by the loss of my mother, the woman's words are still as vivid as they were that day. I've just managed somehow to put my focus elsewhere.

At first, after the funeral, and around the time I came back to Toronto, I managed to settle the storm of emotion I was being bombarded with.

I wasn't so angry with Jax anymore. I wasn't lashing out at the nearest person because I had all of these feelings and no control or place to put them.

Things were beginning to even out. I was starting to feel better.

At least they were until I got the bright idea to go to my father's place. Standing in a home I'd long since moved out and on from and finding it just as empty and devoid of the things that make a place a home as it had been when I was growing up, well, it brought the unsettled feeling back.

An internal chaos that despite putting one foot in front of the other, didn't seem to want to subside this time. Bringing with it the rush of those same emotions from the last day I saw Jax. The day my world stood still. Reminding me of my loss and the collateral damage that came along with it.

Jax's calls, texts and emails only compounding it.

"I haven't talked to Melinda in a year. Not since I called her on what she was doing with Gavin and washed my hands of it all. When I got her text, I was curious. Not curious about a reconciliation the way I'm sure you're thinking, but curious as to why it was happening then. Whether she knew about us or if she was just trying to get a rise out of Fortune and wanted to use me to do it. I let it get to me, Avery. I let her get to me in a way that pulled me away from you. Something that never should have happened. Especially not after what we'd just admitted and shared. It was the worst possible time, worst possible thing, and I'm sorry. You'll never know how much. Please believe me. I just...I need you to believe me."

Click.

I forgave him that day.

Reminders of the conversation box springing to mind and showing me what I couldn't see in the heat of the moment. His words were genuine. His lack of response when it came to Melinda finally doing what it should have done the second I saw the message, and proving what kind of man he is.

Sure, he held something from me, but given the length of time we'd actually known each other, could I really expect anything more? Everything was still new.

Trust. Open communication. Honesty.

They're all things couples want, but also things that take time and dedication in order to achieve. Time that really wasn't on our side given the way our entire relationship came about. We were on a fast moving train with no stops or slowdowns in between. It made sense now that he didn't exactly want to drop this at my feet with us barely a week in.

I understood him.

I forgave him.

So if I did all of that, why after five weeks are we still apart?

Well, that's where the line becomes gray.

We're apart because until I can come to terms with the loss of my mother, the unresolved feelings I have towards the first man in my life to betray me, and the back and forth as it pertains to the loss of him, I can't give Jax what he needs.

I can't give him all of me because I don't trust him.

I don't trust myself.

Twenty-five years I spent being duped by the one man in my life that I never expected it from. Guys that you meet, you expect it from them. Your father? The man you trust with your life and the one that shapes your view on boys and men the older you get?

Not so much.

I don't trust myself not end up in a situation like that again, especially after that text.

If something as insignificant as fourteen words on an electronic device can so easily break my heart, what's going to happen when it's something bigger? Will I be able to sort the truth from the lies or will I do what I seem to have done with my father and just ignore it?

It's not about Jax anymore. He's forgiven. Now it's about me. Love can't fix this. Only I can.

"Avery, this is message number four. I don't even know if you're getting these, but considering your mailbox isn't full, I can only assume you are. Sweetheart, talk to me. Please. Even if it's something as small as a hello or big like you telling me how much I hurt you when I held back. Anything. Just talk. I hate that you're so far away having to deal with everything on your own. I hate that you're probably so wrapped up in your head over everything that's happened that my heart isn't loud enough for you to hear. I hate this distance. Please just talk to me. I love you, Avery. Just you. Only ever you."

Click.

His messages, for as long as I've been getting them, with the way my heart swells and longs for him, should make reaching out easy. But with every day that passes, the unease in my heart and the emptiness in my soul seeming to grow larger instead of smaller, all I can do is love him from afar.

It's better this way.

I've assured myself of that, I believe in it.

I just don't know in the end who it's better for after what happened two days ago.

"So you caught me today. Looked me right in the eyes. The distance between us substantial but my ability to see you clearly showing me everything despite it. The loss in your eyes. The pain radiating from every pore of your body, manifesting itself in your slumped shoulders and sluggish demeanor. You've become one with it now. It's taken you over, the same way that every day we spend apart does to me. Two halves of a whole pulled apart. I can feel it all, Avery. Every ounce of what owns you. It's breaking my heart. It's smothering my will to fight. But I won't give up, you hear me? Your eyes today may have told me that's what you wanted, but your heart, it doesn't agree. It wants time, and even though it pains me to do this, time is exactly what I'm going to give it. I know you don't feel like you're worth it, but you are and if I have to spend the next five, ten, or even twenty years loving you from afar, I will because I'm determined to prove it to you. You're everything,

Avery Davis, and I'll wait as long as it takes. I'll wait until you're ready."

Click.

"If you would like to delete this message, press seven. To save it, press nine."

I wish things could be that simple. Whether to save or let go being decided by a number on a keypad. If it were, maybe I wouldn't be in my office alone, filled with sadness and regrets for words that even though I feel them, I can't say.

But if I could assign a number to Jax and what I still feel for him, it would be a lot like this last voicemail.

A nine.

Every time.

Jax

"What do you think? Everything you wanted or what?"

A few days after Avery caught me in Toronto and I left, I called Tom, my realtor. After listening to me talk incessantly about what I wanted, a few days and a visit with my parents later, he delivered.

Two pages of listings coming over my parents fax machine for places in my price range that boasted every miniscule detail I'd thrown at him. Details that deep down I knew were my attempt at self-sabotage despite knowing that it was something that needed to happen.

Choosing to keep my feet firmly planted in the airport that day, wasting time until the flight to Delaware and then the weeks I'd spent watching Avery since, it called for this. The final time, when she caught me as she made her way out of the office, hammering the final nail in my coffin.

Having been caught, I had to admit defeat. I couldn't very well keep an eye on her when she would now be looking around every corner. I also couldn't walk straight up to her, throw her over my shoulder and steal her away either. My last message to her—the one I made before the flight back to California—having to remain as true as every other thing I've ever said.

I had to give her time.

Time to come to terms with the last few weeks and time to evaluate where she wanted to go from here. With her life and with me.

So back home to my parents I went, even though I knew the second I stepped foot into Pearson Airport, I was actually going to be leaving home.

All of that leading me here as Tom waits patiently on the other end of the line.

"This is whole lot more than everything I wanted, Tom. You weren't kidding when you said this was the place."

There are a lot of beaches in California. *A lot.* So when I set down the beach as a major selling point, I'd been expecting thousands of places to flood the fax lines. Properties both for short term use and long, close to Los Angeles and as far from it as you can get.

Laguna Beach it is.

It's perfect.

"Send me whatever you have on the place, Tom. I want it. I'll sign my name in blood if the owner wants me to. There's not a chance in hell I'm letting this place go."

This two bedroom mobile home overlooking the beach, with the large back patio and garden filled with color and trees that seem to stretch out for miles, needs to be mine. I knew it the second I walked through the door.

All of my troubles and the chaos that seemed to percolate around inside because of them, falling away the second I heard the sound of the waves hitting the shore.

"It's all here waiting, buddy. So get your ass over here so we can make it yours."

That's all I need to hear. Making my way from the back to the front door and slipping out, I bring my fingers to my lips kissing them before pressing them to the door.

Leaving my mark.

Solidifying that the next time I walk through those doors, the only thing allowed in will be the things one experiences when they kiss.

Passion. Warmth. Joy and happiness. A sense of completeness. Serenity. But more importantly, the one thing I felt the last time I kissed Avery.

Love.

This place, whether I stay here a day, a year, or ten, it's only ever going to know love.

I may have only had a little over a week to get to know Avery, and I know for sure that there is a lot more that once we get through this I'll still have to learn, but what I remember is that aside from her house, she hates where she is.

It's not where her heart wants to be and considering she's the beat to mine, this isn't just a place for me. This place; this home, it's my gift to her. What one day I hope will be ours.

This place is going to be our home.

"On my way now. I'll see you soon." I say, ending the call and crossing the street to where my car waits. My head full of possibilities and what is going to have my entire focus until things are finally set right.

Emery wants me to fix this, well, this is a part of it. When I finally stand before Avery again, not only will I fix the mess I made holding back from her, but I would also go all in for our future.

My final words to Tom proving it.

"I'll see you soon, Avery."

Chapter Three

Brady

When you're a kid, the entire world is your oyster.

Life's stresses don't even register. Your actions don't have consequences (at least not until your ass gets caught and there's hell to pay). Every damn idea you have is brilliant and you can really do no wrong. Those dreams you have, you're positive you can live them, completely unaware of the hard work, dedication, time and heart that's needed in order to make them a reality.

The choices you make, you can't be swayed from them because your innocence—naiveté really—has you believing that what you're doing is right.

What anyone else thinks be damned.

Maybe other kids aren't like that. Maybe it's just me. All I know for sure is that the choices I made as a punk ass seventeen year old; the ones that I thought were just so damn smart, are proving to be anything but.

Why seventeen?

I mean, if I got into the business officially at eighteen, married my high school sweetheart at nineteen and those are the things now that are becoming more complicated, shouldn't those be the moments I pinpoint as where my life went off the rails?

They might have been if I didn't know that my stupidity started a whole lot sooner than that.

It could be said and argued that the wrestling business has been in my blood right from the day I was born given my father's ties to it, so I can probably go back even further than seventeen, but until high school, the jury was still out on whether or not I would end up following in my old man's footsteps.

Only I did.

2004.

The day my life both began and ended, but that's taken eleven years to actually see.

Instead of doing things the way some of the guys I work with in CPW do, I'd ridden the Raines name for all it was worth. Being handed things that some of the guys can only dream of and never thinking about just how good I had it.

Where they were living day to day, show to show in their cars, thankful on the random days they could have a warm bed to sleep in and a place to shower, I was jetting from one city to the next on daddy's dime. Five star hotels, running water, access to the gym whenever I wanted to without having to slap down a membership and guaranteed money night after night to step into the ring. Things that on the independent circuit are practically unheard of unless you're dealing in one of the bigger setups.

Daddy's money and name sure did take me far.

Hell, I'm pretty sure that it was his name that got me the girl. Though if you ask Kelly, being a Raines had nothing to do with it given she wanted nothing to do with wrestling back then.

I'll be damned if she didn't enjoy the fucking perks that came along with being with Brady Raines the superstar though.

I swear the more time I spend holed up in the motel with nothing but time to think, I'm starting to see things more clearly. Like for instance, the real reason we lasted as long as we did.

She had to come to terms with what she'd be losing if she walked away.

Not love or devotion and everything else I mistakenly thought we shared. No. Kelly had to make sure that when she walked, she didn't end up back at the bottom of the barrel where I found her.

Using the Raines name for everything it was worth.

She sure learned quickly.

Taking the clueless seventeen year old boy that most days around her had a hard time not busting a nut with how hot I was for her, and twisting him around until he didn't know whether he was coming or going.

Even making me believe at one point that I was at fault for every damn thing that had gone wrong since the moment we said 'I Do'.

What I'm now back in the state to rectify. This time, not lingering and letting her talk her way around our issues, but getting a John Hancock on the dotted line so we can end this charade once and for all.

Accepting what we shared for the time we did, not denying it or running from it, but also not being afraid to admit that it wasn't what we thought it was when we fell in what we thought at the time was a forever kind of love.

Despite all of the animosity of the last six months, the pain that came from being accused of something I didn't even entertain, much less actually do, and everything that came after it, I don't hate her. I've been upset, angry, and filled with rage over what became of us, but not hate.

Kelly, much like the situation a few weeks ago with my father, was a lesson. One that I had to learn the hard way but now that I have, I need to make right.

The first step in doing that, getting her to sign this fresh off the presses copy of our divorce papers so we can stop living our lives on pause.

Pressing hard on the doorbell again and hearing the familiar chime echo through on the other side, I step back on the brick and glance over to where her car sits in the driveway. All the proof I need that even if she's taking forever answering, she's here.

"Brady?" she asks, her eyes widening in surprise when she finally pulls the door back to find me standing there. "Why didn't you just use your key?"

Slipping my hand into the front pocket of my jeans, I hook it around the ring and pull it out, pushing it out between us. Motioning with my hand when she just stands and stares.

"We need to talk." I announce when she finally takes the key and tapping the brown envelope in my hand, I wait for her to react. Her response when it finally comes, exactly what I expect.

"I'm so happy to hear you say that, baby." She purrs, backing away from the door and ushering me in with a sweep of her hand. "When your dad called and said that you two had a falling out, I wasn't sure you'd come, but I'm really glad you're here."

Is that really what my old man is telling people?

"I would have been here sooner," I admit after stepping through. "But I had a couple of things I had to take care of first."

Tapping the envelope in my hand again, I notice her eyes fall to it and the light visible in her eyes when she first saw me, quickly begins to fade.

Good. Maybe this won't be a complete disaster after all. If she gets the reason I'm here right away, what comes next should be a breeze.

You'd think spending the last nine years living in this house would make moving through, straight into the living room that my being on the road furnished and turned into the immaculate display it now is would be easy, but it's not.

As familiar as this place still is despite the months away, I feel no attachment whatsoever and my feet are like stone.

I really don't belong here anymore. It isn't my place.

Part of me wonders if it ever was.

Tossing the envelope onto the table, I throw myself down into the chair and wait for Kelly to do the same. Leaning back and attempting to get comfortable in an effort to take some of the edge I can see in the frigidness of her body away.

I'm not leaving here without her signature on the papers, but it doesn't mean that I have to be a total prick in order to get it. Even if I'm the only one that believes in it, those nine years did mean something and I'm not going to make light of them.

"What happened with Bill, Brady?" she starts in once she's seated.

"Something that should have happened eleven years ago. Nothing for you to worry about and not what I'm here for."

"Then why are you here?"

"Open the envelope and see for yourself." I tell her, motioning to the table. "It's all there."

Thankfully she does what I want by reaching forward and picking it off the table, leaning back as she pulls the papers from their resting place.

Papers that like the ones she originally served me with, are standard, but with a few changes. The reasoning for the divorce one seen thousands of times as marriages all over the world fall apart.

Irreconcilable differences.

"No. This can't be right." She inhales sharply. "Divorce papers? Brady, what the hell is this? Is this some kind of joke?"

I'm known to be a joker, but when it comes to my personal life, my marriage, family and money, I'm nothing but serious.

"What you're seeing is right, Kel. For a little over seven months you told me I needed to let go. Move on and sign the damn papers. Well, I finally did and now it's time for you to do the same."

She's already signed the papers once before, so I know this won't put her out, but these differ from what she originally put in motion. A fact that I know will piss her off once she really delves in and reads the fine print.

Where she wanted it all before, asking for a good chunk of the money I've made all these years on the road, along with the house and everything that came along with it, she was going to sign these and get nothing. Well, nothing besides what I willing wanted to rid myself of.

"I'm not signing this. This is bullshit, Brady!"

"No, Kel. Our marriage was bullshit. The time I spent trying to save it was bullshit. What's in those papers you're holding isn't."

"But we can fix this! I told you I was wrong. I was stupid and let other people get into my head, believing things about you that weren't true. I made a stupid mistake."

All of the pent up animosity I feel toward her, stemming from her original accusations and all the fighting that ensued afterward, it's all there fighting to come out. Throwing my need to do all of this amicably out the window in favor of airing every bit of our dirty laundry.

Everything I took the weeks after leaving my father in order to flush out to guarantee leaving with a signature today. What should have come as a surprise when I learned about it, but felt nothing over.

Keep a cool head, Raines. Don't let her goad you into something you're gonna regret.

Reaching into my jacket and pulling out the pen I'd slipped in there before exiting the car, I lean over in my seat and drop it onto the table. Doing what the clearheaded part of my brain wants me to do and biting my tongue.

Letting my actions speak for me.

Eyeing the pen, she scowls before turning her attention back to the papers, finally doing what I figured she'd have done right from the second she pulled them out and read them over. Her eyes widening as she takes in every stipulation I laid down after walking away from my family and everything that came with them a few weeks before.

My giving up everything of monetary value resulting in her ending up with nothing.

The deepened look taking over her face all the proof I need that I was right before.

It really was about what I could provide her. She never really loved me at all.

"You have got to be kidding! No way, Brady!" she yells, tossing the papers down hard onto the glass table top and focusing all of her ire on me. "I am not signing that load of crap."

"That's where you're wrong." I state evenly, attempting to keep my wits despite the urgency to rise to the occasion and yell back. "You *are* going to sign them. Unless of course you want the last six months of your life dissected and put under a microscope in court."

"You wouldn't dare!"

"Try me."

The reason it took me so long after hitting up my parents to get here, isn't because I was still debating whether or not I could do it. I knew I could. I made that decision after the fallout with Emery.

It's because I knew that when I did it, I had to be armed.

Coming in and asking her politely for a divorce or attempting to make her see that what we had between us had been on life support for far too long, wouldn't work.

Not with Kelly.

I had to hit her where it hurt. Take everything I could get about her life since she told me to get out and use it against her. Force her hand. A fact that given everything I did eventually find out, made me feel a whole lot worse instead of better the way I assumed it would.

I'd given in to my father and the pleas from the woman I married, walked away from Emery, for nothing.

Kelly having moved on long before that day in Delaware when we spoke on the phone.

"Two years, Kel. Two years while I was on the road busting my ass night after night, in order to contribute to the life we promised to build together, you were off building it with someone else. Making me feel like shit when I did get home for having to work with women, when the reality was, you were the one stepping out. Two god damned years I spent missing you, wondering if riding the road, living what I thought was my dream was the right move when the truth is, I was living under the mistaken belief that I left my dream at home."

I wasn't going to get into this, but damn. With the indifferent expression she's wearing and the disbelieving, almost cocky one she had before it, I have no other choice but do it.

She was the cheater. She spent years projecting her own shit onto me and I was stupid enough to fall for it.

Not anymore.

"Brady..."

"Save it. There's nothing you can say that I want to hear. All I want is your signature on the last page so I can get out of here and move the fuck on."

"But—"

"No!" My voice raises into a full blown yell as I hold up my hand at the same time in an added effort to halt her.

The time for hearing excuses is over. She may have been able to pull the wool over my eyes before, but that's over now. The man I was before is long gone.

"Considering everything I found out and could use against you if I really wanted to drag this out, I think if you look deeper at the papers you'll see I was generous. You can have the house, the cars, and whatever money is in our joint accounts. I don't want any of it. It's all blood money anyway. All I want is out. So just take the pen off the table, pick up the damn papers and sign them."

"You're making a mistake."

It's funny what she sees as mistakes. A year ago, hell, a few months ago, the biggest mistake I was making was wrestling. Then, when that didn't seem to get her the reaction she was after, it became me making the mistake of cheating on her with women I worked with. One mistake after another. All my fault.

Making my entire existence seem like the real mistake.

The reality being that we both made the mistake of getting married at nineteen and thinking that what we felt at the time was going to be able to carry us through. The cracks that already appeared in the armor of our relationship getting tossed into the background in favor of our blind naiveté.

A mistake that if she would just stop acting for five freaking minutes, she'd see it's not too late to rectify.

"I've made a lot of mistakes, Kel, you're right. I made the mistake of letting my father rule my life, giving into the Raines name and all of the perks, basically becoming someone I can't stand. I let him with all of his connections run my life to the point that it wasn't even mine anymore. I was a bystander. Taking things for granted, hurting people that I genuinely cared about just because I could. Looking at life as one big joke. I took too damn long to grow up. But this," I motion between us, my eyes cutting to the papers on the table. "This is the one thing that isn't."

"You're wrong. We can fix this. It doesn't have to end like this, baby! Please. Just take a breath."

Nine years of marriage and I can count on one hand how many times she's used that particular term of endearment on me. Usually only bringing it out when she wants something. Another thing that if I'd actually focused on it instead of wanting to do what I thought was the right thing, would have saved us both so much wasted time.

Wiping my hands across the knees of my pants, I stand. Done with her pleas and her delusional belief that what's gone on between us in the last eleven years can be fixed.

It really is true what they say. It's called a breakup because it's broken, and there is nothing more broken than Kelly and I.

Bending over the table and picking up the pen, I steel my gaze, and readying myself for whatever ploy she's about to use next, hold it out between us.

"I've spent the last nine years not breathing. Fighting to keep something alive more out of fear of admitting that I failed than out of genuine feeling. The love I had for you fading long before you told me you wanted out. So you want me to take a breath? Sign the damn papers and set me free so that I can."

"Don't you mean so you can go back to your little side piece in Delaware guilt free?"

Swallowing down the urge I have to go off for the way she's referring to Emery, the one person that despite knowing just how shitty a person I am, still seemed to believe in me, I stay on course.

If Kelly wants to play this game, she can do it with someone else.

My game playing days are over.

"What I do or who I do it with stopped being your business the second you let someone else shove their dick in you, but you know what? I'm not even pissed. Truth is, he did me a favor. He did us both one. We were young and stupid when we got into this thing. Thinking we knew it all when we didn't know shit. We made a mistake and if you would just stop acting like the victim, you'd see it too. This isn't love it's pain. I don't care how much you hate me, but I'm not leaving here until I put us both out of our misery."

Chapter Four

Avery

"Merrick up on the top rope!"

I can't even tell you why I'm doing this. Only that I'm a glutton for punishment. Unable to utilize the ability I have to call him and choosing instead to sit at my desk and watch him from afar.

His athleticism shining through as he hops onto the rope and dives off it, into some kind of somersault move before landing flat on top of his opponent for the night. None other than the other man that's persona non grata in the Davis household.

Brady Raines.

Brady selling it by twisting around and curling in around himself, his face pained before it falls from view as the announcers yell at the top of their lungs about the high flying move that Jackson is paying for just as much as Brady.

Video after video has been watched and devoured in the weeks since we last spoke. A knowledge of what he truly does for a living and just how good he is at it coming along for the ride. A level of respect that I didn't know him long enough to have before, also rearing its head.

Things I wouldn't have known or learned if I didn't make the choice I did while in the pits of my own despair. Making it seem even more like the right one. Knowing that his place was putting on a show for the fans like the one I'm watching now, rather than following me home to Delaware and standing by my side.

God, Avery. Enough already.

Reaching out and running my fingers across the part of the screen where Jackson's body lays frozen in place due to my quick ability to hit pause, I do again what I've done every night since we went our separate ways and run it over the contours of his body.

Committing it to memory the same way that repeatedly listening to his voicemails allows me to memorize the sound of his voice. Somehow lessening the distance both physical and emotional that's between us.

A distance I have the power to fix but am too damn afraid to try. Making the only thing I'm capable of now being how to press play on the video again.

"It looks like the Mojo Master is regretting that decision now!" One announcer calls. "He looks to be feeling the pain more than Raines."

"When have you not known Merrick to put everything he has into a match? This is what he's all about. Putting it all on the line!"

Putting it all on the line.

Even knowing the guys are referring to his ability in the ring and just how unafraid to take risks he is, it still finds a way to hit home on a more personal level as I watch him drags himself across the mat on the outside. Gripping the ring apron before standing and slipping himself back inside.

Whether it's in the ring or in his personal life, he's unafraid to put it all out there. Put himself on the line. Message after message on my voicemail solid proof.

Proving his feelings. Ones I just need to woman up and admit are reciprocated.

I'm in love with him.

"Knock, knock." Markus calls from the doorway. "You got a second?"

I've got all the seconds in the world these days.

"Yeah, of course. Come on in." I tell him, meeting his gaze before lowering it back down to the screen and quickly closing the YouTube window, effectively pulling myself away from Jax for what feels like the hundredth time.

As he makes his way over, I take things a step further, lowering the lid down until I hear the familiar click of it closing, being sure to paste on my best *fake it until you make it* smile before looking up and meeting what I can now see is his concerned expression.

"You didn't need to shut it down on my account, Avery."

"Oh, I didn't. I just wanted to make sure you had my undivided attention."

Or you needed to resist the pull you have to Jax. My always helpful inner voice screams. Causing my fake smile to lose luster as I feel the rise in my cheeks begin to fall.

"When are you going to stop torturing yourself?" He asks, taking a seat and pulling it as close as it can get to the desk before reaching over and patting my hand. "I've tried to ignore it, Avery, but I know what you've been doing and it's not healthy."

Nothing I've done in the last few weeks has been healthy. Absolutely nothing. All of it done while I'm ghosting from one place to the next, just going through the motions and pretending that I'm present and more than that, involved in the day to day functioning of my life, when the truth is I'm anything but.

Watching videos, repeating voicemails, obsessing over my mom's letter and worse, spending every night at home talking to the sky like she's still here with me and not buried six feet underground in Delaware. It's all unhealthy.

"I don't know what you're talking about."

"How many videos did you watch before I got here?" When I start to shake my head in an effort to brush him off, he shuts me down. "I'm not judging you. I just want you to tell me the truth."

"Three." I admit with a heavy sigh.

"Any of those recent?"

"No."

Gripping his hand around mine, he lifts it off its resting place on top of the computer and when I pull it back into my lap, goes to work popping the top and bringing it over into his lap.

About to learn my secret. That it wasn't three videos but five, and that it would have probably been more if he hadn't interrupted.

"Markus, you—"

"Yes, Avery, I do. You haven't been right since you came back from Delaware and while for the first couple of weeks I attributed that to the loss of your mother, after what I caught last night when I dropped off those files you asked for, what you admitted after god only knows how many drinks you plied yourself with, I need to do this."

Oh God. What the hell did I tell him?

Last night is a blur. All I can remember other than waking up fully clothed in my bed this morning, being how sick I felt when I came through the door and how I thought the best way to rid myself of it was to pull a full bottle of wine from the fridge and try and find myself in the bottom of it.

"What did I tell you?"

"You don't remember?" he asks me quizzically. "How much did you drink before I got there?"

Considering the two empties on the counter this morning when I finally managed to clean up and get downstairs to make coffee, I figure I drank a whole lot more than I intended to when I started.

"It doesn't matter how much I drank." I blow him off. "What did I tell you?"

"Other than a whole lot of incoherent babbling, you mentioned something about you and Jackson."

Ugh. It's worse than I thought.

"Did I say what it was specifically?"

"Well...you told me I was right and that you never should have gotten involved with a wrestler, so I'm assuming that whatever went on had something to do with what we talked about before."

Right. The day the doubt started creeping in.

"So all you've got is assumptions?"

"Are you going to tell me they're wrong? That something didn't go down between you and Merrick that involves his ex?"

Nope. Definitely not going to say that because then I'd be a liar, and I'm not Jax.

Wait. No. I didn't mean that.

"I don't wanna talk about it."

"Right." He nods, turning his attention back to my laptop and what I just know my browser history is going to give away. Just what my extracurricular activities have been for weeks. His lips going from an indifferent straight to a painful frown in the seconds it takes me to blink.

"Jesus Christ, Avery."

Great. Here comes another lecture like the one I'd gotten from Emery over the phone two nights before when my hand accidently slipped and I un-paused the video of Jackson fighting a guy named Ron Taylor.

Another lecture I don't need. Especially not from my boss.

"Markus, I know how it looks. I also know that I shouldn't even be here right now with where my head is. You don't need to tell me that what I'm doing is messed up, okay? I already know and it won't happen again."

At least not at work anyway.

I can see it happening right before my eyes and he hasn't even said anything yet.

Everything I've worked for, what I've spent the last five years building is going to be flushed down the toilet because I can't separate my personal life from my professional one.

"You came back asking me for a bigger workload. One that would require you freelance outside of the office a few days a week for other publications, and against my better judgment, I gave in. I never once questioned your need to keep busy and let you have your way. When you didn't slip the way I expected given everything you've been through, I relaxed even more. But this, Avery. I can't overlook this."

"I said it won't happen again."

"That's not what I'm talking about." He says, obviously getting what he wanted from the laptop as he closes the lid and hands it back over. "I'm talking about whatever it is that Merrick did that's causing you this much pain."

"He didn't do anything." I immediately defend Jax. "I did. It's my fault."

"Okay, let's say I believe that. What did you do?"

When I first met Markus, I was green in the publishing world. I didn't know anything apart from what years of schooling had taught me and tricks I managed to pick up along the way with my own writing. Interviews I'd managed to secure. One of which was a mock one I did with my dad before he passed.

A mock interview that even though it wasn't supposed to be anything serious, turned out to be exactly what Markus was after and had led to more than one conversation about my connection to the man behind the myth that was Richard Davis.

If there's anyone that knows the dynamic between me and him, it's Markus even though we never really got into the more personal aspects of it.

So in order to answer his questions, I've got to delve into something I thought was ancient history.

"How much do you remember from when you hired me?"

"A lot." He admits with a soft smile. "Let's just say that when I came out of my office that day and saw you sitting there in your business suit, attempting to look all professional, you stood out."

Okay. It's a little more information than I was after, but I can still work with it.

"Do you remember talking to me about my dad?"

"Of course. As I recall, we talked about him a lot back then."

"Right."

"What does your father have to do with Merrick?"

It's a valid question, but one that even though I'm the one that started it, I'm having trouble actually getting into. My ability to find words to explain this just as screwed up as my inability to just call Jax and end the torture.

"We weren't close, my dad and I. He worked way too much and left me to my own devices a lot. I never abused it. I was the dutiful daughter just the way he raised me to be. I knew he loved me, but he just wasn't as present as I figure most dads should be. I was wrong."

"Wrong about what?"

"He didn't love me. Not the way a real father should anyway. If he did, he wouldn't have kept my mother and sister from me for twenty-five years, making me believe at one point that my own mother was dead."

There. *Phew.* It's out.

"Avery…"

"Even though he wasn't around as much as I wanted him to be and his work came first even when he was there, I loved him. Trusted him. With every damn part of me capable of doing it, I did. Learning the truth; everything that he was keeping from me and how many people he hurt doing it, it's shattered every belief I ever had about the type of man he was."

"What did Jackson do?" he repeats his earlier question when I'm done and again I shake my head. This isn't about what Jax did or didn't do anymore. My inability to let go of him, yet at the same time not allow myself to accept what happened and move on from it, it's on me.

It's all because of Richard fucking Davis.

"He got a text. A text he didn't even respond to. Fourteen words that a rational person would have seen and talked to him about. But that's not what happened because I got Emery's call before I could. Though with how easily I fell apart after seeing it, something tells me that even if that didn't happen, we still would have ended up where we are."

"Which is where?"

"Over."

Liar, Liar pants on fire, Avery.

"I'm gonna go out on a limb and assume the text was from Melinda."

"It was."

"I'm sorry, Avery."

Now this is not what I expected. What in the world would Markus have to apologize for? It's not like he was the person that typed out the message and sent it to Jax.

"Why are you saying sorry?"

"I feel responsible for the way everything played out."

Say what? "Why?"

"When you told me who you were seeing and I talked to you about her and their relationship, I saw the way you reacted. You weren't trying to of course, but I could see that what I said got to you. Maybe if I'd kept my mouth shut and not pushed you to tell me, this wouldn't be happening."

"It's not your fault." I say and even as the words come out, I feel the old familiar fullness that comes with telling the truth. It really isn't his fault. Markus couldn't have known just how insecure I was underneath it all. How on edge I was after what I learned about my dad and his betrayal. He'd just been trying to give me a heads up.

The mess I'm in now is of my own making.

"Have you talked to him?"

"No. Not directly anyway."

"Maybe you need to." He says and before I can argue he reaches across the desk, bringing his hand down on top of mine again, successfully halting me. "Now before you tell me I'm wrong and the best thing for you is to cut your losses, hear me out."

When I make no move to speak or even attempt to move my hand away, the shock of his abrupt movement seeming to completely freeze me in place, he gives it to me straight.

"I don't agree that this is all on you. I think you both have ownership in whatever happened that day. A situation that no matter what way you shake it, won't resolve or let you move on until you've both come to terms with it. Doing what you should have done then, but what Emery's call about your mom prevented."

"We need to talk."

"Exactly. I mean, you could talk to each other and have it still end up the same way. But, maybe not. Maybe if you call him and tell him what you just told me about your father and really listen to what he has to say in return, you could end up turning it into something better. Something that has the two of you together instead of sitting here miles apart."

Talk to Jax. He makes it sound so easy.

"You're better than sitting alone in your office pouring over videos of some guy, Avery. You deserve better. So if you can't get it from anyone else, demand it from yourself. Demand better. Be the one that ends the torture and call him. Win, lose or draw, at least at the end of the day you'll be able to say that you did everything you could."

He's right. I hate that he is, but I'm not going to sit here and deny it.

If I want the hurt to stop, if I want to be able to move on not only from what happened with Jax, but also what happened with my family, this is the way to do it.

"Thank you." I say softly and squeezing my hand and offering up a smile of understanding, he turns to go, making it halfway to the door before I call out to stop him. Remembering him asking if I had a second when he first got here and wondering just what it was about.

"What did you want earlier?"

"It's nothing. It can wait."

If only he understood just how much it can't wait. After the loaded conversation we just had, I need the distraction.

"No, Markus. You came in for a reason, so spill it."

"Canoe Sports called a few hours ago. They need someone to do a write up on an event and asked if I had anyone available. I thought of you first, but after everything...well, let's just say I don't think you'd be the right fit."

There's only one event in the world that after everything we've talked about, I wouldn't be the right fit for, but strangely enough, even knowing that he's probably right, I need to do it.

If I can get through a wrestling show, knowing full well how much it's going to remind me of what I've lost, I'm pretty sure I can get through anything.

Even calling Jax.

"What's the event, Markus?"

"HFWA show."

"When?"

"Friday night."

"What all would I need to do?"

"Avery, I know how dedicated you are to your job, but maybe you need to stay away from this one. Maybe try again when things aren't so raw?"

I know what he's trying to do, but this has nothing to do with me being dedicated to the job and everything to do with facing my fears. If I'm serious about saving things with Jax, this is my chance to prove it.

"Just tell me what I need to do, Markus. Let me worry about what I can and can't handle."

"Just report on the show."

"Call them back. Tell them you've got your reporter, and Markus? I got this. I won't let you down."

HFWA here I come.

Chapter Five

Brady

Starting from scratch or in this case, the bottom.

A position that if I had been asked point blank about a year ago, I would have cracked a dirty ass joke about because there was no way in hell that I would ever end up back there.

Not in the business and not in my life.

The idea of going back to the beginning, wrestling on dirty ass mats in run down gymnasiums and killing myself for whatever spare change I'd make off the gate of the show, not exactly high on my list of to-dos.

Sure, I had daddy's money backing me so I wasn't really struggling the way a lot of the guys I've met over the years did on their way to the top of the industry, but it still wasn't easy. Even if the hard times were fast tracked because of my name. I still felt them for the short period of time I did it.

What I'm not about to feel again after the call I made to Smith and Marie, effectively ending my arrangement with CPW.

The only good thing about the entire experience being, they had nothing they could use against me since while I had signed a soft contract when I started with them years ago, there was nothing ironclad that could prevent me from leaving. I had fulfilled everything asked of me even when I didn't have to and I was free to Fleetwood Mac my way out of there and go my own way.

My own way landing me in Canada with the HFWA— Harbour Front Wrestling Alliance.

Run by two guys that to hear them tell it, would have been riding the same roads I was if it wasn't for injuries. But definitely guys that after talking to them when I landed, seemed to have what I was looking for in this fresh start I was after.

A fresh start that begins tonight as my first match is scheduled. A Cruiserweight title match again the man currently holding the title, the Dragon Master.

A match that the second I stepped through the gymnasium doors, I'd been told I would be letting him go over in.

"So you want to do a springboard corkscrew moonsault for the win?" I repeat back, just to be certain I heard him right. Needing to get over in this match for the guys paying me as much as the crowd that would be attendance. Or considering I'm nobody again, the D Master.

"Exactly. It's a new move I've been trying out. I needed a new finisher and after watching a few of the guys in the big time do it with success, I figure I can adapt it and make it my own."

"Well, let's try it out."

Looking at me like I've just lost my mind with eyes bugged out and the whole bit, I can't help but laugh. I don't know how they do things around here, my only real experience over the last few years being the way Smith ran things in CPW, but if he thinks I'm just gonna run out there blind without a test run first, he's got another thing coming.

I'm all for people debuting new moves, but not without the security of knowing beforehand that they're even possible.

"You sure? I mean, I'm down with whatever, but no one's ever asked me to do that before."

"Really? Reese and Bryan don't have you guys going over matches beforehand?"

"They do, but I've had to deal with a lot of assholes that think they're too damn good to run through a match before the show starts. Like just because they're talented, it means they're invincible."

Now that I'm familiar with. I've met quite a few guys over the years that were the same way and I hated working with them every time. No one, wrestler or not, is invincible and the ones that think they are; going out there and taking moves without knowing the many different ways it could all play out, are just stupid and reckless.

Thankfully, the D Master isn't one of them.

"I hear ya, but I'm not one of those guys."

"Then let's test it out."

After going over the spot three times, along with a few other spots we added, we break and make our way over to the other end of the room where Bryan is deep in conversation with two of the female competitors.

"You two all ready to go?" he turns, looking between us. "I saw some of what you two were doing over there. Looks like we did the right thing putting you two in the main event."

Wait...what?

"We're in the main event?" My partner asks and Bryan grins.

"That's what I said."

"Since when?" I finally enter the conversation, still blown away that my first match in is going to be at the end of the night. A feat I would have achieved easily just based on my name before, but am definitely not deserving of now.

"Since the original main event fell through and what I saw the two of you running when I came in is better. You got a problem with that, Brady?"

See what I mean? He doesn't call me Raines the way everyone in a fifty foot radius does. It's refreshing. Maybe I can do what before seemed so damn impossible after all.

"Not at all, just kind of blown away. It's unexpected."

"Figured as much." Bryan laughs. "But if you keep putting together matches like the one you two are working on, I can see a lot more main event spots in your future."

Main event spots in my future. *Right.*

Take that Bill.

Looks like talent, heart, and drive win out over money after all.

"We won't let you down, Bry." The man known as D Master says, taking Bryan's outstretched hand and shaking it.

"You never do, Kris." He says before extending his hand to me, gripping it hard when I meet him halfway. "Kemper sends his regards."

Matthias Kemper? Really?

"After what I did to his face the last time we squared off, I bet he does."

"He figured you'd say that." Bryan laughs, slapping his hand down hard on my shoulder and leaning in. "He also said payback's a bitch."

Pulling away and laughing again, he moves over to Kris and after leaning in and whispering something to him, starts to head across the room, pausing about halfway through his trek and calling out.

"Blow the roof off the joint tonight, boys! Let's show these motherfuckers what HFWA is all about."

Meeting Kris's eyes and acknowledging his smile with a quick nod, I turn to my new boss and filled with a confidence I haven't felt in years, level my gaze with his.

"Hope you like getting wet, Michaelchuk!" My cockiness earning me the response I'm after when his face lifts and he returns my smile.

"I'd expect nothing less!"

Bryan's words are all the motivation I need.

It's time to bring the pain to HFWA and finally do what I've been trying and failing with for the last few years in CPW.

Making it rain.

Emery

"You're doing what?" I ask, pausing the wine bottle mid pour after Avery drops her bomb. "Since when do you report on wrestling events?"

Filling the glass to the brim, needing the extra after what I'm hearing, I place the bottle back on the counter before slowly making my way out of the kitchen and into the family room. Making sure as I pass by the TV to grab the remote and press play on the DVD player.

Another night of family movie watching all the excitement on my docket. Afraid that if I don't go back and watch every movie my mother made me star in, I'll somehow forget her.

"I told you the last time you were here that I was taking on more freelance work. It just so happens that this time, it's an internet sports site that needs me."

"And you're sure this has nothing to do with *He Who Shall Not Be Named*?" I press, settling back into the sofa and downing a swallow of wine.

"It's not like I agreed to cover a CPW event, Em. It's a new Canadian promotion. They need all the coverage they can get. The bonus being, it's a Merrick and Raines free zone."

"Is he still reaching out?"

Jax, ever since the funeral has reached out to me a few times, letting me know what he's doing and why. The last time, a couple of weeks ago, when after catching him watching over her, he'd left and gone home to California. The devotion he has to my sister even though it shouldn't, making me jealous.

Also making me wish that Brady would reach out and do the same.

"Em, did you hear what I said?" Avery's voice cuts through, and just like that, I'm reminded why I try my hardest not to think of him. Even from a million miles away he's still managing to dominate my thoughts, right now pulling me away from the one person in the world that should matter.

"Sorry, Ave."

"I said that he's still texting me every day, but the calls have stopped."

"Oh. Well, this is a good thing right? I mean, didn't you say the calls were the hardest?"

"Yeah, I did and I guess it's a good thing."

Score one for Jax. Whatever he's doing, whatever his plan is to get back in my twin's good graces, seems to be working. Maybe in their case what people say is true. Absence does make the heart grow fonder. If the soft lilt to Avery's voice is any indication, she's missing him a little more than she wants to let on.

Before I can press her for more though, the doorbell sounding interrupts. Pulling my attention away right as the sound of bare knuckles against the wooden door follows.

"Hey, Ave? Someone's at the door. You wanna wait or can I call you back?"

"You expecting company?"

I choke back a laugh. The last thing I've been expecting since my mom passed is company. The only person that's actually come by the house since the funeral being the mailman.

"No."

"Well, don't keep whoever it is waiting. Call me back when you're done."

"Yeah, yeah. You'll be wanting a full report. Got it."

"You know it." She chuckles softly and after promising her I'll call her back ASAP, I end the call and head for the door.

Forgoing the option of looking out the peephole, I turn the knob and pull it back. Stumbling backwards when I look up and see who's standing on the other side.

Mike.

Seven weeks have passed since the last time we spoke and gripping onto the door now, I can tell time hasn't made it any easier. I feel the loss of him today the same way I did then.

"Hey, Em."

I should be happy he's the one on the other side of the door, but I'm not. I'm not upset either. I'm not feeling much of anything. I'm too stunned to feel.

"Mike."

There's so much I want to say. Ask even. Like, where the hell was he when my mom passed? Why did I have to be surrounded by a bunch of her friends who were honestly more strangers to me than my own twin? Did his love for me prevent him from being a decent human being and putting the issues with us aside for one day?

But the most important one of all, is why the hell is he standing on my doorstep now?

I don't ask him any of those things though. I don't say a word. I'm not even sure I'm breathing. The only real giveaway I'm still alive being the fact that I haven't crumpled to the floor and I can feel the slivers of wood from the door digging into my hand with the death grip I've got on it.

"Can I come in?"

Well, isn't that the million dollar question?

Torn doesn't even begin to describe the way I'm feeling right now. Being pulled toward reaming him out for not being here and the other wanting to reach across the distance between us, pull him in and pick up right where we left off.

Someone shoot me.

"Uhh...I guess?"

Way to use your words, Em.

Stepping through the doorway, his arm brushing against mine since I still haven't figured out how to disengage from my spot, he brushes his boots across the mat near the door and slips them off. Exactly the way he used to.

Turning toward me, acknowledging the awkward way I'm still standing gripping onto the open door, his face dips down into a slight frown before he turns his back and heads straight for the family room.

The room where the movies of me as a kid are still playing. Ones he was more than just a passerby in.

Mike being the second star.

God, I really need to move.

Pulling myself off the door and shoving it shut, I turn and follow him in, arriving just in time to see him pause in front of the television, running his hands over the screen where I can just make out the two midget versions of us on the screen, complete with a sad look in his eye to match the one still on his face.

"Jesus. We were so damn naïve then. Didn't have a clue what we were in for."

"We were six, Mike." I snap, hating how riled his words and him being here has made me. "We weren't supposed to have a clue."

"Yeah. Of course." He agrees. "You're right."

Usually I'd be all for someone telling me I'm right, but now? Not so much. I don't need him coddling or placating me. We've passed that stage in whatever this new version of our relationship is.

Making his way over to the sofa and throwing himself down, he keeps his eyes trained on the television, not so much as twitching when I take the spot on the other end and turn toward him.

"What are you doing here, Mike?"

"I honestly don't know."

Sure he doesn't. He forgets how long we've known each other. He doesn't do anything without having it all planned out first.

"Try again. I know you too well to believe that."

"Not as well as you used to."

"Can't exactly argue with that."

Running a hand through his hair he finally tears his eyes away from the screen and turns toward me. "It was just another day. I went to work and was heading home like always, and of course, I have to pass by your place. I've done it a million times it seems since things fell apart, but this time, I turned into your driveway instead of just driving past."

"And why do you think that is?"

"Honestly?"

"Always."

"I had a shit day and I wanted to tell your mom about it."

Another way we're alike. When we both ended up getting jobs when we were younger, I wasn't the only one that would climb those stairs and talk to my mom about the day when it was rough. Mike did too. Sometimes even more than I did. With her being gone for so long now though, his bringing it up now just stings where before it would have probably made me smile.

"You missed hearing her tell you to slap on your big boy underroos that much?" I lamely joke and he laughs. The first genuine laugh I've heard from anyone, much less him, since before I lost her.

"Something like that."

"If it helps, I can do it for her."

Shaking his head, but his face betraying him as his lips lift in the faintest trace of a smile, he starts tapping on his knees.

This is what we've become. We're nervous around one another. Even a happy memory like the one I just joked about not helping ease it.

"Em, I miss you. This shit isn't right. The truth is, tonight wasn't the first night I turned into your place. It's just the first that I've admitted to. I've done it a lot. For the first couple of weeks I actually had to pull the car to a stop before I even made it onto our street because my body just wanted to turn in here out of habit."

What the hell am I supposed to say to that?

He's the one that made the choice to walk away from our friendship. Sure, I led him on not putting my foot down about our relationship before Brady came into the picture, but I didn't tell him to go.

He did that all on his own.

"When Rebecca died, I wanted to be here even more. I didn't want you going through it alone, but after the way we left things, I didn't want to just assume and show up either. I mean, you had Avery so you probably didn't even need or want me here."

"I always want you here, Mike."

Swivelling his head up, his gaze lands on mine and what I catch looking back at me just breaks my heart all over again.

He's surprised by my response. All of those years being attached at the hip and because of one moment in time that I hated even having to happen, he's doubting what should be a no brainer.

I don't care where I go in life, I'm always going to need my best friend.

"Even after everything?"

"Especially after everything."

We mean different everything's, but I don't care. Right now, what I said encompasses them all.

Looks like my heart and my head finally picked a side after all. The side where I admit that my best friend, no matter how many times he walks away or how often I screw the pooch, is always going to be my best friend.

Slipping his hands off his knees and laying them down flat on the sofa, he shifts and in the time it takes me to blink, he's bridged the gap between us and his arms are coming around me. Just the way I imagined them doing so many times since the night he walked out of my life, but didn't think I would ever be deserving of again.

"God, Emery. I was a total ass. I knew the way you felt about me. I always have. I just hoped I could change your mind.

Leaving the way I did, turning my back on you and then every damn day I spent alone after it, it was so damn wrong."

Freeing my arms from their place inside his embrace and bringing them around his back, I pull him tighter to me, holding on for dear life.

"I screwed up with you, Mike. I didn't deal with things the right way. You're not the only one that messed things up."

"I'm sorry I wasn't here for you." He apologizes. "There's only one place I need to be when I'm not with my folks or working, and that's with you. My place has always been with you."

"I didn't exactly make it easy to be with me, Mikey. How can you be there for me when I make it impossible?"

Silence dominates the space as he pulls out of the embrace and leans back. Moving away from me but not so far that I feel the same distance I did when we first sat down.

We're not at opposite ends anymore. We're definitely not where we were, but at least it's an improvement. I didn't realize just how badly I wanted to be this close with him again until I was actually living it.

I'm happy he was the one on the other side of the door.

"How are things with Raines?" he asks lightly, glancing at me, but pulling away before I have a chance to meet it. The awkwardness of our last time here together obviously still eating at him.

"Things are..." I pause, wanting to come up with just the right word for exactly what Brady and I are to each other. "They're complicated. Non-existent really."

The man dominates my heart more than the one sitting beside me, but I'm still sitting here trying to talk myself into him meaning nothing. Obviously not taking anything my mother said in her letter to heart.

"That bad, huh?"

"Yeah..."

Tapping on his legs again, Mike tuts under his breath before finally raising his head and turning back to me with a soft smile. One he's used a lot over the years and one that I just know means that while we're not going to talk about it, he does understand.

"Well, rich boy's loss is my gain."

Shifting his body closer, my heart catches in my chest. Flashbacks of the last time we were here together springing to life so vividly they're impossible to ignore.

Please God, don't make me have to do this again. Please don't make me lose my best friend right when I get him back. I don't think my heart can take it.

"Mike...I—"

"Shut up, Em." He says smiling even brighter than before. Throwing his arm over the back of the sofa, his hand falling against the back of my neck, he pulls me closer to him. Confusing me all to hell in the process.

Just what the hell is this?

"It's not my gain because of the way I feel about you. It's my gain because I get to spend the rest of the night with my best friend watching our greatest hits and honoring a woman that was just as much my mom as my own was."

This. His answer. It's all the proof I need that what she said in her letter is right.

Rebecca Davis really is here and this time, she came bearing gifts. My best friend.

Thanks Mom.

Chapter Six

Jax

"You know," the no nonsense rasp of a man I thought I'd never see again interrupts at the exact moment the paint brush in my hand touches the wall. "When word got back that you'd pulled out and gone domestic, I called bullshit. There's no way the god damned Mojo Master had given it all up to become a homebody. Looks like the jokes on me."

I've had quite a few people stopping in since I officially moved into the place and begun renovations, but the last person I ever expected to grace my doorway was Smith.

Especially since the last time we spoke, I screwed him over.

"Well, believe it." I shrug before turning my attention back to the paint brush and the touch up demanding my attention.

Hearing the scuff of his feet across the hardwood floor, I do my best to focus on the task at hand and not on the surprise of him actually being here. Knowing deep down what him standing here is for and as determined as I was the day I slapped down the payment on this place not to fall victim to it again.

Wrestling, no matter how much I loved it at one point, is in my past.

"What do you want, Smith? Figured we said all we needed to when I didn't show up in Vegas."

Truth is, we said everything the day after that when he called and spent the better part of an hour ripping me a new asshole, but I don't exactly feel like getting into that again. Shit was said that if I was grudge holding man, I'd want to pound on him for, and that's not allowed here.

"I came to try and talk some sense into you, boy."

"Well in that case, you wasted a trip. And I'm not your boy."

"So that's how we're gonna do this, huh? Fine." He grumbles, making his way over to the wall to the left of me and leaning against it.

Annoyed by his presence, but even more so with the way I seem to just be okay with what I know is the real reason for him standing here, I huff out a breath, blowing the stray hairs that had fallen out of my half ass ponytail from my face before stomping my way down the ladder. Making sure to move across the room to where he stood when he came in and started playing this game.

A game that if I don't go along with, will have me breaking the promises I made for the place. Something I can't have happen because they're the only thing with all of the time on my hands I've got to hold onto.

What seems to be the only thing keeping me upright without her.

"If you came here to go off again about what happened, spare me. You said it all back then and contrary to popular opinion, I heard you loud and clear. I'm not really in the mood for a repeat. I'm too hard headed for your 'sense'."

"Merrick, for every ounce of talent and heart you have, you've got double it in stupidity."

Just like I suspected, he's starting off with a bang. If he's here to get me back the way I assume, he would have been better off sending Marie. At least her way of doing business isn't going directly to insults. You'd think with the amount of time they've been married and running this show together, he'd have picked up a thing or two by now.

Looks like I'm not the only stupid one in the room.

"Maybe that's why we always worked so well together, huh?" I joke, but as expected by the way his mouth caves, it falls flat.

"How many years we work together?" he asks, shifting back off the wall and moving toward me. "Five years? Ten?"

"About seven." I begrudgingly admit. "What's your point?"

"My point is, you don't spend that amount of time with someone, working relationship or otherwise, and not end up knowing them almost as well as they know themselves. Whether you want to admit it or not, I know you, Merrick. And this," he motions around the room. "This isn't you. This is beneath you."

He's wrong. Wanting to lay down roots, live out of something that isn't a duffel bag or a suitcase, that's not beneath me. It's not beneath anyone. It's what half the guys that are still working with him want for Christ's sakes, even if none of them have the balls to admit it. We all want a place to call home. Someplace the rest of the world and this damn business can't penetrate.

"No, Smith, it's not beneath me. It's just me finally doing something that's right for me."

"So what's right for you is locking yourself away from everyone and everything, working on a house for some chick that probably won't ever see it? All those years training and busting your ass in the piece of shit promotions for scraps just so you could entertain the masses with your god given talent, that was all for nothing?"

"No." I answer quickly, biting my tongue on what I really want to say. What his pot shot about Avery was supposed to get out of me given the smirk he's wearing.

Too bad, old man. You're not winning this round.

"Two months, Merrick. You've been away from the ring for almost two months. I've checked. Not even one of those matches for scraps is on your record. What the fuck you been doing with yourself all that time besides turning yourself into some kind of biblical carpenter?"

"Something tells me you already know what I've been doing so I'm not gonna waste my breath. Now, like I said when you got here, I'm not in the mood for another speech. I do have parents more than willing to give me that if and when I need it. So put your cards on the table or leave. I've gotta get this wall finished."

It's a lame excuse. Having ample time on my hands means I can get to the walls and all of the other tasks I've taken on since buying the house whenever the hell I want, but if it gets rid of him, I'm prepared to be even lamer.

"You're right, I do know where you've been or rather who you've been spending all of your time on, and you know how I feel about that shit. I think you're wasting your time. Time that could be served rising to the top of CPW where you belong and being the man at the top of this industry."

For a married man, there is no one more anti-relationship than Radley Smith. Sometimes I'm amazed he even took the plunge at all with how dead set against it he is. My time in CPW proving on more than one occasion just how far he would go to eliminate relationships between people on the roster, let alone creating the very drama he hates so much in an effort to get his guys heads screwed on straight.

He's one hundred percent business, one hundred percent of the time.

It's also a one hundred percent failure now.

"You telling me that. Is it supposed to get me to crumble and admit that not heading to Vegas was a mistake? Or do you want to go even deeper than that? Admit that once upon a time, wrestling was all I lived for, all I thought I was good at, and I've been wasting away every day since making the decision not to show up? Because, Smith, I gotta tell you, if that's what you came for, you really are wasting your time and your airfare."

Having had enough, I pull myself out of the entry way and make my way around into the kitchen. Yanking the fridge door open and pulling out a beer, I turn my back completely to him as I twist off the cap and bring the bottle to my lips.

A break that I need, but that in true Smith form, he doesn't let me have for long. Following me in after the first swallow and motioning to the fridge with a grunt.

Prolonging this any longer is the last damn thing I want, but exactly what I give into as I reach back in and grab one of the cans on the shelf and toss it to him.

"In all my years doing this," he starts after cracking the top and taking his own swallow. "And I'm talking back when I was the one in the middle of the ring, there's only been a handful of guys that I knew beyond a shadow of a doubt had what it took to succeed in this business. That were able to put up with all the sacrifices wanting to do this for a living causes you to make."

"And I'm one of them?"

"Yeah, but you already knew that. You're aware of how good you are. That's never been in doubt, though there was a time not that long ago when situations you found yourself in made you begin to question your place."

Situations. That's funny. I suppose if I was going to bring up the Melinda Era, I'd want to call it a situation too. Makes it sound a whole lot better than what it actually was.

"I was doubting it long before that so called situation you're talking about." I admit and I'm taken aback when he nods like he's aware of it. Considering how long I went not admitting to myself just how disconnected I'd become from the one thing that up until that point I'd claimed to love more than anything, his awareness makes no sense.

"I'm aware of that, but given how quickly you seemed to shake yourself out of it and put your head back in the game, it wasn't something I needed to concern myself with. Not the way I did with Melinda anyway."

And there it is. My situation finally has a name.

Bringing the bottle to my lips, I don't stop until I drain it dry, putting my entire focus into the way the liquid feels as it makes its way down my throat. Anything that keeps me from having to acknowledge the only thing worse than having him berate me.

Melinda is not only a reminder of one of the worst betrayals in my life, but also everything I've managed to lose since.

"I'm not..." I pause, placing the bottle down on the counter. "I'm not that guy anymore, Smith."

"Like fuck you're not." He barks out in disagreement. "You might not be the snot nosed baby face you were when you walked into my gym all those years ago. I'll give ya that, but in every other way, you're exactly the same. You've got this in your blood, boy. You were born for this and no chick, no matter how magical her pussy may be, is gonna change it."

There's strike two. I'd let the first one go, but the more he opens his mouth and lets the shit fall out, the less peaceful I become. I'm willing to take a lot of crap, especially when it's basically him just calling me the biggest screw up on the planet, but he's not gonna make light of Avery.

I refuse to have her treated like a piece of ass.

"I can tell by the fire I just lit up under your ass that you don't agree with my assessment." He laughs as I flex my hand, balling it into a fist and stepping toward him. "But I didn't come here for your agreement. I came here to prove a point."

"So you want me to take your damn head off?"

"If that's what it takes, you're damn right."

Having bridged the short gap between us, there only being maybe half a step before I'm right up in his face and handing his ass to him the way he deserves, I pause. The reality of what he's doing and what I was about to willingly give him shooting straight into me, leaving me scrambling for control.

"I don't know who this chick is or what went on between the two of you, but if I have to use her to get rid of the dead look you've been wearing since I got here, I'll do it."

"She's everything, Smith. She's fucking everything. So whatever nasty comment you've got lined up next in order to piss me off, I suggest keeping it to yourself. I respect the hell out of you, but I won't hesitate to lay your old ass out."

Grinning like I didn't just threaten him, he takes the half a step between us, slinging his arm around and slapping me on the back. His boisterous gravelly laughter filling the space.

"That's the Merrick I came for. Now what do you say you grab us another couple of beers and we take them out back? I've got a proposition for ya."

*****

After the run in with Smith, the offer he placed on the table, and what he was expecting my answer to by days end, the last place I wanted to be was the house. With as badly as I wanted to fill it with love, it was the last feeling that came to mind as I made my way around after he made his exit. So freeing myself from the vice his visit put me in, I jumped behind the wheel and drove to the one place in the entire world that would give me the relative peace I was after.

My sisters' place.

"Uncle Jax!"

Running full steam at me after Denise opens the door is the little ankle biter I've spent the last several months away from and missing. Making good on his nickname by wrapping his tiny body around my leg and making it impossible to move.

"Logan! You've been told about doing that." Denise admonishes, making Logan's grip tighter.

Shifting my leg to get used to the extra weight, I laugh when he makes no attempt to get off after I've taken a step. Waiting until I've made my way halfway to the kitchen before finally releasing the hold.

"Did you feel how hard I was holding on? I'm getting stronger, right?"

Right from the time he was born, my sister never hid what I did for a living from him. Choosing instead to embrace it and take her support a step further by bringing him to the shows. Most of the time, she didn't get to stick around very long, but her trying went a long way. Those shows, she likes to tell me, being what sparked Logan's eventual interest in wrestling and his need to show off for me every chance he gets.

"Yeah, buddy, you are. When you tightened the hold you actually made me lose feeling." I offer up in confirmation, there being more truth to what I said than I like to admit. "You get a little bigger and I won't stand a chance."

"See, Mom! Told you!" he smirks smugly at Denise, causing her to shake her head before turning to me and rolling her eyes, silently telling me off with the words she mouths.

This is all your fault.

"Not that I'm complaining about my little brother stopping in for a visit, but don't you usually call before you pop down?"

"Yeah, sorry. It was a spur of the moment thing."

"Something else I have no familiarity with. Since when do you have time? Doesn't that promoter you work for keep you pretty booked?"

Damnit. She really has the target in her sights this time. I'm screwed. She'll probably figure everything out about Avery before I even get the chance to say her name.

"Usually yeah. That's kind of why I'm here."

Motioning to the table when we finally make our way into the kitchen, I take her up on the offer and throw my weary body down onto the seat as Logan runs to the fridge, grabs a juice box and with a yell that he'd catch me later, books it straight back out.

Great. Even he knows the shit is about to hit the fan.

"Alright, Jackson." She starts, pulling out a seat across from me and settling in. "What's going on?"

"Something happened a month or so ago. Things are different now."

"Okay. Since you wanna play the vague game, I'll bite. What happened?"

"It's actually been longer than that. I don't know anymore. Time's kind of gotten away from me."

Reaching across the table, something in my words or maybe even my expression giving me away, she squeezes my hand. Her silent way of letting me know that she's here and listening.

"What happened, baby bro? I didn't catch it at first, probably because Logan jumped you, but what has you looking so sad?"

"I met someone." I painfully admit, wanting to tell her more but needing more time. This isn't easy, even when I'm sitting with the person I trust most.

"Okay..." she drawls. "Does this someone have a name?"

"Avery."

Mulling over the name, she hums to herself before smiling softly my way. "That's different."

"Yeah."

"So if there's a new person in your life, why do you look like someone backed over your board?"

Leave it to my sister to think of my most prized possession and use it to get her point across. I'm a morose mother fucker and she wants to know why.

Instead of answering and letting the entire thing pour out, though, I take a different route.

"What's the one thing that could come between me and happiness?"

"Oh god damnit, Jackson! Don't tell me the she-witch put herself in the middle of things!" Denise exclaims, bringing her hand down hard on top of mine. "Better yet, don't you dare say that you let her do it!"

"I didn't let her do shit, Deni."

It's not lost on me that I just lied to my sister. Something that no matter what kind of crap I got caught up in when we were younger, I've never done.

"What did she do this time, huh? Call this new lady and threaten her? Show her video of the two of you that she taped without you knowing? What tricks did she pull out of her bag and screw you over with?"

You would think that me being the guy, I'd be the super protective one when it comes to my sisters, but that's not how the Merrick family works. I was always the softer one. Always the one that needed the backup instead of being it. Denise coming to my rescue more times than I can count and apparently, even though I'm edging closer to thirty, still doing it.

"I told you I got rid of the video the last time she tried pulling that, Deni. She didn't do anything like that this time. Just sent a text."

Settling back into her seat, she sighs.

"What kind of text? Was it this sexting crap that Travis's buddies keep trying to talk him into doing with me?"

"Gross, Denise. I didn't need to know that." I gag. The last image I need one of my sister sexting with Travis. It's called privacy for a reason.

"Spill it, Jax. You've never held back before, so don't start that shit now. No changing the subject either. What the hell did Melinda do that's got you so twisted?"

"She sent a text saying she missed me." Seeing the wheels turning in her head, I cut her off at the pass. "And before you ask, no. I didn't respond."

"Then what exactly is the problem? If you didn't text her back, no harm no foul."

"Except all there is harm and foul."

"How so?"

"I didn't delete it. Avery…" *Shit. This is hard as hell.* "I got it and didn't do a damn thing with it. No response, but no delete either. I kept the damn thing on my phone and every time I went into the messages, even when I was texting you, I saw it. I let it twist me up and she caught on. Called me on my change in attitude and instead of telling the truth, I blew her off. Kept telling her it was nothing and she was reading too much into it."

"Holy shit, Jax."

My sister doesn't curse often. Usually it only happens when she's pissed. She's cursed more since I got here than she has in the last ten years, I'm sure of it.

"I know, alright. I should have said something the first time she asked if I was alright, but I just thought it would pass. Whatever the hell it was with me and that text, I'd get over it, delete it and move on."

"Why did you keep it in the first place?"

"Curiosity?" I lamely answer. "I don't know, honestly. I was trying to sort out why it was happening. What had changed or if she knew about Avery. Instead of telling her to screw herself, I let it eat at me until Avery, in an attempt to find out what was really going on, found it."

"Have you tried telling her this?"

"Yeah, but just in messages since she won't pick up when I call. I want to be able to sit down and tell her everything face to face, but she's not—she doesn't want to hear it."

Pushing the chair back from the table and standing, she makes her way over to the coffeemaker on her counter, pulling down two mugs and proceeding to fill them before turning her attention back to me.

"What are you doing?"

"Something tells me that there's a whole lot more going on here that you haven't told me yet and if I'm gonna hear it, I need coffee."

Can't fault her for that. If she drank, I'd tell her to go ahead and spike it with all of the crap I still have to say.

"You still take yours black?"

"Yeah."

Reaching into the fridge, she pulls out the milk, pouring even amounts into both cups before placing it back in, picking up both mugs and making her back way to the table.

"Alright, little brother, let's have the rest."

"I could tell something changed when I came back downstairs. We were supposed to head out into the city and spend the day together, but when I walked into the living room, she was curled into a ball on the carpet. She was crying so hard I swear you could actually make out stains in it.

"Over the text?"

"No." I shake my head, wishing it was that easy. "Right before I came down she got a call from her twin sister. It's a long story, those two, but her sister called because their mom passed away."

"Oh my god." She gasps and on that note, I let her have the rest.

"I could tell there was something brewing between us, but because all I wanted to do was console her, I pulled her into my lap and let her cry it out. Putting the rest of it out of my head. We must have sat that way for an hour or so before her entire demeanor just changed. She pulled away, got on her computer right after to book the first flight out and honestly, everything is a blur after that. We didn't say so much as two words to each other the entire time we ran around packing and I didn't get the chance to hold her again after either."

"Why not? Jackson, what aren't you saying?"

"I was going to change my flight to Vegas so I could be with her, but when we got in the car, the shift I was telling you about, it hit a head. She confronted me about Melinda and I didn't say shit. I froze. I was so wrapped up in making her understand that what I felt for her was real, that what we shared wasn't a one off thing, and focusing on the loss she suffered that when the question came, I sat there blank."

"Okay, wow."

"There's more."

"What else can there possibly be?"

"The days off. I had to sign a termination agreement in order to have them."

"I think I'm gonna need something a little stronger than coffee."

My thoughts exactly. An entire bottle of scotch sounded great right about now.

"I couldn't let her go through this alone, Deni."

"So you thought you'd what? Blow up your entire life instead?"

"It's not like that."

"It's not?" she asks, glaring. "From the time you were old enough to walk, all you wanted to do was wrestle. When it came on the TV you were glued. So none of us were shocked when you announced you wanted to do it. It made all the sense in the world. We believed in you. We still do."

"Things change." I lamely argue and she just shakes her head.

"Not with you they don't. Hell, half the reason you dated the she-devil to begin with was because she understood what it was like. You two were in it together. Even disliking her the way we all did, we liked that about her. She got you. Wrestling is who you are, Jax."

"No!" I bite out angrily. "Wrestling is—*was*—what I do, Deni. Not who I am. Not anymore."

"Since you met Avery, you mean."

"Wrong. Since before Melinda. I just didn't give it the focus I should have."

"Jackson, how bad are things, really? Are you still with CPW or did you end up following the girl home and throwing it all away?"

This was a mistake. No matter how much I missed her and Logan, I never should have come here. She thinks I made a mistake and no matter how much I wish I could agree, it's something we won't ever see eye to eye on. Avery wasn't a mistake.

She's the only damn thing in the last five years I've done right.

"What part of *I couldn't leave her alone* aren't you hearing? She just lost her mother. Twenty four hours before that, I told her I love her. Something that even though the rest of you can throw it around like it doesn't matter, I can't do. I meant it. She got under my skin. Even deeper really. She's in my bones. You don't leave someone you love like that to fend for themselves. Even when you're part of the reason they're messed up."

"Jackson..."

She wants to tell me off, I can hear it in the way she says my name, but I can also tell that something I've said is getting through too. She's being reminded of who I am away from wrestling. Who I was before I let the sport dominate my life.

Denise sees her little brother.

"I love her, Deni." I choke out through a swell of emotion so strong it threatens to make my entire chest collapse under its weight.

"I see that."

"I changed the flight Smith booked and god damnit, I followed her to Delaware. Even if she didn't want to see me, I was determined that I would be there for her. The same way that you always were for me."

"And where is she now, Jax? I mean, you're sitting here practically breaking over a cup of crappy coffee, pouring your entire heart out. Where is this girl you love so much that you're willing to throw everything away?"

"She's at home. What does that have to do with anything?"

"It doesn't, other than her not being here with you. Where, if she loves you half as much as you obviously do her, she should be." She says bitterly and even though I see her point we're at odds again because all I want to do is defend Avery.

Make my sister understand exactly what happened and why she can't be here.

"It's not her fault, damnit. Didn't you hear me before?"

"Yes, Jax, I heard you loud and clear, but I don't see it the same way you do."

"Melinda's text. Finding it. My change in attitude over the two days we were together, all of it starting the night after we made love for the first time. Then her sister's call about her mother. A mother that until the day she met me she had never so much as spoken a word to. How the hell is she supposed to be reacting right now?"

"I don't know! I'm not her!" Denise snaps, finally raising her voice to match mine. "But unless there's something I'm missing, you didn't do anything wrong apart from being a bonehead that was too afraid to man up and admit he'd gotten a text from his ex."

She makes it seem so simple.

"Which in case you think I'm sitting here wanting to attack the woman you love, means that yeah, I do think you screwed up. But everything else, Jax. I love how you want to take it all onto yourself like this, but it's not your fault. You didn't cause her mother to die. Life sucking major ass did that. Stop taking all of this on yourself."

"How do I do that, Deni?"

"Give her time. Go back out on the road, do your thing and move on."

The only moving on I'm planning on doing is with Avery. End of.

It's just too bad I don't get the chance to tell her that before she's starting again. This time moving her chair in and reaching across the table to bring my hand into hers.

"If she loves you, and yes, I said if, she'll come to you. I know you want to be there for her and make sure she doesn't have to go through any of this alone, but sweetheart, you can't force it. She's going to have to come to terms with her loss and what happened between the two of you on her own. Do you understand that?"

I do understand it, but in understanding, I can't help feeling like I'm letting Avery down. That if I do what Denise says and take a step back, it will be the end of us.

An end I'm not ready to accept.

"I hear you, but now it's time for you to hear me. There is no if when it comes to Avery. She loves me, I love her, and I'll wait or fight for as long as it takes. She's been doing things on her own for so long she doesn't know how to depend on someone. I want to be the one that changes that. I want to be the one that changes everything."

Chapter Seven

Avery

Alright, Ave. You got this. Just follow along with the people in front of you, grab a seat and you're set.

Sounds easy enough, but it's not.

I mean, who exactly am I trying to kid here?

My boss? The people at Canoe?

I'm not the right person for this job, no matter how great my summarizing skills are. I'm out of my element here. Hell, this is something Emery would be able to do blindfolded. She should be the one entering this run down gymnasium and doing a write up on this show. Not me.

Following the flow of people and doing exactly as the voice commanding the pep talk I gave myself when I pulled up and got out of the car, I take my seat and glance around nervously.

Almost positive as I do that all of the hardcore wrestling fans all in conversation with the people surrounding them can spot the one person that doesn't belong.

I may have poured over videos of Jackson over the last seven weeks, learning a bit about what he does for a living, but doing that does not a real wrestling fan make. I'm just as green as I was the night Emery dragged me to the show in Delaware.

Take who's on the card for instance.

I have no idea who any of these people are. If they're like Jackson and are labeled risk takers and high flyers, or they're more grounded like Brady, where a lot of his skill is mat based. I don't know the champions from the jobbers (thanks for that Markus) or who the person to beat is.

All I really know is I've got a front row seat to the mess that is about to be me and HFWA.

Reaching into my purse and grabbing out the notepad and pen I stored there to keep track of the matches, highlights, and winners and losers, I lay them across my lap and toss the bag to the floor. Lifting my head just in time to hear a throat clearing to my left.

"Oh, I'm sorry." I blush in embarrassment when I acknowledge the guy sporting a set of the grayest eyes I've ever seen. A guy that if I had to guess is a pretty hardcore fan given the shirt he's wearing emblazoned with the promotion logo.

Shifting my legs to the side and letting him pass, I lower my gaze to the notepad filled with notes I'd taken before making the drive across town. Attempting to make sense of as much as possible before the lights dim and the show starts.

A move that the guy I let pass doesn't seem to want to let me do as he lifts and turns his chair toward me before sitting down and coughing to get my attention.

"First time at a Harbour Front show?"

Cheeks heating, hating the fact that yeah, despite all of the research I'd done once I accepted the job, I'm still a newbie, I nod slowly.

"Figured as much. You definitely don't fit here."

Gee thanks, asshole. Like I didn't already know that.

Wishing I had the balls needed to be able to say what I'm really thinking but failing miserably in that department with how out of my element I am, I just paste on the same lame smile I've been doing for weeks when I have assignments.

"Who are you reporting for?" he asks softer this time, motioning with his hand toward the pad in my lap when I stare through him, confused.

"Canoe."

"Ahhh, right. I asked Adam to send someone."

He asked Adam to send someone. Hmm.

Maybe this guy isn't some hardcore fan after all. Especially not if he's on a first named basis with Markus's contact.

Given his size and the way he fills out the shirt he's wearing, I can't believe I didn't catch on to it sooner. He's one of the guys on the card tonight. He has to be.

"Looks like I'm that someone."

"Pretty attractive someone." He admires and I don't even attempt to hide my eye roll.

It figures the person that sits here is one that's gonna spend the night hitting on me.

What was I thinking agreeing to this?

I can barely handle one of the girls at work telling me my hair looks great when I run a damn brush through it. I'm definitely not in the mood to get hit on by a sleazebag wrestler.

A wrestler that's apparently gonna keep up the charade since he's holding his hand out between us for me to take.

"I'm Bryan Michaelchuk."

Slipping my hand into his and shaking it, alarm bells start going off in my head.

Shit. Shit. Shit. I just called the co-owner of HFWA a sleazebag.

"Avery...Davis."

There's a second when I drop my name that I'm waiting for him to recognize me. Like the week with Jax had been more public than either of us were aware of. But when Bryan displays no recognition at all, just returning my tight smile with a much brighter one, I put it to bed.

Thank God. I'm not sure what I would have done if my name somehow preceded me.

"Can I be honest with you about something, Avery?" he leans in whispering as more people join us in the seats to his right.

"Sure." After thinking he was a wrestler and calling him a sleazebag, he can tell me whatever the hell he wants. It's the least I can do.

"This is the third event I've reached out to Adam about in an attempt to get coverage and he's never sent anyone that remotely looks like you. Dude with a beer gut. Check. Bald guy with tattoos in place of his hair. Check that one too. But a woman? No way."

I'm starting to see why he commented on me being attractive earlier. With what he's had to work with, I have to be a step up.

"Are you saying this isn't a place for women?"

"Fuck no. What I'm saying is, women that wear blazers with jeans and a blouse don't normally come here. You stand out, sweetheart."

Heart seizing the second the endearment falls, I pull away and lower my gaze to my lap again. This is too close to home, even if the guy is a stranger.

"My boss told me the same thing when he hired me." I mumble and even with breaking eye contact and looking away, it doesn't seem to stop Bryan as he laughs.

"I can see that. Look, I'm sorry about the comment I made earlier. I'm not perving on you, I promise. It's like I said. You stand out."

Standing out is the last thing I wanted to do when I got here, preferring to just melt into the background and let the others around me take over. But given that this isn't my scene and I knew it even before I took the job, it's not surprising.

A wrestling fangirl I'm not.

"Sorry about that. I didn't really think about the way I was dressed before I came."

Shaking his head, he leans his body back into the seat and sighs.

"I'm messing this whole thing up, so let me try again." Turning back toward me, he extends his hand again. Looking up and meeting him head on, this time a smile on my face that's surprisingly natural, I take it and he does what he promised.

He starts over.

"Hi. My name is Bryan and I'm horribly inept at talking to people. I'm also the guy that should have followed up his standing out comment with what he really meant to say. I like the fact that you aren't like anyone else here, and when I head to the back in a few minutes to go over things with my guys, I'm definitely going to be ringing Adam and thanking his ass for sending you."

"Nice to meet you, Bryan." I play along. "I'm Avery. The reporter that you've successfully embarrassed with your incredibly kind words."

"Ha! Embarrassment! Now that definitely beats offending you, which I'm pretty sure I was dangerously close to a minute ago. I'll take it."

Maybe this wasn't such a mistake after all. If Bryan can make fun of himself like this, basically throwing himself at some unknown reporter's mercy, maybe I can make it through the show unscathed.

Well, I can if I use his being here now to my advantage.

"I thought you were a wrestler when you first sat down." I tell him, affectively throwing myself under the bus. "I also thought you were hitting on me."

"Ahhh, I see this isn't your first rodeo after all. You, Avery Davis, have gotten around."

If falling in love with a wrestler is getting around, then you're damn right I did.

"That would be my twin sister, actually." I say instead. "I guess I just know guys."

"If I had feelings, you would be hurting them, sweetheart." He jokes. "But you're not exactly wrong. Evolution didn't quite take with a few of us Neanderthals. We see a woman, we grunt, slam our chests and then proceed to act like our bottom ends and let the shit fly."

Alright, it's official. I'm really glad I took this assignment. That has got to be the best damn explanation for guys acting like asses I've heard in a while. If ever.

"But not you."

"Basically. Don't know about most guys, but I like my balls where they are." He motions down with a wiggle of his brow. "And on that note, I think I'm gonna head to the back and make sure everything's ready to go. I hope you enjoy the show."

Reaching out when he stands and brushing my hand across his arm before he can excuse himself in order to leave, he turns those gray eyes of destruction back on me again with a dip of his head.

"Before you go, do you think you can answer a question?"

"Sure."

Slipping the colored program out from under the pad in my lap and flipping it open, I tap the bottom of the page and he grins like he already knows the question I'm going to ask.

"Why is the main event slot empty?"

"If I told you that," he answers playfully. "I've have to kill you, and I don't think you need me to tell you that doing that would be a crying shame. What I will say is that you picked a good night to be here."

"Why's that?" I ask, curious. "What's so different about tonight?"

Pointing to the ring, his playful grin still firmly in place, he laughs before filling me in.

"Because tonight after you see the main event, I have a feeling your twin won't be the only wrestling fan in the family."

"That sure of yourself, huh?"

"Always, sweetheart. Mark my words. Tonight, after you see what we've got lined up, you'll be a believer."

"A believer in what, exactly?"

"Magic."

Brady

Six matches. All of them running anywhere from ten minutes to twenty. Six matches I've watched play out from behind the curtain, and six damn matches that in watching them, have made me question just why the fuck I'm in the main event.

The women's match, the second of the night, exceeding all of my expectations. A match that given the way Smith ran his own women's division in CPW, is what I figure to be the gold standard. A performance so strong it could have very well been the main event.

Bryan and Reese may only be starting out with their promotion, but the level of talent they have and how dedicated everyone seems to be for the peanuts they're going to make tonight, speaks volumes. Serving to make me feel even more inadequate.

I'm confident in my ability. That's not in question, but with what I'm witnessing here, I've got to step it up tonight if I want to come across half as good as the people that went before me.

"You ready to do this?" Kris asks and keeping my eyes glued to the ring and the match currently running, I swallow down a lingering lump of nervousness and nod.

"Don't sweat this, Raines. We got it. Bryan wouldn't have given us the spot if he didn't think so."

Sure. I get that. If the owner didn't believe in what we could do together, or even what we could do separately, we'd be stuck somewhere in the middle of the card. It doesn't shake the first night jitters I've got though. Wanting to prove myself and their support of me right by being even better than what came before me.

I have to summon up some of the Raines cockiness from earlier if I want to make it out of this night alive.

"You ever have nerves this bad before?" I ask him, lifting my hand and letting him see the involuntary tremor. "I went out for air, paced around a shit ton, tried jogging it off. Hell, I even went into the school and beat off in the shower in an attempt to calm myself and still, this is happening."

If he's even remotely offended by the fact that I damn sure gave him too much information, he doesn't show it. He just nods his head in understanding before slapping me across the back.

"I was worse. I used to puke three to five times before every match. It's gotten a lot easier since I came to work for Bry and Reese, but every once in a while, it still hits me."

"It hitting you tonight?"

"Yep. Where the hell you think I've been for most of the night? This is my first main event slot. I'm scared shitless. I'm just better at hiding it than you." Motioning over to the two guys now passing through the curtain, he frowns. "Took getting hazed for months by those two jerkoffs to toughen me up."

Interesting. Maybe the D Master and I aren't so different.

"So basically you're telling me to slap on my big boy tights, go out there and own the show?"

"Pretty much, but making sure to sell me before you steal it."

Steal the show. Hmm. I like it.

Catching Bryan's signal from across the room, I return Kris's slap on the back and when he tosses me a look, clue him in with a quick motion to my new boss.

"Looks like we're up."

"See you out there." He grins and giving myself one final shake, even more determined to shake off not only the few weeks of ring rust I'd gained, but the nerves that are still dominating my mind, I nod and make my way over to where any second, the music I chose earlier in the night will announce my arrival.

Bowing my head in reverence once I reach the curtain and bringing two fingers to my lips, I aim to the sky the exact way I did before every match in CPW and bounce from one foot to the other. All of the people around me, the noises other than the beginning bars of my music all shut away. My focus right where it always is when I'm in this position with my face officially steeled for what comes next.

It's just me, my opponent, and the ring.

Time to make it rain.

Ears tuned into the ring announcer as he calls for the final match of the night, one that is for the HFWA Cruiserweight Title, I reach for the curtain and step through as my billed location and weight are announced.

"Hailing from Wilmington, Delaware, weighing in at two hundred and eighteen pounds, the number one contender for the Cruiserweight Title, Brady Raines!!"

The billed weight total bullshit since the weigh in I'd done after arriving earlier is at least thirty pounds larger, is barely a blip on my radar. The way it feels hearing me use the place where my heart resides as my hometown, all I can seem to focus on as I make my way up the aisles.

Slapping the hands of those fans that seem to know who I am based on the name and smirking much the way I did during my 'rich boy' run in CPW, I strut the rest of the way to the ring steps cocky, the confidence I seemed to be missing the entire time I stood waiting for my match to start, finally coming back in full force.

Surveying the crowd as I slip in between the ropes, the familiar rush of being here and entertaining the masses surging through and lifting me even higher, my face lifts into a smile. The first genuine one that has nothing to do with character development and storyline that I've worn in what feels like forever.

But a smile that once I turn and look to my right, is wiped clean away when I see the pair of eyes staring back at me from ringside.

Eyes I've been dying to get back to since I stupidly walked away a little over six weeks ago. Eyes that have haunted every single one of my dreams since I took up this plan to work my way back to her.

Eyes that as they raise and take me in, I realize aren't the ones that haunt me after all, but those belonging to her mirror image.

Avery's here.

Dividing my attention between the music belonging to my opponent and the woman now grabbing her purse up from floor and pulling her phone from it, I watch as she brings it all the way up and forgetting all about my role for the night, I do what in any other place would be the unthinkable.

I break kayfabe and blow a kiss directly to her, knowing exactly where it's going to end up.

With Emery.

Chapter Eight

Avery

Bryan wasn't kidding when he said I was going to experience magic by the time the main event rolled around. Because this? What's happening? It shouldn't even be happening at all.

The magic he spoke of, it's the kind that travels you back in time. The kind that erases the last seven or so weeks of your life and brings you back to the moment when everything changed.

That is what's happening after all. Me sitting at ringside, only this time in a more official capacity than last, making me realize that I didn't actually time travel and watching as the man himself, Brady freaking Raines slips through the ropes and makes his way around the ring like he owns it.

We're not in my city anymore. We're back in Delaware, and he's doing the same damn thing, only this time, not for an entire audience, but for one.

Me—err, well Emery.

His in ring presence not all that different from the one I first met him with that day at the gas station. Same familiar smirk in place as he now stalks back and forth as the guy he's going to be facing tonight runs to the ring.

Yeah, you heard me. This guy is running like his pants are on fire. But given the mask he's wearing, along with the rest of his ring attire, I've got a feeling that's the point.

My online video stalking of Jackson not only limited to his time in CPW, but also all of the other little gems that the internet holds onto forever and showing a few matches that took place south of the border in Mexico.

Watching the two of them stare each other down from opposite ends of the ring as the referee makes his way to the center and holds what I have to assume is the Cruiserweight belt in the air for the entire place to see, I take in their differences.

The champion looks like he weighs about fifty pounds less than Brady and is about a foot or so shorter. Both of them are jumping from one foot to the other, but the Dragon Master seeming to fly based on the air he's catching, while Brady stays pretty much planted.

I can't believe I'm actually sitting here dissecting this. Breaking down their random movements like all of that is going to go into the basic results posting I write up for Adam at Canoe.

You know why you're dissecting them, Avery, and it's got nothing to do with the match. It's for Emery.

After Brady blew the kiss and I snapped the picture, I wasted no time sending it to her. Not wanting to cause issues given what happened between them, but wanting her to see that while she's all Team Jackson, I'm firmly in the Brady camp.

Wanting nothing more than for the man to handle his personal issues and get back to loving my sister the way I know deep in my gut that he does. His letter, much like Jax's texts saying everything that based on outside influences and a serious case of bad timing, he hadn't gotten the chance to tell her.

Go figure. I can't fix my own shit but I can sure as hell be the best damn cheerleader Brady Raines has ever had.

How screwed up is that?

Focusing my attention back on the ring, ignoring the relationship, however minimal that I have with one of the combatants, I focus on the real reason I'm here.

The first thing I notice is just how well timed it is. Their bodies seeming to work in perfect sync with each other. One move turning into another so flawlessly that it doesn't even feel like I'm watching a fight at all, but a dance.

A fast one for sure, based on just how quickly Brady seems to be able to turn over the Dragon Master's moves and execute his own. Along with just how quick they are capitalize on certain moves and execute new ones off the ropes.

They're most definitely dancing, but the ring is a third partner.

Magic. It's more than just my being here and Brady being the one performing. It's the entire thing. Each match before the main one displaying little pieces until the entire thing explodes in a sea of movement, color and perfect execution at the end of the night.

I'm starting to see what Emery sees when she goes to shows. This is cool.

"It's magical, right?"

Jumping back at the blast of warmth against my ear, I grab onto the metal chair. Looking up just in time to see Bryan Michaelchuk's eyes dancing with the laughter he's smart enough not to let fall out.

Jackass.

"Thanks for that." I hiss, making sure I'm loud enough for him to hear and he just grins even bigger before sliding his way into the aisle and throwing himself down into the seat beside me, pointing to the ring as he does.

"So what do you think? Was I right? Have I made a fan out of you, Miss Davis?"

"I'll never tell."

Pouting at my answer, I laugh and focusing on where he's still pointing, watch the Dragon Master hit the top rope again. Recreating some kind of somersault move I could have sworn I'd seen Jackson use in one of the dozen or so videos I'd painstakingly watched over the last few weeks. Jumping to my feet with the rest of the crowd when after catching even more air, he lands it.

"You just told me." He grins when I take my seat again and the embarrassment at being caught floods its way straight to my face. Reaching up, I do my best to block it as I hear the slapping on the mat coming from the ring and the bell sounding as the Dragon Master is declared the winner.

Brady, when I finally let my eyes fall to him, selling it for all he's worth as his eyes still remain shut but his body is curved into itself in what looks to be pain.

"No I didn't. I just recognized the move."

"Sure you did. Sorry to disappoint you, Miss Davis, but not even that excuse is gonna erase the way you jumped out of your chair."

"Careful, Mister Michaelchuk, or I'll make sure to include my thoughts on the owner of HFWA when I write up my summary."

Mouth dropping into a deep oval shape before his hand slaps over his mouth dramatically, I laugh. "Not even those theatrics can save you."

"You wouldn't dare."

Before I can respond, I feel the hairs on the back of my neck rise and turning toward it, come face to face with the man who despite losing had put on one hell of a main event match.

"Hey…"

Forgetting about Bryan altogether, I return his smile with one of my own. "Hey, Brady."

"Wait. You two know each other?" Bryan says, eyes flicking between us and I nod as Brady just stands as still as stone, his eyes never once leaving mine.

"You got anywhere to be now?" he whispers after a few seconds of awkward silence and I attempt to divide my attention between the man sandwich I find myself in.

"Not unless you count home. Why?"

"If you give me ten, I'd like to take you for coffee."

"Sure." I say softly, nodding for emphasis, which when he catches it, seems to make the weak smile he'd been wearing finally reach his eyes. A look that if I had to guess, has probably been on my face since everything happened too.

"Great."

Taking his leave as the people surrounding us seem to pick up on him lingering a little too long after the match and attempt to get to him, I turn my attention to Bryan and the smirk waiting.

"Seems like there's a story there."

"There's a story everywhere. Some are just better off not being told."

"Fair enough, but if the look in Brady's eyes is an indication, I'd say he doesn't feel the same."

Of course he assumes there's a romantic angle to what just happened between us. Brady's eyes, which I'm sure have been nothing short of hard and focused since he got here turning decidedly softer when he noticed me, how could it not be seen that way? Too bad he'd be wrong.

"Looks can be deceiving."

"That they can." He agrees. "Now before I let you get back to the next chapter in whatever the story is, I'm gonna need something from you."

"And that is?"

"The truth."

Considering that not two seconds ago, I was determined to not tell him the truth, content to let him believe that something was really going on between Brady and me, I'm not sure how comfortable I am with this.

"Did I make a fan out of you?"

Laughing to disguise the very real breath of relief I take, I lean in and gifting him with one of the only genuine smiles I've been able to manage before tonight, I give him what he's after.

"HFWA fangirl at your service."

*****

"So, I gotta know." I start the second we've grabbed our drinks and made our way to the back of the coffee shop and taken our seats. "How is it that you end up in Canada, Toronto no less, and this is the first I'm hearing of it?"

I'm not familiar with a lot of guys showing their emotions past Jax. Most of them are hard to read, but with the deer caught in headlights look Brady is sporting, it looks like he's another exception.

A look that quickly turns a completely different shade as his eyes seem to lose some of their luster and darken in what looks to be sadness, but when he finally does answer, I realize might just be guilt.

"Yeah, sorry about that. I guess I could have reached out, but after everything, I wasn't exactly sure you'd be open to it."

"I'm not Emery, Brady."

"No, you're not. I know that. You are her sister though and for all I knew, you hate me as much as she does."

Shaking my head, not willing to sit and let him think that Emery hates him when I know it to be the complete opposite, his eyes seem to lighten again as he sees it.

Much better.

"So, I'm pretty sure your new boss thinks we're dating." I attempt to lighten the mood.

"Yeah, I should probably apologize for that too. I just didn't want you to leave before I had a chance to catch up."

"Don't worry about it. I'm pretty sure I'm the reason he thinks it anyway."

"How is she?" he asks, switching gears. "I've wanted to reach out so many damn times but what I said when I wrote her, I meant."

I know what he's getting at, but I don't let on. Emery showing me his letter was her choice and I'm not entirely sure how happy Brady would be to know that it wasn't entirely for her eyes only.

"There's two Emery's right now. Kind of like there seems to be two versions of Avery running around."

"How do you mean?"

"There's the one that we show the rest of the world. The person that's got her shit together despite losing one of the most important people in our lives. We appear happy and alright on the surface, but it's only skin deep because deep down, we're still pretty broken."

"And the other version?"

"The busted up one. The one that stays behind closed doors. Though with Emery it seems like she's coming out of that one more as time goes on. I seem to be stuck there. We cry, we scream, and fall apart. But mostly, we drown in the memories we have of her and the other people that we've lost."

"I wish...I don't want her going through this alone. I hate that I'm not with her."

"She's not alone. I've made sure of that."

"You don't get it." He says, realizing a little too late how he must have sounded and slapping a hand off his forehead before trying to rectify it. "Wait. I didn't mean it like that. Shit."

"It's okay, Brady. I think I know what you're trying to say."

Jax's messages over the course of the first five weeks giving me a hell of a lot of insight into what Brady must be feeling right now. He wants to be there for Emery the same way that Jax wants to do with me.

"Can I tell you something and have it stay between the two of us?"

"Brady, uhh…I don't know."

"Right. Sorry."

I don't want him thinking he can't trust me, but if whatever he's about to say has something to do with Emery or what happened between them, I can't promise I'll keep it from her. All things considered, with everything she told me about her talks with Jackson when she really didn't have to, I want to be the same. No secrets.

"I'm pretty sure you know what happened with us, the same way I know a little about what happened with you and Jax— which, I just wanna say is bullshit by the way."

Right. Bullshit. Even Brady thinking what's going on with us is crap.

"I know some, yeah." I tell him honestly, swallowing down the urge I have to press him for what he knows about Jax.

"Then you know that I chose my family, wrestling, and by default, my ex-wife over her, right?"

I nod because I do know that much, though the way Emery described it, Brady was going home to his wife, which definitely doesn't match with what he's telling me now.

Since when did the wife become the ex-wife?

"I wrote her that letter while I was sitting outside my parents place. I knew I made the wrong choice not even two minutes after I made it. It didn't really hit me until I was on the flight, though. What I wanted to tell you, it was just…" he pauses and I use the time it takes before he starts talking again to bring my coffee cup to my lips and drink. Needing to keep myself busy and appearing to be oblivious for whatever he's about to say next.

"I'm making changes, Avery. I meant what I said. I want to be the guy she deserves and the one she met in her kitchen the day she told me to go? That wasn't someone that deserved her."

"And now?"

"I still don't. Not yet, but I swear to god, when we do see each other again, I will."

Pulling a page straight from my sisters book; I ask him the question that she asked me when I finally broke down and told her the reason why I couldn't reach out to Jax the way it seemed like the world wanted me to.

"What happens if Emery isn't the same person when you see her again?"

"Then I'll have to work even harder to be the man the new version of your sister deserves."

Emery can roll her eyes and tell me off for my support of Brady all she wants, but what he's just said, is the reason why I'm so behind him.

Brady Raines right now is the poster child for determined. Knowing what he wants and going after it, even knowing that in pulling himself completely away, he could end up biting himself in the ass in the process.

It makes me want to put my money where my mouth is.

If Brady is willing to throw himself at the mercy of my sister no matter what the cost, then it's time for me to do the same.

I've gotta talk to Jax.

Chapter Nine

Jax

It's strange being back here.

Even stranger that after the way I wanted to take his head off a week ago when he showed up at my house, I even agreed to it in the first place.

But with everyone telling me what they thought was best for me—being back in the ring and doing what I love—it seemed like the right thing to do at the time.

What I hadn't expected was the blow-up I was going to have with Denise on the phone the night before over it. Going into it under the impression she'd be happy with the news that I'd taken her advice, but on the receiving end of the complete opposite.

*****

Picking up the envelope and tracing a line over the outside, I pull out the ticket inside and study the printed words across it.

A one way ticket to Illinois for the show there tomorrow night. Foxlake, Illinois to be exact. A town that with all of the ones I've been to, is a first for me.

What Smith had come armed with a week ago when he showed up unannounced in an effort to get me back. Also what I'd tried fighting for as long as I could before finally breaking down and agreeing to.

Dropping the ticket to the counter and reaching for my phone as it chimes and vibrates across the marble counter, I press talk and bring it to my ear. Armed and ready to thank the person on the other side for the momentary distraction.

"Yeah?"

I stopped answering my phone the proper way weeks ago. The emotion needed to get out a standard greeting too much. Choosing instead to go about it this way, regardless of who it was on the other end.

Probably not the best thing to do when it's your sister though.

"Jackson, geez. Did you forget how to say hello?"

Yeah, actually, I did. Seems the only thing I'm good at doing these days is saying goodbye.

"Guess so. What's up, Deni?"

"I just got off the phone with Mom and Dad."

That can't be good. After chickening out calling Avery, I'd called them next, filling them in on Smith's visit and what had been decided. After the better part of an hour listening to my old man tell me what a good move this was and how I'd start feeling like myself again in no time, I'd let them go, content I'd made the right move. Something that if they're filling in Denise about it, I'm starting to have serious reservations about.

"Yeah? How are they?"

"They're good, but you already knew that, didn't you? I mean, you're the reason for how upbeat they're sounding."

Yep. It's what I thought. They filled her in on what I'm doing.

"So they told you about me going back to work?"

"Yes, but it was a little bit more than that, Jax. Wrestling is more than just work and you know it."

No, see. We're right back where we were the day after Smith popped by. After I'd dumped everything with Avery at her feet and had to sit there and listen as she tore it all down under the umbrella of caring about me and wanting what was best.

Wrestling is *work. Whether it was a dream of mine as a kid or not. It's still at the end of the day something that I have to put my entire body and focus into on a day to day basis, just like every other working person on the planet.*

She needs to get that wrestling isn't everything. Not anymore. Especially not after I got a taste of what it could be like away from it.

"Are you calling to tell me how happy you are that I took your advice? Because if that's it, save it. I already got it from Mom and Dad."

"Actually, I was calling to ask you what the hell you were thinking."

"Say what?"

"When I told you to get back to doing what you loved, I figured you would have started with a random local show here and there. Not throw yourself right back into being on the road twenty-four seven."

Okay, now I know she's lost her mind. Maybe all the time she's spending alone with Logan while Travis works is finally wearing her down. That's not at all what she said to me the last time we talked. She wanted what I'm doing now.

"You're gonna have to refresh my memory here, sis. Because as I remember it, we almost came to blows in your kitchen over your need to get me back on the road."

"I refer you to my earlier statement." She says with a sigh. "Buying a house and putting down roots in Laguna, you did all of that for a reason. Spending all of your days running from state to state and not having any at home, it's like your place in Los Angeles all over again. So as happy as I am that you're taking my advice, you're also screwing yourself over in the process."

Money. She's talking about money. This house if I had to get rid of it would probably sit on the market for years waiting to sell the same way my condo did. Effectively making me eat all the money I'd spent years saving and put down on it.

Too bad this house isn't like the last one.

This one's not going anywhere, just like when it comes to the person I want sharing it with me, I'm not going anywhere either.

"I get what you're saying, Deni, I do, but you need to stay out of it."

"And let you throw yourself under the bus again?"

"That's not what's happening."

"Yes, Jackson, it is. You might have taken the advice we all gave you, but the way you were torturing yourself over what happened with Avery, you're still doing. You're just going about it in a different way with the same end result."

"And you're putting your damn nose where it doesn't belong, like usual." I snap, finally having enough of the brow beating I seem to be getting from all ends. This is the final straw. I've listened to my parents tell me that I'm making a mistake, Smith has told me I'm acting stupid and making mistakes and now it's Denise's turn.

Well, since I didn't tell them what they could do with their words last week, I'm damn sure going to do it now, no matter how much it pains me.

My choices. What I choose to do with my life, it falls on me. It's not a mess they need to insert themselves into and attempt to clean up.

I know what I'm doing.

"No, Jackson, I'm not." She argues softly, her voice dejected and losing a lot of the steam she started off with. "I'm just looking at this from all angles. Seeing it for what it is. You've always done things in an extreme way, going all in with everything and this is no different. I just want to make sure you know what you're doing."

"I know exactly what I'm doing, and I'd appreciate it if you'd stop seeing everything I do as a giant mistake and actually let me get on with doing it."

"So I should just let you continue hurting yourself?"

God damn. She's making it seem like I'm suicidal. The way she used to watch over me when I was ten or eleven is one thing. I'm twenty-seven now. I've grown up. As much as I love her, I don't need this.

"You're blowing this out of proportion, Deni. Maybe you should focus your attention on your own damn life and stay the hell out of mine. Better yet," I offer up spitefully. "Maybe you can call Jennifer and tell her every damn way she's screwing up hers. I'm sure she'd appreciate it almost as much as I do."

Pulling the phone away from my ear, I hear her gasp before slamming my finger down hard on the screen and ending the call.

Let the entire damn world think I've been pussy whipped or whatever other vulgar shit they want to call my feelings for Avery and my choices for my life. I no longer care. When I do finally get to set things right, I'll prove them all wrong.

Until then, Illinois here I come.

*****

You would think after everything I'd been through, watching my life seemingly implode around me on more than one occasion, I'd be used to the way things went down with Denise. The problem is, fighting with my sister isn't something I've got familiarity with.

It's something we just don't do and sitting here in the makeshift locker room, remembering the call and the anger fueled words I'd spoken, has me feeling even more out of sorts than I was when I first found out Melinda was cheating.

Even worse than having my heart ripped out when Avery exited my car at Pearson Airport and walked away from me and what we had.

It's not right, but it's also not the only thing I managed to screw up in the last twenty-four hours. That happening when after catching my flight and landing in Illinois, I'd come across the other very real change that had taken place in CPW in my absence.

Not only was my road partner persona non grata, but apparently Smith had gotten the bright idea to bring back the very last person I wanted to share space with.

Melinda.

Her returning after such a lengthy absence should have had me turning on my heel and stalking back out the same way I came in, but that's not what happened at all. Because instead of just walking away, I'd called and told Avery all about it instead.

*****

Don't hang up this time. Just let the rings go through and when the machine kicks in, do what you've done with her in the past and just tell her about your day.

Pep talk aside, with the trembling in my hands and the firing squad seeming to go full throttle in my head, I should probably hang up. The last thing I want her hearing is how completely destroyed the last twenty-four hours has made me.

Or the reasons why.

The person I'm turning into now that I've lost her.

"Jackson." Her voice murmurs softly, the sound of it like a punch to the gut as all the air seems to be knocked clear out of my lungs.

This has got to be some kind of sick joke. My mind torturing me after the day I've had. I'm dreaming her voice saying my name. I've gotta be.

"Avery, shit. Is this really you or am I going crazy?"

That's what crazy people do right? They ask the figment of their imagination to confirm or deny their delusions?

"It's really me."

She sounds so good. Her voice, just like it was all those weeks ago, feeling like home. The softness of it mixed with the lift near the end, clearing the haze of the last few weeks just like I told her.

God, I've missed her. Missed this.

My heart hammers in anticipation of what comes next. How easily we can fall back into the routine we'd promised to keep when I went back on the road and she ended up back in Toronto. Before things took a tragic turn.

Before the text. Before her mother passed. Back when things were perfect.

"Sweetheart...shit. I don't even know what to say now. I was preparing for the machine again." I admit, knowing how lame it's going to sound.

"Jax."

"Don't say anything."

When her laughter filters over the line, I'm pretty sure I've died and gone to heaven. The ache that's permeated straight into my soul after she left, lifted the moment I capture her laughter.

"I missed that sound."

It's not a lie, but I really want to tell her that I miss all of her.

"If I don't say anything, it won't be much of a conversation."

"Okay, I take it back. Talk. About anything. Everything. Don't stop."

"Why did you call?"

"The truth?"

"Always."

"Today was harder than I was expecting. Words were said. Not so nice ones. Things happened. Heavy things that have me sitting back and doing a lot of soul searching and well, as stupid as it sounds, I needed your voice to clear the haze."

"But you said you were expecting the machine." She repeats back my earlier admission.

"I said I needed your voice, Ave. I'll take it however I can get it."

There's no missing the catch of her breath, but it's one she obviously doesn't want to give much focus to as she wastes no time changing the subject. Taking what could have been a pivotal moment for us—for me—and putting us back on a safer track.

"What happened today?"

"I got into an argument with my sister. It wasn't pretty. We don't usually fight, or say anything remotely antagonistic toward each other. I don't know what to do with it—about it."

"And the things that happened, what were they?"

"Work stuff." I admit casually, but remembering my earlier promise to keep things honest no matter what the response, I don't let her get in a word edgewise before getting down to specifics. *"Melinda is back."*

✶✶✶✶✶

Something told me I was going to lose her after that so when Smith called through, wanting to know if I'd landed and I went back over to the line to find her gone, it wasn't surprising.

Definitely hurt like a bitch though.

How am I supposed to fix this when it seems like the second I get close, my past seems to come back to haunt me? Can it even be fixed? Or was my sister right?

Pulled away by the sound of the locker room door swinging open, I look up just in time to meet my opponent for the night's overeager expression. His excitement over his spot on the card tonight the way I should be, but after everything that's happened, I can't seem to summon up the energy for.

Cameron Wilson.

The one guy I've worked with since I got here that actually took the angles we had to be a part of seriously. Probably so excited because he can go out there tonight and win or lose, give me the beat down he thinks I deserve for putting him and Brady out of commission a little over a year ago.

This is going to be a long night.

"Look," he starts, crossing the room and throwing himself down onto the bench beside me. "That shit that went down a year ago, I was an asshole. You lipped off once and I took it too far. So before we go out there tonight and blow that crowd away, I just wanna be sure we're cool."

We were cool back then, so what he's attempting to do, while impressive considering I know it can't be easy for him to admit he was the one acting like a child, he doesn't actually *have* to do.

"We're good, man. Ancient history."

"Awesome. We're on after Ron and Manny. You still cool with me going over?"

Maybe the history isn't as ancient as I think if he has to ask me that. I know I've been gone for a few weeks, but there's never been a time in the years since Smith took me on that I've ever argued the way a match was booked and even if it is Cameron, I'm not gonna start now.

"Yeah. As long as we use the fifteen minutes we're given to put on a hell of a match that makes us both come out smelling like roses, I could care less about who's going over." I tell him, earning a giant grin.

At least I can make someone happy.

"Alright. Well, I guess I'll see you out there."

Standing from the bench and making his way to the door, he salutes me before heading out and following his lead, knowing that with Ron's match going on now we don't have a whole lot of time, I push all thoughts of what happened with my sister and Avery to the background.

CPW re-debut here I come.

Brady

Two weeks.

That's how long it took for word to make its way around about my working in HFWA and for Radley Smith to come a knocking.

Two glorious freaking weeks of being at what looks to most outsiders like the bottom of the damn barrel, but given the way Reese and Bryan seemed to make me feel at home and a part of things, more like the top of the line.

My job, even with the pay not being the best since the gates are still low, consisting of running programs with a variety of different guys a few days a week instead of the straight seven I was working before. Matches that we got to run through multiple different times and different ways for maximum impact in front of a crowd. What in the end seemed to revive my love for all things wrestling.

The best part though being the serious lack of travel. I mean, other than hopping in a car and travelling a couple of hours out of Toronto to some small suburb, we stayed in a block of motels the guys bought out for months in advance.

Giving me time to not only do my own thing, but also spend a bit of time catching up with Avery. Time that even though I'm not sure I could ever get her to admit, has been as good for her as it has for me.

Both of us giving the other something that for the last nine weeks or so, we've seriously been lacking.

Her a connection to the sister that even though I would have wanted to do all of this anyway, was the catalyst for all of the real changes taking place in my life and me, well, me being the connection to the man that even though she's denied it on more than one occasion, Avery can't seem to move past.

Having been summoned to Reese's apartment by Bryan with only the grunted reply of Radley Smith to go on, though, I just know everything is about to change.

I'm going to end up leaving yet another Davis woman hanging.

The only difference being that when I leave here, end up having to leave her, I'm doing it armed with a plan.

One that if I have my way will end all of the distance once and for all.

For all of us.

"Thanks for coming, man. I know I was pretty cryptic on the phone." Bryan says, extending his hand when he pulls the door all the way back.

"I'm only used to cryptic, remember? I'm more concerned with the name you dropped before you hung up."

"Yeah, figured that." He admits before turning and heading down the short hall and around the corner.

Keeping close on his heels and rounding the corner, the apartment seems to open up as a kitchen comes into view on one side and on the other, what looks to be a combination of dining area and living room. A living room that the deeper I step in, I can see Reese and Smith both utilizing as they sit across from each other on a loveseat and sofa respectively.

Both sets of eyes firmly planted on me.

Well, this isn't nerve wracking at all.

Throwing a look back toward Bryan and seeing his brow bunching before he grimaces, I know that what's about to come next, no matter how civilly they're all sitting together, isn't going to be good.

"Okay, someone wanna fill me in on why I needed to be here?"

"Nice to see you again, son." Smith begins, his voice as raw and rough as always.

"I'm not your son, Smith. Let's clear that misconception up right now. I was a cash cow for you. Nothing more."

Clearing his throat, Reese pulls my attention away from my rising anger at how damn smug the old bastard looks, putting my focus where it belongs.

"Before the two of you end up tearing each other apart, how about we get down to business?"

"I've got no business here."

My business with Smith and CPW ended weeks ago and considering how much better I've been feeling since I landed in Canada, more importantly under the umbrella of Harbour Front, its business I'm not looking to repeat.

Even if it means living off raw potatoes and greens for the rest of my life.

"Brady," Bryan interrupts, moving up and pausing beside me with a motion to the chair to the right. "Why don't you take a seat and hear us out."

Okay, I get why Reese reacts the way he does. The two of us haven't exactly spent a whole lot of time together, what with him actually on the road looking for the next big thing for his promotion, but what the hell is this shit with Bryan?

We've talked at length about what my life was life before CPW, during it, and the way it all differs from what I've got going on now. He knows how pointless this is. So why is he trying to get me to sit in order to feed me bullshit?

"What gives, Bry? I don't need to take a fucking seat. Just spit it out."

Here's the deal. Harbour Front Wrestling Alliance, while an independent promotion a lot like CPW, doesn't have nearly the level of exposure that Smith has spent the better part of twenty years building off his name. There are no contracts. We're all working on a night to night basis and it's pretty much a given that the only coin you'll see is going to come from whatever tickets and merchandise are actually sold. What I'm sure if I was given access to their books, isn't all that much.

Sure, they're not doing horribly, but until they employ someone with a big enough name to garner the attention they need, or the matches I've spent the last couple of weeks putting on along with the others take off, they're going to be running in the same sick cycle. Limited in what they can do for the people they bring in and definitely limited in what they can offer on a long term basis.

What the bigger promotions, ones like TNA and WWE, don't have issues with.

Financially able to offer the guaranteed contracts with stipulations that would make your head spin in terms of what you can be given during your tenure. Exactly the type of thing that Smith, with his nose and head for business, is hoping to one day achieve with CPW. Exactly what he will achieve if his current business plan continues to soar.

It's also the last thing I want. Been there, done that. Not looking to repeat having my life and my choices dictated by the allure of cash.

"You know how things are with us, Brady. Hell, you know the way things are run around here better than half the guys on the roster." Bryan starts to explain, but shifting in his chair and standing, Smith takes over.

"What Michaelchuk is pussy footing around telling you is this, Raines. I'm running a showcase in a few weeks when we roll through New York City. Two nights of non-stop action from the best performers that CPW and the world have to offer. Only the best of the best need apply. We've even lined up MSG as the venue, complete with a full court press."

That's great for him, really it is, but I'm finding it hard to figure just what the fuck that has to do with me. Compliment of being considered one of the best aside.

"Let me guess what that means. Because I'm under no obligation with Reese and Bryan, you want me to be a part of it. To come back and play the part of company bitch boy for you again."

"Yes and no."

Doing what Bryan suggested before, I pull out the chair closest to the table and swing my legs around it leaning my arms across the top and setting my head down. Settling in for whatever bullshit my old boss is planning on slinging next.

"I want you to be there, but not as a company boy, and not because of the long standing relationship I've got with your old man. I want you there because of your god given talent. A talent that while I'm sure has been of some use to both of these guys, is better served with a larger audience."

"I'm assuming you both agree?" I look between Reese and Bryan, the former nodding almost enthusiastically while Bryan lowers his head, neither confirming nor denying.

"It's not like you're under a contract here, Brady. You're making pennies sticking around here considering how much of a ring general you are. We're happy to have you here, don't get me wrong, but this opportunity seems more your speed."

Five years ago, hell, maybe even ten, I would have agreed with Reese's assessment. I am good. Damn good in fact. But I'm a lot older and wiser now, and my priorities, especially in the last couple of months, have changed dramatically.

Shit. I'm at the point now where I'd gladly work a job some of the boys would consider menial just for the sake of feeling somewhat normal.

"You know it's not about the money, right?" I ask Reese, but when no response comes one way or the other, I turn to Bryan and repeat it.

"Of course I know that. But I also know that you need more of a challenge. Something that while we could eventually give you, we can't right now. I think you need to give this some serious thought."

Give some serious thought to Smith and New York. Full press coverage and two nights of nonstop action on what is considered the grandest damn stage of them all.

I'd be stupid not to do it, but what everyone seems to forget is that I've already done it. Send up one of the other guys I'm working matches with every night, they'd benefit more from it than I would.

I'm content where I am.

"I'm good where I'm at. I don't need to think about it."

"Merrick already signed on." Smith announces with a smirk. "Since you two were damn near attached at the hip not that long ago, I figured you'd want to jump on board too."

Jax did what?

I can't have heard him right.

Jackson Merrick; the guy more destined to settle down away from the ring. The one that actually chose love for a woman over what he spent years perfecting in the ring, actually agreed to this bullshit?

Damn.

Losing Avery must have fucked him up more than I thought.

That's what you get for not keeping in touch, dumbass.

I'm definitely rectifying that when I get the fuck out of here. I need to know just what the hell Jax is thinking.

It's time for me to act like a certain reporter I know. Even if in the end, all I end up with is another boatload of regrets to add to the ones I've already spent the last two months racking up.

Smith wants me back for this CPW showcase? He's got it. Just not for the reason he thinks. Because not only am I going to get answers from Jax about just what the hell is going on in his head, I've also just been handed exactly what I need to put the plan I have to get the girls back in motion.

"Fine." I announce loud enough for the entire room to hear. "I'll do it."

Chapter Ten

Emery

After the pictures Avery sent me, three of them showing Brady in various stages of his match against a guy she called the Dragon Master and the forth being one I'm sure was just him embracing a new layer to his character and not the way it actually looked in blowing a kiss directly at my sister, the last thing I'd been expecting was to hear from him.

Avery sure. She hasn't stopped talking about the show when she calls, and she definitely doesn't let up in text. But Brady? No way.

Badaboom! Sexiest girl in the room. How you doin? ;)

He gets points for being funny, but those same points definitely get taken away for originality. I mean, does he really think I wouldn't notice that he totally just ripped of Enzo Amore? I might be more into the independents than the bigger companies, but come on.

Everyone knows who Enzo Amore is.

Fail Rich Boy. Try again. This time with your own lines.

Considering that other than pictures from my sister, this is the first conversation I've had with Brady since the letter he sent telling me not to give up on him, I'm pretty much expecting more of the same silence in return. So when he answers back almost right after I'd gotten the sent message with the time stamp, to say I'm shocked is an understatement.

I'm not really in the position to make it rain for you, babe. Sorry. If I was in Delaware though, you can be damn sure I would be using a whole lot more than my lines on you.

What is this? What is he playing at?

Let's ignore me for two months and then come back on the scene when I'm just starting to get a handle on everything and screw it all to hell again?

What do you want Brady?

There, asshole. Take that. I'm not playing your game.

You mean, what do I want besides you? Or....

No. I mean what I said. What do you want?

This is ridiculous. I've got like fifteen minutes to get ready for work and I'm sitting here hands gripping my phone with my eyes stuck to the screen wasting it. A little too invested in hearing what his response is going to be when I should be telling him to go fuck himself and turning the damn thing off.

Damn you, Brady. Why do I have to keep giving a shit? Why after all this time do I still feel this annoying pull to you?

I want you, but I don't deserve you yet. I will soon though.

That's providing I even still want anything to do with you, which if you haven't already figured out, I don't. So save your lines for someone stupid enough to believe them. Like, I don't know, your wife.

Way to lie your ass off and sound like a total bitch at the same time, Emery.

...

Stupid phone showing me when he's responding. I knew I should have kept my old android. Being able to see that he's responding to my message is not helping me pull away from the conversation.

What if I said I was reaching out because I wanted to help two people find their way back to each other?

"I'd say you're a complete moron if you think I'm gonna fall for that!" I scream, like losing my shit on my phone is going to make it all the way to wherever he is.

God, I really have lost my mind.

I don't want to get back together.

Lie number two.

Wasn't talking about us darlin'. I told you I don't deserve you yet. I still got some shit I gotta fix first. But I am talking about your reflection.

My reflection? What the hell?—*oh wait.*

He means Avery.

Okay fine. If Avery is what he wants to talk about, maybe I can have this conversation after all. The only thing mattering to me these days apart from keeping myself upright being her happiness.

Okay, I'll bite, Rich Boy. How do you plan on bringing them back together?

The dots filter across my screen again, but instead of only lasting a few seconds like they did a few minutes ago, they seem to last forever. When his text finally does come through, it being so long it damn near takes up the entire screen.

I've gotta hand it to him, he's come a long way. Getting a text, let alone one this long would have been unheard of before.

Smith is running a CPW Superstar Showcase in NYC in a few weeks. Full press coverage, which means backstage interviews with the guys, a tour of the Garden, the whole bit. Considering Jax is a part of it and your sister is a reporter, I think it's the perfect place for the two of them to "meet" again. That is, if a certain cliff diving hottie I know can work a little bit of twin magic and secure her being there.

Cliff diving hottie nickname aside, it's not a half bad idea. If the issue between Avery and Jax right now is distance based, which given the fact that they're nowhere near each other it obviously is, getting them both in the same place under the guise of work is the perfect way to eliminate it.

You can't keep running from your problems if you're thrown into them head on.

Not bad.

I'm all good, baby. You know that already. ;)

Cue eye roll. Well, cue it when I wipe the damn smile that his stupid text brought on off my face. Damnit. I really need to get a grip here. I'm gonna be a love sick puppy in a matter of seconds if I keep reacting to him this way.

Whatever. The idea is good and considering I'm heading up there in a few weeks for a visit, it could work.

So you'll help?

Help Jackson fix what he broke and force my sister to admit what's really going on with her so she can finally be happy?

You're damn right I'm gonna help.

There's no question, especially after what my mom told me before she passed.

If you pay attention, you'll see that everything in life is a serious of signs all coming together to lead you in the direction you're meant to go in. From the day we all met in the hotel lobby in Wilmington and gone our separate ways, all signs have been pointing to Jax and my sister. Every damn thing about them speaking to what our mom said.

Everything being in the blue. It's them to a tee.

From Jax's car, to the color of sweater Avery chose to wear that first day in an effort to make things easier on him, to something as basic as the color of Jax's eyes.

The road to them getting back together, the blue my mom was speaking of in her letter to my sister, it was loss. Both of Richard and her. If Avery wanted to be happy again, she was going to have to go into the sea of blue known as loss in order to come out the other side.

To Jax.

Like you expected any other response. :P

There's my girl.

Damnit. Things were relatively calm and then he had to go and say that and turn what was supposed to be all about my sister and his friend, about us.

No way. I can't go there. No matter how much my heart wishes that it could.

Eyes on the prize, Raines.

If you say so, Davis. His next text filters through right on the heels of mine, but before I can respond to it, offer up some equally snide remark, the dots signaling him writing filter across the screen again.

So I was thinking you could shoot me a text when you're heading up there and I'll reach out to her boss. If everything works out the way I hope, especially with all of the information I managed to dig up on Markus in order to secure his cooperation, he'll drop it on her when you're there and you can sway her to go.

Considering how eager Avery is to take on assignments these days, affectively keeping herself too busy to do much else, whatever info Brady has about Marcus, I don't see him needing to use. She'll take this job the same way she keeps taking on the others.

Even the ones that seem to make her heart break more.

Don't think that's going to be a problem. What about Jax? Are you going to fill him in or bring him in as blind as Avery?

Something tells me that while I don't exactly want to keep a secret this big from my sister, I'll handle it a lot better than Brady. I might not have spent all that much time with him before things seemed to blow up between us, but I did see that he's a horrible liar. His face tells more than he thinks it does.

When he finally texts back, he confirms it.

Are you kidding me? That sorry son of a bitch needs something to hold onto. I'm filling him in the second I see him and I'm not taking no for an answer.

Then it looks like everything settled. We're really doing this.

Brady and I are actually going to forgo our own personal shit in order to work together toward the common goal of getting the two people we seem to care about most back where they belong.

I'll be damned.

What proves too good to be true when the familiar dots begin their movement across the bottom of my screen again and a few seconds later a message drops, showing me why.

I miss you, Em, but I just keep telling myself *not too much longer*. In just a little while we'll be together again and I'll finally prove I can be the man you deserve. I just wasn't telling the person I should have been, so I'm going to tell her now.

Emery? Soon, okay?

I'll be home soon. <3

Chapter Eleven

Brady

Three months.

All the time it took once I finally dug my feet in and made a decision for myself, for everything around me to change. What standing here now, I'm forced to acknowledge my amazement over.

How much things can change, how different people can be and how aware you can become about the things that really matter. Along with just how much time you wasted believing in the things and people that at the end of the day, didn't.

The only constant the entire time being the promise I whispered in my car, hopefully making its way to Emery the way I know my letter did.

A promise that standing here outside the locker room, I've done everything possible to adhere to and one that now that I'm here and free of all of the ties that bound me before, it's time to make good on.

Bringing my heart and home together again.

It's time for me to get everything I want. My career—what I love to do—falling in line with the only person that even three months later, I can see myself living it with.

It's time to get Emery back.

The next step in doing that waiting for me on the other side of the door.

Pushing my way through, heading straight for the back and tossing my bag down before lowering my body down onto the bench beside it, I don't say a word. Just take it all in. Breathe the air that for the last twenty years, has been stifled by someone else. Air that is now clear, even if it is just as nasty as I remember it.

"We meet again." The familiar voice of my old road partner says, making his way over until his shadow is looming over mine.

"That we do." I agree, slapping his outstretched hand.

"When I heard they were bringing you back in, I gotta say I was blown away. Didn't think I'd ever see you gracing this place ever again with the way people said you left."

"Could say the same about you. Last we spoke, you walked away. Gave it all up."

"I'm starting to think when it comes to this," he motions around the locker room and the guys now making their way in. "There's no such thing as walking away."

Truer words were never spoken. From as far back as I can remember this was all I wanted to do. Sure, it started because of my dad, but it quickly morphed into something more when after attempting it myself for fun, I found I was good at it. What quickly became my dream from that day forward and one that even with the chaos, I don't think I'd ever be able to live without.

A sentiment it seems he and I share.

"You might be right about that."

Throwing himself down onto the bench beside mine with only my bag separating us, he turns toward me and it doesn't take him long to get into what we're really both focused on.

"So if you're here does that mean all the shit you said you were gonna do back home got straightened away?"

All that shit being my father, Kelly, who at the time had been my wife and was now settling into life as my ex officially, and starting from the ground up with my career. The Raines name this time around having no connection whatsoever with the legacy before it.

"Yeah. It took a lot longer than I expected, but I can finally say that the guy sitting here now isn't the same one that was riding the road with you before. Different set of priorities."

"Priorities you're gonna fill me in on, right?" he asks and I laugh, knowing exactly what he means. I made no secret of the fact that I would be coming back for Emery, the same way Jax made sure I knew that the feeling was mutual with Avery.

"You know it, but before we get into all that, why don't you fill me in on you? What have you done with yourself the last three months?"

"Besides stalking the woman I love, you mean?"

I laugh again, knowing the lengths he went to in order to be near Avery, at least for the first little while after they seemed to implode. Avery having filled me in during our visit together.

"Yeah, besides the obvious."

"I went back to California. Slapped down most of my savings on a beach house in Laguna and just spent whatever time I wasn't checking in on Avery, with my sister and surfing. Even got myself a regular job for a few weeks."

A regular job. *Huh.* I didn't think we were capable of shit like that. The pull to put on a show engrained in our DNA. This is news.

"What kind of job are we talking about?"

"Working at the surf shop. With as often as I was out there, the owner roped me into being an instructor."

"You enjoy it?"

"For a bit. It wasn't the same. Helped replenish some of what I lost on the house though, so can't complain."

"So how'd you end up back here?"

"Smith came calling, same as he did with you I bet. Flew out to my place for a chat and well, here I am."

He's right about that, though, with me he'd landed in Reese's living room and gave me an offer that based on what I wanted to do, I couldn't refuse.

He godfathered the shit out of me.

"And Avery?" I ask even though something tells me with the weeks we spent visiting during my time in Canada, I know more about her then he does.

"Still in Toronto working at the magazine and as far away from me as she can get."

"You talk to her at all?"

"Once." He quietly admits, his eyes falling away and travelling out over the room.

"How long ago?"

"Right before I came back. So, a few weeks I guess?"

"And how did that go?"

"I'm here, Brady. How the hell do you think it went?"

"That good, huh?"

"Yeah. She's still closed off. I mean, I think I made a little bit of headway with her judging by the way her tone changed toward the end of the call, but not being there with her and able to see it for myself, it's all just a guess."

There's something else I know is playing on his mind as much as it is mine now that we're both back. Something that even though I don't wanna bring it up, I need to know the status on, given everything I've heard through the grapevine since the news broke.

"What about Melinda?"

"What about her?" he snaps, his head swivelling rapidly until his glare is leveled straight on me.

"She's back, right?"

"Yeah." He huffs out a breath. "Fortune put in a good word for her and Smith brought her in before I came back. At least that's what I'm told."

"And how do you feel about that?"

It's a valid question. From everything I remember about the last time we spoke and the bare minimum Avery gave me, Melinda was the reason he wasn't with his girl the way he wanted to be. One text she'd sent for god knows what reason had been dropped in Avery's lap at the same time she got the call from Emery and everything had blown up after because of it.

"She's tried talking to me a few times, but I'm not having it. I swear, Brady, it's like being in the same room with her, even if it's just for a meeting, feels like a betrayal."

"Does Avery know about her being back?"

"Yeah. I told her that night on the phone. No secrets. Not anymore. I made the wrong choice once before. If I'm serious about getting her back, and I am, I can't do it again."

"And her and Fortune?"

"Done as far as I know. He's moved on to some other chick now."

Well, at least three months away doesn't change the way shit is done around here. Things still sounding like a bad episode of daytime television. One aspect I definitely didn't miss during my time away.

"Well, good for him, I guess. Though with the way he was even before him and Melinda started hooking up, I can only see this one ending badly too. Fortune never could settle for one. He had to have them all."

"Sometimes he has to have them all at the same time too." Jackson jokes and I laugh, at least until the very person we're talking about slams his way through the door and glares at us.

"Judging by that look, I guess I don't have to ask how things are between you two."

"No you don't. But let him keep the stick up his ass. I'm over it. All I want to do now that I'm here is put on the best damn show I can. Everything else is bullshit I don't need."

Another way that the last three months has changed things. Jax now appearing more focused than ever before. A focus that only comes when you've got nothing left to lose.

"So you ready to hear the plan I came up with to get our girls back?" I change the subject and pulling his attention away from Gavin and turning back to me again, his shoulders lose their tightness as he relaxes against the wall nodding. Doing the one thing that since I made my way in and he came over I haven't seen him do.

For the first time since I got my ass back here, Jackson is smiling.

Operation: Get Our Girls Back is a go.

Jax

I've gotta hand it to Brady. When he plans something, he really does go all in.

There are a lot of ways this can fail, but I'm not gonna be the one to bring it up. Not with the way it seems to have lit a fire under his ass.

A fire under both our asses now that I've heard him out. One that hasn't been there in so long I almost forgot what it feels like when it does appear, and what it brings with it.

Hope.

It's a tricky thing, hope. Believing in something when leading up into it, all you've felt is the sting of disappointment. Loss. It's hard to grasp onto something and have hope in it working out when that's the hand you're consistently dealt.

But it's what I've got now. That is, if it all goes off the way Brady seems to think it will.

"I did a bunch of research on the flight down. You gave me the basics months ago, so I just took what I had and ran with it. As it turns out, not much has changed on her end since everything got blown to shit." He explains and of course, he's being as cryptic as always.

"Care to be more specific?"

"Avery. She still works for Markus, only now, I have more to go on than just a first name. Funny thing is, I learned so much about this guy that if he doesn't buy into what I want him to, I'm not against using it to get my way."

Now he's got my attention.

What could Brady possibly have found out about Avery's boss that he's not against using as leverage? Better yet, is it something that could impact her job?

"Like what?"

"Did you know that five years ago our magazine owner was brought up on charges of sexual misconduct? It was all swept under the rug of course, but not so much that it wasn't readily available once I did a little bit of digging around."

"Are you sure you and Avery didn't swap places over the last few months?" I ask, ignoring the way my heart seems to constrict with the news about Markus and instead focusing on just how bizarre Brady sounds. "Since when did you become an investigator?"

"Since my dumbass friend had to go and make me one." He quips and I resist the urge to punch him. Like I'm the only reason he's doing this.

"Whatever. Seriously though, how did you manage to come across all this?"

"The internet. You told me to become one with technology, so I did. Pretty good, right?"

"Not bad." I admit easily, definitely more than a little surprised with just how deep his need to get Emery back has made him go.

Maybe there's hope for him after all.

"So you're gonna use what you found on Markus against him if he doesn't agree to your plan to get her here?"

Nodding, he reaches over into his duffel before turning back and tossing his phone over. "Go into my texts and the first two conversations listed, read over them."

Making quick work of his lock screen, the password the same as I remember from our time together riding the road, I head into the messages and sure as shit, as I read over the two conversations he told me to, I see just how far he's taking things.

The first, what looks like a back and forth conversation between him and the lady Markus was accused of harassing, and the second, one he started with Emery. Not exactly thrilled at having to read what should be a private conversation between him and the woman he so obviously loves, I skim past the sweeter ones until I find what I'm sure is what he wanted me to see.

"Leaving out the amount of times you were a total pervert, how the hell did you get her to agree to this?"

"Easy, Jackson." He grins. "The one person she loves more than anything in the world is still hurting and I have the ability to end it. Love is a powerful motivator, wouldn't you agree?"

Nudging me when I don't answer, he does it again until I release a tight breath and shove him back.

"So she's going to head up there and do what exactly? Talk her into taking on the job?"

Nodding, the smirk on his face only seeming to grow more, he takes his phone back, throwing it into his bag.

"She's going to be there anyway. I got her to tell me that much. You missed it in your scrolling. I'm just going to time it so she's there or someplace near when Markus asks Avery to do it."

"Okay, I get what you're saying. Planning to get her here for the full court press that Smith is riding out next week is great. What I don't get is how the hell this is going to work for you."

"Because Avery isn't going to come alone, dumbass. Have you heard anything I've said?"

Going back over everything he'd told me about the plan and still not being able to place where he mentioned Emery's coming along for the ride, I shrug. All I can really see is another way this can go wrong.

"Providing Emery agrees."

"Jax, I get that you're preoccupied lately, but you really can't be this fucking slow. You do remember Emery, right? The girl you practically jumped at the show in Delaware?"

Great. Like I needed the reminder of that mistake.

"Yeah, I remember Brady, though I was really trying to forget. Thanks for that by the way."

"You're welcome." He smirks. "If you remember Emery that night, then you also remember what Avery told us about her at the bar. How she wasn't the fan of wrestling, but her sister was. There is no way in hell that Emery is going to talk her sister into doing this and not attempt to go with her."

Now it makes sense.

I'll be damned. He really has thought of everything.

"There's only one issue I see."

"All ears, man."

"What if Markus says no and then doesn't go for whatever kind of blackmail you're planning on using? That was a long ass time ago, even with the conversation you had with the woman involved. Shit is probably sealed up tight. She's probably gonna pay for even talking to you. What then, Brady?"

And again, the man has an automatic answer.

"In the unlikely event that happens; which it won't, Senor Buzzkill, we'll go to plan B."

"Which is?"

"Simple, Jax. We get our asses on a plane, go there, and get them ourselves."

Chapter Twelve

Avery

Looking up and toward the door at the sound of the knock, I groan.

So much for a day off.

Pulling myself off the sofa, my legs groaning nearly as much as I did at the intrusion, I head for the door. Pausing before opening it and looking through the peephole.

Seeing the one person standing on the other side that I'm willing to come out of my self-imposed exile for, I waste no time flipping the locks, throwing the door back and grabbing to pull into an embrace.

The last few weeks since we've seen each other wasting away now that she's here.

"Glad to see you too, sis." She chokes out. "Finding it a bit hard to breathe, though. You think you can loosen the grip?"

"Sorry." I say, releasing her as a warm flush of embarrassment floods my face.

"I wasn't expecting anyone."

"But you're happy I'm here, right? That was what the stranglehold was for?"

"Of course." I laugh softly, motioning for her to come in and shutting the door once she follows me in and slips off her shoes. Making a beeline straight for the fridge just like the last time she visited, she grabs the corked bottle of wine and heads for the sofa. Moving at a speed that even though I'm attempting to follow her, has my head spinning and makes me want to crash the second my ass hits the sofa cushions.

"Are you get a glass this time?" I joke, referencing the last time she was here.

"What for? After the flight I had to endure in order to get here, I need the instant buzz that drinking it straight gives me."

"That bad, huh?"

"Five hours of listening to some guy switch between snoring, choking, and growling in his sleep. You tell me if it was bad or not. God," she sighs. "I would have preferred a screaming kid to that guy."

Patting her on the knee with all the sympathy I can muster, which isn't much with the amount of travel I've had to do with the same kind of people, I reach over when she laughs and hug her again.

"I'm so glad you're here. I don't really think about just how much I miss you until you're standing here."

"I missed you too, Ave. So much. It's harder than I thought it would be being in that house alone."

When I went back to Delaware for the funeral and stayed for two weeks after, I actually brought up the idea of staying there permanently because I didn't want her to be alone, but as I learned the more time I spent with her, stubborn was her middle name and she wasn't having any part of it.

Hearing her admit how hard things are though, it makes me wish I'd pushed her harder then. She shouldn't be alone. Neither of us should.

We were all we had.

"I'm just glad it was you and not Markus."

"Is he still trying to get into your pants?" Shaking my head, not at all agreeing with her assessment, she groans. "Avery, I know he's your boss and you think he's just being nice and all, but you have to see everything he's doing for what it is. The man is trying to get into your pants."

Fat chance of that happening. Not after the disaster that took place the last time I let someone near them.

The only person getting into my pants from now on is me.

"Not happening. I already told you that the last time you were here. Besides, he's just being understanding. He knows how hard things have been since we lost Mom."

"Yeah, I just bet he does. I'm sure he's being *real* helpful."

Truth be told, Emery isn't wrong. I'm just choosing not to focus on it. Markus and his intentions are a sore subject. Especially given how closely we've had to work over the last several months. Even if my heart didn't completely belong to someone else, it wouldn't ever go anywhere.

I can't see anyone the way I see Jax and the more time that passes, I'm starting to realize that I never will.

"He called me yesterday." She says after a few minutes of silence and it's all I can do not to plug my ears. She never has to say who called. I already know. I just don't know what she expects me to do about it.

Reaching over and grabbing the bottle straight from her hands and ignoring her protests, needing the shot of liquid courage for whatever it is she's bound to say next, I bring it to my lips and take what has to be the world's biggest chug before handing it back over and leaning my back all the way into the cushions.

"He's a mess, Ave." *That makes two of us.* "He told me that the two of you talked a couple of weeks ago. Is that true?"

A couple of weeks ago. Right. The night that after talking with Brady, I'd come home and answered one of his calls. Actually picked up because I needed—no—wanted to hear his voice. The voice that's done nothing but haunt my every waking moment since I lost my shit on him and walked away.

"Yeah, we talked."

"About?" she inquires lightly and swallowing heavily, I shake my head. I can't get into this. I don't know when I'll be able to do it, but it's definitely not now. Jax is an even sorer subject than Markus. "Avery, come on! You gotta give me something here."

And just like that, I'm right back in that night. The night that if it weren't for an incoming call he said he had to answer, would have probably ended with us back together.

Giving my heart what it wants.

What *I* want.

*****

"Mom, today was one of the hardest days yet." I whisper up to the sky, where just like it's been the last three nights, the moon is

there to greet me. Familiar like an old friend. Or a parent you'd given anything to have standing with you.

"I had to interview this couple. They've been married seventy years. They're both in their nineties. The way they looked at each other was like seventy years hadn't passed at all and they'd just that day admitted their love. The depth in their eyes, Mom. It was too much. A reminder of what I could have if I could just get past the pain."

I've been doing this for weeks. Talking to the moon and for a few brief minutes believing that my mom is behind its glow. Telling her every truth in my heart that I wouldn't be able to speak otherwise.

For a little while it helps, like it is now.

Just like she said in her letter, I can feel her here. The difference between this conversation and the others, is that I'm almost positive with the way the water seems to rush the shore that she's letting me know she's pissed off at me too.

I'll take whatever she's willing to give, even if it's her upset.

Imagining as I stand here what she would say back to what I've admitted. Especially with what she told Emery before she passed about accepting the love I deserve.

Accepting Jackson.

Her words something to the effect of, 'Avery, my sweet girl. What you don't realize is that you do have it. You just have to let it in. Give it a fighting chance.'

But how do you give something a fighting chance when you can't seem to give yourself one?

You pick up the phone.

The voice comes through clear right at the moment my phone shines a spotlight over my back porch, ringing before the vibration sends it moving across the plastic chair. The name one that's called so many times I've lost count, but that until now, with what I'm sure is the sound of my mom's voice guiding me, I've never answered.

This time is different. This time I have to answer.

"Jackson." I murmur softly, his name falling like a prayer from my lips.

"Avery, shit. Is this really you or am I going crazy?"

"It's really me." I tell him, swallowing down the lump of guilt that rises with the realization of just how many times I've made him go to voicemail.

"Sweetheart...shit. I don't know what to even say now. I was preparing for the machine again."

He's not the only one that doesn't know what to say. I may even be at a bigger loss than he is with how completely locked up I am now that he's actually on the other end. Live. As live as he can get over a cell phone anyway.

"Jax."

"Don't say anything."

Letting the laugh bubbling inside of me loose, he sighs and the moment is lost. Another sound to go along with the other hundred or so I've missed since everything went to hell between us. Jax when something makes him happy. The lilt to his normally strong voice, doing what it did during our week together and warming me from the inside out.

"I missed that sound."

I miss you period. *I think but don't dare allow my lips to utter.*

"If I don't say anything, it won't be much of a conversation." I respond instead and it's his turn to laugh softly.

"Okay, I take it back. Talk. About anything. Everything. Don't stop."

"Why did you call?"

"The truth?"

"Always."

Even if it hurts. Which with Jax, I think it always will.

"Today was harder than I was expecting. Words were said. Not so nice ones. Things happened. Heavy things that have me sitting back and doing a lot of soul searching and well, as stupid as it sounds, I needed your voice to clear the haze."

"I saw you then, the same way I'm seeing you now. Clearly. You're the only thing that is."

His words from three months ago coming to the forefront of my mind so easily, as if he'd just uttered them for the first time.

This is too much. I don't think I can do this after all. I'm still not ready.

Too bad my heart has other ideas.

"But you said you were expecting the machine."

"I said I needed your voice, Ave. I'll take it however I can get it."

All of the missed calls, the ones that messages aren't attached to, they make sense now and they just chip away at the block of ice surrounding what's left of my heart.

"What happened today?" I change the subject, my realization definitely not something I can touch on, no matter how badly my heart wants me to.

"I got into an argument with my sister. It wasn't pretty. We don't usually fight or say anything remotely antagonistic toward each other. I don't know what to do with it—about it."

"And the things that happened, what were they?"

"Work stuff."

Wrestling. He doesn't need to say any more. Despite all of the hours spent pouring over any video that his fans saw fit to post to social media and YouTube, we're not anything to each other anymore. Which means any right I have to know what's going on in CPW is gone.

"Melinda is back." he practically whispers and the name, same as it has the last few months sends shivers down my spine.

I definitely don't have any business knowing this.

"Today was hard for me too." I admit, again flipping the topic around in an effort to deflect away from what I feel.

"How so?"

"I interviewed a couple." I tell him easily, like no time as passed between us at all. "I've been doing that since I came back in order to keep myself busy."

"I understand. What was it about the couple that made it hard?"

"Truth?"

"Always." He repeats my earlier answer back. "You know that."

"How in love they were. How they met. What they seem to have even after seventy years. What I just can't..." I fade off as another sigh filters over the line. This one different from the last. Sadder.

"I love you, Avery." He whispers. Three simple words and my name capturing me the same way they had the first time. The way I think they always will.

"Jax..."

"You don't have to say it back. Not until you're ready. I told you in my letters and calls. Only when you're ready."

I'm ready now! *My heart screams as loud as it can. The words slamming against my chest and causing it to ache with their need for freedom.*

"I miss you so much, Avery. I hate the way things went down with us, but I hate myself even more for letting it happen. For not deleting that stupid text message the second I got it."

"I miss you too, Jax." I finally give in and admit, hearing his intake of breath before things go silent, but not silent enough for me to think we've lost our connection. His next words, how shaky they are, proving just what my admission had caused.

He's crying.

"Tell me what to do, Ave. I'm trying to give you time, but its killing me. I need you. I hate this distance. I hate the finality I saw in your eyes when you caught me there a couple months ago. I need to fix this. I just need you to tell me what to do."

The list of ways this could be made better is short and none of them can he really fulfill. They're up to me to handle. It's all on me.

Jax can't erase the fact that he got a text from Melinda. He can't go back in time and make it so my mom didn't die. He can't take away the hole in my chest that just seems to grow infinitely larger the more things I lose.

"You need to let go."

"Never." He answers almost the second the words slip out. *"I'm never letting go."*

Closing my eyes and attempting to catch my breath, handle the pain and pleasure that come in equal measure to what he's said, I stop fighting it and give in to it. To what I feel.

To what I need.

"Jax, I lo—"

"Fuck. Not now." He curses. *"Avery, its Smith. I need to take it or he'll just keep calling back. I'll never get rid of him."*

"Okay. Do what you have to do."

"I'll be right back. Please don't hang up."

Mumbling a half-hearted acceptance of what he's asked of me, I wait for the line to go completely silent, signalling that he's clicked over to the other line and despite the plea in his voice as he asked me to stay with him, I do the opposite.

I end the connection.

✳✳✳✳✳

"Nothing, Emery. Nothing happened."

If it's possible, reliving the memory of that call was even harder than the call itself.

"Jax didn't seem to think it was nothing."

Of course he didn't.

"Why does it even matter, Em? It's not like anything's changed. Besides, with everything I've managed to read on CPW lately, it seems like he's back with Melinda anyway."

"Looks can be deceiving."

"Is that what you tell yourself about Brady?"

Damnit. All of the progress I've made in keeping my emotions in check since our mom died, it's like it all falls away with the way I go on the attack now. Bringing up Brady, taking a shot at her, that's not me at all.

"Sorry. That was stupid of me. I'm just reacting."

"Avery, I get it. You're allowed to be a bitch sometimes. For what it's worth though, yeah, that's what I tell myself about Brady. That it's not the way it looks and I just need to hang in there a little longer. Sad reality is though, we're not you and Jax. It's been almost three months already and other than his letter, there's nothing to go on."

While Jax on the other hand is still reaching out.

Message received loud and clear.

Before I can respond, the doorbell rings, shaking the both of us away from our conversation and making us both stare at each other in confusion.

"You expecting someone?" Emery asks with a motion with her head toward the door that again, is ringing off demanding to be answered.

"No."

"Well, since I showed up unannounced, the least I can do is answer the door for the next person trying to do it." She says, slipping off the sofa and handing me the bottle before heading for the door. With each step she takes, my heart picking up pace, hoping the person on the other side isn't who I think it is.

With how raw that memory left me, the last thing I need is a repeat. Especially one of the up close and personal variety.

My fears when I hear the door open and Emery greet the person on the other side lessening, but not going away entirely.

So much for a work free day.

It's Markus.

Emery

"No thanks, we don't want any." I say before attempting to close the door. Wanting nothing more than to see it through, but what his hand coming out across it prevents.

I can't believe this guy doesn't see how onto him I am.

"She here?"

"No. Bye now." I lie, putting more of my weight into the door, wishing he'd just get the message and screw off already. I don't care what Brady is attempting to do for Jax and my sister. I don't want this sleazebag anywhere near her. Boss or not.

"Why don't I believe you?" he smirks and I swallow down the urge to smack it straight off his face.

I wasn't always this bitchy, but ever since I made my first trip to Toronto and to Avery's work and came across this guy, everything in me screams to keep him as far away from her as I can. There's a look in his eyes whenever he's in the same room with her that he thinks he's keeping under lock and key, but that is so blatantly obvious it turns my stomach.

He wants her, and something tells me that it's probably been going on long before Jax and my sister split. That's the kind of smarmy douchebag he comes across as whenever we're in the same room together. He's just amped his game up in the months since.

"Today is supposed to be her day off, which means no bothering her. Don't you think you own enough of her time?"

Clearing his throat, he finally lets a bit of his true colors show as his eyes harden and he scowls. "Time you're forgetting she asked me for. Now, are you going to let me in or not?"

That's gonna be a no, asshole. I answer silently, about to make it the answer he actually gets when I hear shuffling from inside the house and Avery's voice following it.

"Emery, let him in."

Not even attempting to hide my distaste for that response or him, I groan before releasing the hold on the door and pulling it open, allowing him entrance. One that once he's made his way in, earns me a cocky grin before he turns his attention to the living room and the person he's really here to antagonize.

"Sorry to just drop in like this, but I need to talk to you about something. You got a minute?"

"As long as you don't mind Emery being here. Come in and make yourself at home."

Avery. Always hospitable, even when she'd much rather be alone. One of the ways I hate that we're not alike. If this was my place and he was attempting this bullshit with me, he wouldn't have even gotten in the door, let alone get to ask the question.

I sure as shit hope what Brady is planning is worth this or the next time I see him, he's a dead man.

Making his way into the room and sliding down onto the lounge chair across from the sofa, he leans forward as his face takes on a pained expression.

Another one I know is as fake as the guy wearing it.

He might have my sister under some kind of spell where his intentions are concerned, but he damn sure doesn't have me.

Purposely taking the long way around the table in order to slip past him, I bump into him hard, smiling when he grunts his disapproval before falling back into my spot on the sofa.

"I hate to do this to you, but there's an assignment. Two day freelance work for one of our subsidiaries."

"What would I have to cover?" Avery asks and I send up a silent prayer that whatever Markus is about to say next has to do with Brady and not something else, otherwise everything he said he wanted to do in text is going to be blown to crap.

"Sporting event. One that would take you Stateside."

Thank the freaking lord. It's Brady.

"What kind of sporting event, Markus?"

"Something that I'm sure once I tell you, you're going to want to kill me for. But before I tell you, I need you to know that I tried getting someone else to cover it. I reached out to every contact I have, but they're all tied up or unwilling."

Way to give it away, idiot.

"Just spit it out, Markus. I'm a big girl, I can handle it."

Avery is a lot of things, but stupid isn't one of them. She might be acting like she doesn't have a clue what he's talking about, but I know better. It's there in the subtle tensing of her shoulders and the way her eyes flicker from me to the floor and back to me again before landing on Markus.

She knows its wrestling related. Probably that it's CPW too if I had to hazard a guess.

"I need you to cover two wrestling shows. Also, in the hours before show time, interview the superstars."

"Where and what promotion?"

Here it comes. The CPW bomb. One I'm sure that this piece of crap is actually enjoying given the history he knows she has with one of their performers.

"Not far. New York City."

"Markus…" Avery sighs before rubbing her temple. "What promotion?"

"Combat Pro Wresting."

There it is. The reaction I knew was coming.

Avery's lip trembling slightly before her eyes sink and she melts back into the sofa, her face crestfallen. Looks like it's my turn up at bat.

"Markus, I can't believe you're even asking this." *Way to go, Em. Sling the bullshit.* "You know she can't do that even if she is the only one you've got left to reach out to. It's too close to home."

Gifting me a grim smile, Avery slips her hand over until it's wrapping and squeezing mine gently. No words even needed to get the point across. She's thankful that I'm there and going to bat for her.

What she'll kill me for when she finds out I'm actually one half of the team throwing her under the bus. As much as I dislike anything to do with Markus, he's actually being the innocent party here.

"Why don't you let Avery tell me that, Emery? It is her I'm directing this at, after all."

Good God. I take it back. There is nothing remotely innocent about this douchebag. Especially not with the smile he's throwing Avery's way now. One I seriously need to knock off his face and make sure never appears again.

Brady, you freaking owe me.

"You really couldn't get anyone else?" Avery questions and I'm torn between being happy she's doing it and hating it because if she keeps it up, the truth might end up pouring out.

That can't happen. Not when we're so damn close.

"No, and trust me, I tried. I'd take it on myself but I'm already booked for a conference that week."

Biting into her lip, she looks away from Markus, but instead of lowering her eyes to the floor, she lingers on me. The truth I'm holding back from her threatening to spill out the longer she holds my gaze.

This is not supposed to be happening. I'm no good with secrets, even worse when they've got something to do with someone I love as much as I do Avery. Damnit. If she doesn't look away soon, I'm gonna break and tell her everything.

"I'm willing to sweeten the pot if you take it on." Markus interrupts, giving me the out I'm after when she turns her attention back across the room.

"How?"

"Since like Emery said, this is close to home and I'm not exactly fond of throwing my best employee under the bus; what would you think about having some company on the trip? If of course she can manage to get the time away from her own job." He offers up, turning his attention to me.

Wait, what?

This wasn't part of the deal I worked out with Brady. What the hell is Markus playing at and what does it have to do with me?

"I'd say you've got my attention."

"This has to happen, so if it makes it easier, take Emery with you. She can even help out. You can run point and she can be your gopher." Turning to me he plasters an even bigger grin on his slimy face. "So what do you say, Emery? Will you go with Avery to the CPW shows?"

Chapter Thirteen

Brady

Whatever you said, it worked. She accepted the job and will be in New York for the shows. You did a really good thing, Brady.

It's not exactly her undying love and gratitude, but considering the plan wasn't just about Avery and Jax, but her too, I'll get that when her cute butt lands in New York with her sister.

"Hey man, wake up!" I call out, throwing my body down onto his bed and smacking him with the book I'd been attempting to occupy time with before Emery's text.

One that once it makes contact, he grabs a hold of before turning it around on me, shoving it hard against my chest with a groan.

"Five a.m., Brady. We were up until five." He whines before turning over and shooting his arm toward the window. "And since I can't see the sun, it's not time to get up yet. Go back to bed."

"Jax, it's the middle of the fucking afternoon and considering that I just got confirmation that the plan is a go, I figured you'd wanna be awake."

"Say what?"

"I said, I got confirmation that the—"

"Yeah, Yeah. I heard that the first time." He cuts me off. "What I want to know is what kind of confirmation."

"The horse's mouth kind, my friend."

"Emery?" he deduces and I nod. "Well, shit. It actually worked."

"You really doubted I'd be able to pull it off?"

"Brady, you're not exactly the poster child for plans. Do you need me to remind you how well your last big plan worked out?"

No thanks. I don't need the reminder that the last time I put a plan in motion it blew up in my face and landed me right where

I am now. I've been living with the daily reminder of that for three months too long already.

"No, jerkoff. I remember."

"But, buddy, it's my pleasure. I mean, you'd do the same for me right?" he smirks. "Oh right! You already do. Every god damned chance you get."

"Would you just get your ass up already? There's still another part of this thing that I gotta nail down."

Sitting up in the bed and rubbing at his eyes, he grunts before looking over at the time, groaning louder when he sees just how right I was about the time.

"We're supposed to be at the gym in thirty minutes. What the hell, man? Why didn't you wake me up sooner?"

"I get enough of your sunny ass disposition when I let you sleep in. No way am I waking you up earlier. You'd probably decapitate me or something."

"Yeah, you're probably right, but that's on the days when we don't have matches to prep for. Jesus. Guess I'm gonna have to screw the shower."

Resisting the urge to flip his words around on him, I slide off the bed and head over to my own. Grabbing my gear bag, I sling it across my neck and turn back just in time to catch him slipping into his pants, complete with a string of curses being delivered under his breath with what sounds like my name attached.

"What exactly is the next stage in your plan?" He asks once he's pulled his shirt on and slung what's needed into a bag of his own.

"You know how the guys like to bar hop after the show, right? Well, since Avery is going to be going around interviewing them, I figured we'd get their help in inviting her along."

"No. Brady, what the hell are you thinking? You know the way they get."

He's right, I do, but it's not going to stop me from seeing it through. Not when what I have planned for Emery depends on it.

I suck at planning and I'm even worse with big gestures. I like to make jokes that the reason I'm like that is all the head shots I take, but the truth of it is, I've just never cared enough to try before now. This, though. This is different. Emery is different.

This calls for me amping up my game in more ways than one. I can take care of the first thing I want to do on my own, but the last part, the real grand gesture, that's gonna take some help.

"Right. I'm actually banking on them being like that."

"So you want them to come on to Avery?"

"No, Senor Buzzkill. I want them to get Avery and Emery where they need to be."

"Even if when they do, they start hitting on them? God, Brady. You can be the world's biggest idiot sometimes."

"So what if a couple of the guys hit on Avery! It's you she's gonna be going home with at the end of the night, right? So settle it."

"Right." Jax laughs, confusing me. "So when Gavin, Max, Dave and the rest of them start getting touchy feely with Emery, trying to seal the deal and get her in bed, you're not going to want to rip them limb from limb?"

Shit. He's got a point. Emery made a joke about Matthias Kemper in passing months ago and I could already see his death in my head with the level of anger it brought alive. No telling what I'll do when the real thing happens right in front of my eyes.

I'll end up in prison for sure.

"Fine, you've got a point. But I'm not really planning on them actually spending any amount of time with the girls. Just putting out the offer and getting them there."

"Good luck with that, but Avery isn't going to be a part of it."

Alright. I'll admit it's not the best idea, but I don't see what real harm it can do. It's not like we're gonna leave the girls with any of the assholes we work with. Odds are they'll be off trying to nail other chicks anyway. So what's Jax's deal?

"Come on! It won't work with Emery if Avery isn't there!"

I'm not against whining at this point. Whatever it takes to get him on board with this.

"Brady," he sighs, finally finishing with his bag and flinging it over his shoulder. "I know this is going to be hard to believe, because well, you're you and all, but just because you want to do something huge for Emery doesn't mean I'm going to be the same with her sister. They're the twins. We're not. I don't even know what we are at this point. We're too absurd to define."

"Bullshit, Jax. You're my brother. End of."

Call it knowing the guy better than he knows himself, some kind of psychic ability I seem to have picked up in the last twenty minutes or so, whatever you like really, but I know that what I just said to him is what is going to seal his participation in what comes next.

When all else fails, tell the truth.

"Can you swear that I won't have to wrestle one of those pervs off her?"

"I swear to you. They won't even get close enough to try."

"Then come on, *brother*." He points to the door, his obvious attempt at being a smart ass failing with the smile he's now sporting. "Let's go set the next phase of this plan of yours in motion."

Jax

"Jackson. A moment?"

No sooner do I finish my workout, go to follow the rest of the guys out then a thick meaty hand is slapping itself down hard on my shoulder, followed quickly by a familiar gravelly voice.

Smith.

"What can I do for ya?" I ask, making sure to plaster the most compliant looking smile I can manage on my face before turning around.

"There's something I've been meaning to talk to you about. Been putting it off for a few days, but thinking with the week we've got coming up, the attention we're going to be drawing from the media, we need to hash it out now."

Nothing he said sounds remotely like something I want to hear. If he's been putting something off, it's a sure fire bet I'm not going to like it. But because I'm all about doing what's best for business and towing the company line again, I'm going to end up agreeing.

"Shoot."

"Now I know you two don't have the best track record, but with her back and putting her best foot forward, I think it's time to revisit things between you."

Melinda.

Of course this is what he's been putting off. No one wants to talk to me about her. Not if they have any hope of living afterward anyway.

"Revisit things how?"

Rubbing his hand across his chin, he meets my eyes and smiles. A genuine one. Whatever he's thinking about doing for me and Melinda obviously something that pleases him greatly.

I suppose I should be happy he's not rubbing his hands together in money making glee. I've been privy to that one more times than I can count and it might just make me sicker than the thought of Melinda and I being together in any kind of capacity does.

"It's no secret that the two of you have chemistry. Quite frankly, son, you two damn near set the ring on fire with the passion between you. With her back, I think it's time we go back to that. Really give the fans a couple to root for."

When people crack jokes about our business reading a lot like a daytime soap, for the most part they're right. There's something about two performers together that just seems to translate well to the crowd. The WWE taking full advantage of it over the years and feeding straight into the need for some loving that the audience seems to clamor for.

It makes sense that Smith would want to capitalize on what works. I just don't see the point. I want to make my mark based on what I can do in the middle of the ring, not by what I can pretend.

Maybe that's another reason walking away wasn't so hard when I attempted it months ago. I just didn't have it in me to be an actor. I still don't.

But if he's silent now because he's waiting on me to argue his point, he's gonna be mute forever. I can't deny what Melinda and I can do in the ring together, performance wise. We did translate well the last time it happened. The difference between then and now though, is we were dating at the time.

I couldn't grab the new girl Kimber and grind on her and make it work. There's no chemistry because there's no love. No feeling. There's nothing but our individual dedication to what we're doing, and that alone is not enough to make a story like what I've done in the past work.

"Why now, boss?"

"Because if you haven't been keeping up with the times, boy, sex sells."

Sex has been selling long before I was even born, so I'm not really getting the point in him bringing that up. Surely there are two other people under Smith's employ that can pull this off better than I can. He doesn't need me.

"And there's no one else you can use?"

"Correct me if I'm wrong, but I hear reluctance. Wouldn't have something to do with any residual feelings you might have for the girl, would it? Would have thought by now you'd have gotten over that."

If by residual feelings he means the urge to throw up whenever she's in the vicinity then yeah, I've got them. But what I've also got is the empty feeling in the pit of my stomach, the one that feels a lot like betrayal that rises every damn time we're so much as mentioned in the same breath together.

She's already messed things up enough and we're not even together. Why bother giving her the chance to do it again?

"There's nothing between Melinda and I anymore, Smith. That's historic shit."

"Then you won't have a problem being put in a program with her."

Statement, not a question.

Great.

If I wanna stay here, which after making the choice the night he showed up at my place in Laguna, I obviously do, it means I'm gonna have to suck it the fuck up.

It's time to do business.

"Can I ask you something, boss?"

"Shoot."

"If I said I didn't want to do it, would you strip me from the Middleweight Title spot?"

"In a heartbeat."

Well, at least he's honest.

"One more question."

"I ain't looking for questions, boy. Especially since you're not the one calling the shots. What I want is your answer."

Oh he'll get my answer alright, but not before he gives me this one thing. I need to know if that little pop in visit he pulled was for real, or if this has been his end game all along.

I need to know just how deep I got played.

"You'll get it, but just give me this one thing."

"Fine," he huffs out, motioning with his hands for me to continue as he starts tapping his boot against the floor impatiently. "What do you got?"

"Was this the plan from the start? When you hired her back, did you come for me because you wanted things to play out this way?"

After a couple beats of silence, his face not giving away one way or the other what the truth is, he's not the only one tapping their boot on the floor. His silence enough of an answer, but one I'm still not prepared to settle for as fact until I hear him speak it.

"Yeah, son. I knew when I flew down to Laguna for you that this was how I was going to play it."

There it is. Brutal honesty. Right from the jump, I was a game and just like he knew I would based on my desire to do what I do in the ring, I fed into his bullshit like a chump. I walked right into this and now, unless I want to up and quit, there's not going to be a way out.

I'm going to have to work with Melinda.

"When do we start?"

Smile back in place, he releases his arms and slaps one of them across my back, my answer as torturous as nails on a chalkboard to me, but seeming to make him the happiest promoter on the planet.

"I'm so glad you asked that, Jackson. We're gonna be starting next week when we ride through the east coast."

East Coast. Which in other words means New York.

Avery.

Two words and just like that, I feel my luck running out. Brady's plan, it's going to blow up in my face, I just know it. Instead of having my girl walking toward me, come next week, I'm going to be reliving history and having her walk away instead.

I'm screwed.

Chapter Fourteen

Emery

"Okay, I know I agreed to this when you said you had a stop to make, but you wanna tell me why out of all the places you could have taken me, we're here?"

Here is actually Resthaven Memorial Gardens and it doesn't take a brain surgeon to know who's buried here. What I don't get is why she feels the need to visit now.

Sure, a lot of her issues with Jax, at least to hear her tell it have to do with what our father did, but he's been dead for a while now. What the hell is confronting him going to do?

If that's even what she's here to do.

Hell, this could be her way of bringing the two of us together for the first time for all I know since she's been pretty tight lipped since she sprung this drive on me when we got in the car.

"Aren't you the one that keeps telling me to face my demons so I can finally be happy? Well, here," she pauses before walking a few steps and pointing out over the massive space laid out in front of us. "Or rather over there, is where my biggest demon lies."

So she is here to face her fears.

"So, how are you going to play this exactly? Just go up to his gravestone and yell at him for being a complete asshole?"

"No." she chuckles. "Though that's not a half bad idea either."

"Then what are you planning to do when we get there? I'm not sure how comfortable I am having a heart to heart with Daddy."

Truth is, I don't know how comfortable I am with anything that pertains to him. Even knowing how our mother felt about him, the only feeling I can summon up when I think about Richard is the urge I have to dig him up and smack him around. For me, my mother and Avery.

Richard Davis deserves nothing less for what he put us all through.

Taking my hand in hers, she drags me down the path, moving at a brisk enough pace to allow me to take in all of the marble slabs we pass, but unable to make out just who any of them are. The farther we seem to go, the more I realize just how many people have actually died and ended up here.

This is the last damn place I need to be with the loss I'm still trying to figure out how to live with.

My days since she passed and we laid her to rest consisting of waking up, watching old movies and letters she left behind, along with her journals. Heading to work from there, and going through the motions of standing behind a cash register with a smile on my face when all I want to do is run to the back and break down.

The only thing keeping my afloat the visits to Avery.

Maybe I should have stayed back at the house. I'm not going to be any use to Avery when I'm as stunted by grief as I was the day I got the call that she was gone.

"I know this is probably the last place you want to be, so if it's too much you can go back to the car. I won't be long I promise." Avery says when she finally pulls us to a stop to the left of the stone I can make out as our fathers.

Her fathers.

"You're right. I don't want to be here. It's a reminder of Mom and it hurts. I get why you need this, though. I just don't think it'll be much help."

"Maybe not, but all things considered, it also can't hurt."

She's got a point.

"You want privacy?"

"Normally I'd say yes, but having you here is making what I've got to do easier, so I'd really like it if you stayed."

What she doesn't get is that the same way she was with me when she was in Delaware after the funeral, I am with her. If I had my way, I'd never leave her.

It's what sisters do.

"Then here is where I'm staying." I tell her, squeezing her hand. It may have taken us twenty-five years but now that we're in each other's lives again, she's never going to have to face anything alone again.

Slipping her hand out of mine, she steps toward the stone and kneels, but before she can say whatever it is she's put together in order to move past the damage he caused, I'm speaking.

"You know, I wasn't going to say anything and I'm sorry that I'm interrupting you in order to do it." I move toward Avery, meeting her eyes when she looks up to my place behind her. "But I can't leave here without saying my peace."

"Richard Davis," I turn and face down the headstone. "You are a selfish piece of shit. You had no problem meeting and falling in love with our mother, but when the time came to expand on that love, make it something even more meaningful than it was to the both of you, you did what I'm sure you always do and you ran. Taking the heart and soul of the most devoted woman on the planet and my sister with you. Never once thinking about the damage doing that would do. And it didn't end there because you spent the next twenty-five years, even knowing that the love of your life was out there looking for you and Avery, running. Keeping her away from the people that would have given up their lives for her. Loved her more than a selfish piece of garbage like you was capable of. I hate you for that. I hate you for breaking the woman you claimed to love and not fixing it. But most of all, I hate the fact that you had to go and die before I could say any of this to your face the way you deserve."

"I'm sorry, Avery." I repeat once I'm done and with tears falling from her eyes, she just nods slowly, reaching out before I can move away and slipping her hand over mine. A hand that once hers makes contact, I shift around until our fingers are entwined together.

The only thing left in the moment that needs to happen with where we're standing.

Richard needing to see that despite everything he selfishly did, we still managed to find our way back to each other. Creating a bond that no matter what or who comes into our lives from now on, will never be broken.

Take that, Dad.
Love always wins.

Chapter Fifteen

Avery

"When we get in there follow my lead, okay?"

"Follow your lead. Got it." Emery repeats and I use the time before reaching the door to explain the rest.

"If for some reason we get separated, or worse, one of us gets lost, flash the press pass at the first person you see. It will say everything we need to about what we're doing back there. At least it will until the actual event starts."

The first time I did this, the fear I have for Emery tonight happened. I'd gotten lost. At the time, I was also too damn green to remember to flash the pass. It's only because the security guy seeing it sticking out of my pocket that I wasn't hoisted out on my ass.

A performance I definitely don't want repeating itself tonight and something tells me that Emery feels the same.

"Who exactly are we interviewing? And are they going to be in a specific area or are we going to have to hunt them down?"

"The last time I did something like this, we had to go to them. Catch them in their element. Something tells me that this time, it's going to be a lot more rigid."

"How do you mean?"

"From what Markus told me before we left, we're not going to be the only reporters here, so I'm pretty sure that means we're going to be all shuffled into the one area."

"Is it wrong that I'd rather have it be the way it was before?"

This is where Emery and I agree. Walking into a room and shutting the door, asking questions I'm sure are repeats of ones that have come a million times before, we're getting nothing but robotic responses. Being able to capture them doing other things, preparing for the show, their matches and even getting their gear on, there's a wealth more knowledge that can be picked up and questions born from.

"Not at all. I kind of wish it was that way too."

Slowing down when I realize Emery is no longer keeping up, still standing a few feet back seemingly frozen in place, I head back and grab her by the hand.

"Not as easy as you thought it was going to be, huh?"

"That obvious?"

"To me, yeah. I mean, I freaked out before we even got in the air. Figured it would end up hitting you sooner or later."

Pulling Emery over to where a behemoth of a man in a black shirt with **Security** emblazoned on the pocket stands leaning against the wall, I flash my pass at the same time Emery does and his demeanor at seeing us, tense and alert, falls back in line with what I can only assume is his nature away from what he's here to do. Relaxed. Even regarding us with what I believe to be a rare smile.

"Would you mind telling us where it is we have to go?"

"No problem." Pulling himself off the wall, he points down the hall, a look I can't quite place crossing his face as he looks between Emery and me before it falls and he's again focusing his attention to where he's pointing. "First door before the blue ones at the end of the hall. Smith wants ya'll there."

"Thanks a lot." Emery blurts and brightening even more, this time his smile flashing teeth, he wastes no time responding in kind.

"You're welcome."

With a curt nod, we follow the security guard's instructions, my attention pulled back after we've taken the first few steps when I hear the same voice we just encountered mumbling something into his walkie talkie.

What, if I'm right, sounded a heck of a lot like an announcement of our arrival.

Weird.

Pulling Emery to a stop, I lean in and as quietly as I can manage while making sure I'm heard, I check to see if she's heard the same.

"Did you hear that?"

"What?" When I flick my thumb back toward the security guard, she shrugs. "If you mean did I hear him talking to someone, yeah. Just couldn't make out what he was saying. Why?"

"Nothing." I say, putting what is probably just my paranoia at being here and having to interview Jackson out of my head. "Never mind."

"No, Ave." she reaches out before I can start walking again. "If it was enough to make you stop and ask, it's a lot more than nothing."

"I could have sworn I heard him say something about us. That we were here or whatever. I mean, it's probably nothing and just me imagining things, but..."

"But it's got your reporter senses tingling."

Leave it to Emery to get it.

"Yeah, kinda."

"We can go back and ask him what he said or we can head into the room he told us we need to be in and get to the bottom of it ourselves."

Tempted to go back and ask, but knowing it would probably get us nowhere, I motion down the hall toward the room closest to the side exit. "Let's just get this over with. The sooner we run through these interviews, the sooner we can hit the crowd and put this entire thing behind us."

"Sounds good to me. Lead the way, reporter lady."

Laughing softly, she slips her arm through mine and we make quick work of the rest of the hall, only coming to a stop once we've reached the entryway inside and caught sight of all of the performers and the reporters that had beaten us to the punch.

Thankfully, Brady and Jackson nowhere in sight.

"Alright, who the hell do we hit up first?" Emery asks after she's done a once over of the room and its occupants, snatching the list of superstars from my hand and scanning over it before handing it back with a grin.

One that makes a whole lot of sense once she lifts her hand and points to the left corner of the room where a lone person sits staring into space. Looking as uncomfortable at being there as I do just standing in the doorway.

"Fortune is free."

Gavin Fortune. Pulling facts from the back of my mind, things I've learned on the way down here with all the information Markus plied me with, along with the tidbits I'd managed to catch during my Jackson video stalk fest, I'm confused.

He's the current CPW Heavyweight Champion. Why is he sitting alone? Given his position at the top of the company and holding their most prestigious belt, shouldn't half the room be lining up to talk to him?

"I'm going to explain all the ways that sentence is wrong later, but since he does appear to be lacking in attention, why not? Might as well hit up the champion first. If you're sure you want to that is."

Turning into me, eyes widened in confusion, her brow tightens. "Why would you ask me that?"

"Didn't Gavin and Brady used to be a tag team?"

Releasing the death grip she's taken on my arm, she laughs.

"No. Brady tagged with Cameron. Gavin was just scripted to be their leader for a little bit. Though to be honest, I never understood it. I mean, sure, Gavin is great, but Brady was the one with the family background. It should have been the other way around."

"Focus, Em." I snap my fingers and say once I catch her starting to ramble. "I promise you can ask him about that, but we actually have to go over to him first."

"Right."

Slipping our way around the seats filled with competitors, Emery guides us to the back, her confidence center stage again as she grabs and pulls the two chairs out when we reach Gavin and proceeds to slip her arm out of mine in order to fall into it. Choosing the moment that my butt firmly plants itself in the vacant chair beside her and he's looked toward the interruption to as always, blurt the first thing that comes to mind.

"If it isn't the biggest asshole in CPW."

"What she means is," I quickly interject as my cheeks begin to heat in embarrassment. "We're from Canoe Sports and we'd like to ask you a few questions."

Meeting my eyes, the simple pink shading I can feel across my face deepening under the intensity of his glacial blue irises, he nods before turning his attention to Emery and smirks.

"You. You got a name?"

"Emery, and this here," she points before shoving her elbow into my side. "Is Avery. But she's wrong. I meant what I said before, just like I mean what I'm about to ask."

"Which is?"

"Are you always this pretty?"

Eyes softening, he leans back into the seat and laughs heartily, shooting me a look of understanding when he catches me shaking my head.

This is definitely not the way I imagined this going. I'm out of my element here, while it looks like Emery found hers.

"I mean," Emery continues to speak, digging me even further into a hole. "Moderation is key. If you're sitting here all pretty now, what the hell are you going to do in a couple of hours in the ring?"

"Emery, God." I hiss under my breath and again Gavin laughs. Thankfully not the least bit bothered by her verbal assault.

"It's alright. Let her go. This is the most fun I've had since they forced us into doing this."

Motioning with his hand and a smile toward Emery, I inhale sharply, praying that whatever she says next is actually something I can use for the actual job I'm supposed to be here doing.

"How awesome does it feel to be interviewed by twins? And better yet, ones that look as good as we do? Does it make you jealous?"

"Gavin, I'm sor—" I attempt to apologize, but he holds up a hand, completely shutting me down.

"I'm gonna go out a limb here and say that you're not the actual reporter." His attention again solely placed at Emery's feet, just like the smile that seems to only get larger the more she speaks.

"You'd be right. I'm just the eye candy."

"Damn." He curses before shifting his attention back to me, his expression flipping from the cool one he displayed for Emery and turning hard when our eyes finally meet. "As much fun as I could have with this, we really should get on with it since I've got a match to prep for."

Finally! Something we can agree on.

Throwing a quick glance at Emery, more than willing to eject her from the room in order to get the interview I'd been sent here to get, I see the smile still firmly in place. Something about Gavin Fortune obviously doing what nothing else had been able to in the months since her and Brady parted ways.

Turning her back into herself.

Happy.

Looking down toward the paper in front of me, pulling away again from the intensity that whenever he looks my way Gavin just seems to exude, I prepare to ask my first question. Shut down before I can even get the first syllable out when he speaks again.

"Some of us are heading out after the show. I know we're not supposed to be doing this and I'd catch a ton of heat from Smith if it ever got back, but what do you think about joining us?"

Looking up, expecting to find the question directed at my sister, I'm surprised to find his eyes still on me.

What exactly is this?

"Sure, why not?" I agree, when I feel Emery's eyes burning a mark into the side of my face. "That okay with you, Em?"

"Count me in."

With that out of the way, Gavin seems to relax back into the chair, motioning toward the paper in front of me, ready to get on with what we're really here to do.

Question after question pours out of me after our exchange, with not one instance of having to look down at the paper for prompting. All ones tailor made for him and what after the reading up I've been doing, I know about his career leading to this point.

Not once does he scrimp on his answers, either. Some of them even spanning minutes instead of the seconds I assumed he would give us. Giving me an insight that had I not done this, I don't think I ever would have had about the profession, let alone the man across from us.

After a quick glance at my watch, and the realization of just how long we've sat here talking, I wrap it up. Reaching across the table and shaking his hand with a soft smile before pushing my chair back and standing. Watching and waiting as Emery wastes no time following suit.

Only instead of turning and following the way I expect when I start to move, I hear the sound of Emery's laughter before she seals our plans for the night. Ones that I'd been hoping I would have a little time to work up a good excuse to get out of, but am now officially stuck with.

"See you after the show, pretty boy."

Just what the hell have I gotten myself into?

Chapter Sixteen

Jax

Bidding another reporter goodbye and desperately in need of a break, I push the chair back from the table and stand, making my way for the nearest exit. Craving the solitude I knew I would be given if I could just make it through without being stopped again.

Being back here is strange enough on its own, especially with how determined I'd been never to do it again. Having to sit here after only a couple of weeks and give interview after interview all because during my time away, it seemed like CPW had become an even bigger force to be reckoned with, is another thing altogether.

Even worse because almost from the time I set foot back in the fold, Smith had seen fit to throw me straight into the lion's den in the form of a long standing feud with Matthias Kemper and his Middleweight Championship.

Some of the reporters even claiming there was more interest in how that would play out then there was for the Heavyweight belt. An acknowledgement that should fill me with pride, but that only seems to add to the already overwhelming stress I'm under.

Reaching the door that leads out into the parking area and praying no rabid fans in desperate need of a selfie are lying in wait, I push my way through and the second I'm out, fill my lungs with the longest breath of cool air I can.

That one blast doing more for me in a second than I've been able to do for myself since I landed here hours ago.

The reason for that makes sense given that I'm having to spend the entire time before the show even gets underway talking to reporters and there only being one of those that I really want to sit down and talk with. One that even with the distance and the lack of communication, is still the first thing I picture when I wake up and the one I ache for when I finally allow my eyes to close at night.

Tonight though, surrounded by all of these people and their stupid questions, she was there front and center in my mind. Like she'd never left. But unlike what people say, I don't remember the bad times we shared more than the good ones. All I seem to be capable of is reliving the good.

Like the way she'd looked that first night in the hotel bar. The way her body felt curled into mine while we watched movies, and the way she fit so perfectly when we danced, both at the hotel and her place. Treasured memories that lead me into the most important one of all.

The feeling of utter completeness I experienced when I slid inside her for the first time. The connection that was made when our bodies came together into something stronger than the sum of our individual parts.

When I made good on the words I said and she really did capture me.

Sensing movement out of the corner of my eye, I pull my attention from the ground and lifting my eyes, catch it making its way across the sky. Leaving a streak so long in its wake that it seems to go on forever. My body filling with warmth at the sight before the full weight of what's happening floods the one organ that for the last three months has been dormant.

My heart.

Having given up on wishes when my life seemed to take a serious nose dive, but not wanting to let the chance pass me by, I close my eyes as tightly as I can and give into the magic. Focusing on exactly what it is that I want and putting everything I've got into it, bringing it—or rather her, to life in my head.

God, let Brady's plan work. All I want is for Avery to show up here tonight.

Hearing the click and turning toward the door as it cracks open enough for the sound of voices to filter through, I move to the side and listen. The intrusion affectively pulling me away from the wish that probably won't even come true and bringing me slamming straight back to reality.

"I'll be right back, I swear. I won't leave you to fend for yourself with the trouble you've already gotten us into tonight. I just need some air. That level of testosterone is smothering." A woman's voice says and even though it's muffled, I hear whoever she's talking to laugh in response.

Letting out a relieved breath that it's not Melinda cutting into my private moment, I notice the door being pushed back further and feet coming down onto the ground as whoever it is steps out around, bringing themselves into focus.

Taking her in, my heart begins hammering in my chest as I realize who it is as she attempts to get her footing on the cement.

As her hand falls away from the door and it closes behind her, I watch as she steps out and inhales deeply, her similar movements to mine only making the effect of her standing here now even more powerful.

My heart both stilled and wanting to jump out of my chest in the same breath.

She's here.

Giving her another minute of peace, as taken by her now as I was the first time I watched her this way back in Toronto when her gaze, just like now had gone straight to the sky, I step forward and clear my throat.

Jumping back from the sound, she loses her footing and before she has the chance to fall, I dive forward in time to catch her. On instinct wrapping my arms around her body without so much as a negative thought about what she was going to think once she realized it was me. My entire focus on keeping her safe, no matter how complete having her in my arms this way again feels.

"Holy shi—" she calls out, stopping herself mid curse when she finally looks up and her eyes land on mine.

The way it feels seeing her again after all this time nothing at all like I thought it would be. The rush from all of my senses gripping me tightly. Awareness awakening in me so rapidly that I'm having a hard time keeping up. Both of us locked on each other, without so much as a blink between us. Our connection as alive as it was from the start.

"What do you know? It *does* work." I mutter softly.

"W-what does?" she stammers as she moves her body in an attempt to right herself.

"The wish."

"What are you talking about?"

Releasing my arms from around her when I'm sure she's back on solid footing, I point up to the sky in explanation. "You just missed a shooting star."

"So if it worked, what did you wish for?"

It all comes down to this moment. Three months apart. Long horrible months where I hadn't been able to make good on the first wish I made and instead had to mourn the loss of her from afar. It's all been leading me to this exact moment.

This is my chance to make things right and win her back.

And if I have my way...never let her go again.

"You, Avery. I wished for you, and it came true because just like I wanted you to be, you're here."

Chapter Seventeen

Emery

This is ridiculous.

I should have stayed where I was when Avery after like our fifth interview said she needed air, but *nooo*. I'd had to head out into the hall and then start a little investigating of my own.

I've been to *a lot* of wrestling shows.

I'm not bragging or anything, but for a long time going to these shows, especially after mom got sick was the highlight of my existence.

There was just something about watching two people lock up in the middle of the ring and then proceed to put their bodies on the line in order to entertain a few hundred of us that spoke to me. The guys and girls really no different than us in the crowd. Just people living their dreams, just doing it on a larger scale than most of us ever get the chance to.

I even met a lot of the guys at the shows. Doesn't matter what the promotion was. WWE, ROH, TNA, or CPW. I was all over them all. Getting my shot to meet them, at least with the bigger places, by putting down the extra bit of cash that would secure me at least a minute in their presence.

It's larger than life and every meeting and every show has always stuck with me.

Being backstage though, this was new. So with Avery gone, this was really my shot at seeing how the other half lives. At least how things go down before they walk through the curtain anyway.

I was officially behind the velvet rope.

Only what did I do with that access once I had it?

Gotten lost.

The very thing Avery warned me about when we first got here was happening. I had no idea where I was, much less how to get back to the room the interviews were supposed to be in, and more than that, I had no idea where I was supposed to find the next victim, what with him not being where he should have been.

Great. Just freaking great.

This *is not* the way things were supposed to go tonight.

It also doesn't help that the longer I spend out here lost and alone, the more open and exposed I am to the one meeting I've been trying to avoid since I got here.

You see, Avery isn't the only one that doesn't want to run into someone here tonight. I'm the same way. I'm just a better bullshitter. I can pretend seeing Brady doesn't bother me when the reality is, just thinking about it now is giving me goose bumps.

What I just know the longer I focus on it will end up having me breaking out in a severe case of hives.

Please don't let Brady be the one that finds me stumbling around like this.

When did basic fascination and fan adoration turn into something more? When he beat me at the bowling alley? Or was it when he took me in the water?

And why, after twelve torturous weeks of only a letter and a random text conversation that surrounded my sister and his buddy Jax, am I secretly wishing that it is him that comes around the corner and finds me?

Get a grip, Emery. You're better than this.

"And we meet again."

Spinning at the sound of the voice and stumbling back into the wall, my hand instantly flying up and over my heart as it threatens to beat straight out of my chest, I take a deep breath and release it when I realize who it is.

Gavin.

"You alright?"

Talk to the man, Emery. Let him know that while he scared the living shit out of you while you'd been lost in thoughts of Brady, you're better than okay. Sell it.

"Y-yeah. I'm great." I manage to stammer out and just like he'd done during the interview, he smirks.

"You lost?"

"What makes you think that?"

"Well, for one," he grins before turning and pointing down the hall. "The interviews are back that way."

"And two?"

"I was actually watching you for a bit. I saw you turn down here and then mutter something about not knowing where the hell you were."

Busted.

The only thing to do now is admit defeat and ask for help. That is if I ever want to make it back to interview the rest of the people on the card tonight. If Avery hasn't already come back and done it.

"Avery said she needed air so when she took off outside, I decided to use the time to stretch my legs and well, the more I walked, the farther away I got until I ended up here. This place is bigger than I was expecting."

"Wanna know a secret?"

With the way his eyebrows raise I can only imagine what kind of secret he's about to drop on me, but given that right now he's the only thing standing between me and possibly becoming even more lost, I'll bite.

"Sure, why not. On one condition."

"I don't really think you're in a position to be making conditions."

"Humor me."

"Fine. What's your condition, firecracker?"

Firecracker. *That's new.*

"You have to drop the 'I'm better than everyone' shtick you've got going on right now."

"Who says it's an act? What if I really believe I'm better than everyone else?"

"Then you really are a prick and I called it right earlier."

"Alright, princess. I'll give you what you want. No more cockiness. But just until I get you where you need to be." He appeases me, which when I smile, earns me what almost feels like a natural one back. "Wanna hear the secret now?"

"All ears, Fortune."

"My first night in CPW, I ended up locked out of the building."

"You're kidding!"

"Afraid not. I was so green back then and like you, I wanted to step away and check out my surroundings. Before I knew it, I was lost. I think I took like three or four turns that turned into more until thinking I was so smart, I went outside."

"And you couldn't get back in?"

"You got it." He laughs. "It was pretty bad. After calling out until my voice went hoarse, I figured I'd just head around to the front and go through that way."

I'm not a wrestler and I'm not well versed in how they handle moving from one place to another without getting bombarded by fans, but I do know that the last thing you do is walk around to where they're all lined up and waiting to get in and hope to get by undetected.

"Let me guess what happened when you did that. You got jumped by about fifty or so fangirls, right?"

"Don't tell me you were one of them."

"Afraid not. Hate to burst your bubble, pretty boy, but you don't really do it for me."

Bridging the space between us, he leans himself back against the wall as he laughs. "Now it's my turn to guess."

"Guess what?"

"Who does do it for you."

There's this part of me that wants to back off of the wall, turn and run given who he is and the role he plays in my sisters' life even if he's not entirely aware of it, but playing with Gavin Fortune is a whole lot better than pining after Brady. So even if it earns me shit with Avery later, I keep playing his game.

"Let's hear it."

"Kemper. Dude seems like your type."

Matthias Kemper is a pretty good guess all things considered, and has on occasion been one of the reasons I've slapped down money on a show, but what Gavin doesn't get is that when it comes to the ones I don't even have to think about putting money down for, he's lower on the list.

"Try again." I tell him, grinning when his brow furrows.

"You're kidding me, right? I thought all women went panty dropping crazy for him."

"Well, not this panty dropping woman. So try again, pretty boy."

"Fine." He groans his annoyance. "If it's not me and it's not that lunatic Kemper, I'm gonna have to go with Merrick, Taylor, Wilson or Raines."

I've gotta hand it to him. He's four for four. Though there are a few more he didn't mention, but considering the ones he did name, he's forgiven for forgetting the rest.

"Much better."

"Figured I'd nail one in that list. For the record though, you're on the wrong side."

Funny he should mention sides. Sides to me when it comes to wrestling fall into three categories.

You've got your heels, which are the guys you just love to hate because they're jackasses during any of their matches. They do anything they can to make you hate them. Ripping up signs, talking shit about you, they'll do it all. Even taking it a step further and doing the same in the ring. Willing to do or use just about anything to win. Including people.

Then you've got your faces. Those sweet cherubic and often times pretty faces that you can't even go there with. The ones that bleed good guy and want to win the right way, though not against using underhanded tactics in return in order to make that happen.

They're the ones that have the taglines that people always throw into hashtags, the kids sporting their merch, and the names that get hollered the most during their time in the ring.

The faces of the company. *Get it?*

Last but not least, are the antiheros. The ones that walk the tight line between good and evil. Darkness and Light. Guys that if we're talking national level, are like Stone Cold Steve Austin and sometimes even the Rock. Those are usually the ones I feel more of a kinship with, but all things considered, I'm not going to turn down a pretty boy.

As long as his names not Gavin Fortune anyway.

I think I'll enjoy turning that particular pretty boy down a lot.

"Raines is a heel, Merrick is a face that has the potential to be a pretty wicked antihero if they used him right, and Ron is an antihero. So you're wrong. I think I've covered all sides pretty nicely."

"No, see. You don't get it. Where you need to be is my side."

Bye-bye normal guy, hello jerk face.

So much for his 'not gonna be an ass again until later' bit. I knew he didn't have it in him. Gavin is as he appears.

A complete and utter jackass.

But a fun one.

"In your dreams, Fortune."

"After meeting you, it's a guarantee every night."

Reaching out and laying a hand across his chest, drawn to it when he flexes under my touch, I offer up the sweetest smile I can before leaning in as close as possible, pressing my lips against his ear.

"Down boy. No one likes having their leg humped on the first date."

Pulling back, expecting to be met with a scowl or some other means of his disapproval, I notice him smiling instead.

"Emery Davis, I think if you keep this up, I might just fall in love with you tonight."

"Been there, done that. I chew up and spit out pretty boys like you all the damn time. It's the not so pretty ones I really want."

"Oh really?"

"Yes really." I tell him, pulling myself off the wall and putting a few feet of distance between us. "And you're going to help me get it."

"How do you figure?"

Slipping the paper Avery made up with the names of all the superstars we're supposed to interview from my pocket, I hold it out and wait until he takes it to fill him in.

"You're gonna tell me where I can find River and Ross."

"Damn. When you said not so pretty you weren't kidding." He snickers as he unfolds the paper and takes in the names on the page, both crossed and still waiting to be seen. "Most of these you've already talked to from the looks of it."

"Right. But those two weren't in the room and trust me, I looked. So since they're half the reason I took off to begin with, and you not being the total jackass I think you are, you're gonna help me find them. Any idea where they might be?"

"If I had to guess, they're in the locker room since they're up first tonight."

The locker room. Right.

Where we're not supposed to be and even if we were, I'm not entirely sure I'm equipped to handle being. Familiarity with the sport aside, I'm still a woman. Walking into a room filled with half naked men, some of which have actually starred a time or two in some of my fantasies, well, I don't see that ending well.

Rage, pain and upset. Those things I can mask pretty well.

Lust? Well, that's a whole other bag of nuts.

"Any idea when they'll make their way out to the press room?"

Offering up a shrug, he pulls himself off the wall and moves toward me, stopping when he falls in line to my left, gripping his hand around mine.

"I can't tell you when they're gonna hit the room, but I can take you to them."

"Isn't that against the rules?"

"Probably, but you don't exactly look like someone who enjoys following rules. So Emery, do you want to take a walk on the wild side with me?"

Brady

Having blasted my way through every reporter within a thirty foot radius of the space Smith set up to be the press room, I head out and down the hall, making quick work of the hallways until my destination lands in my sights.

The locker room.

Where I can now officially sit back and wait until it's my time to head to the ring.

Shoving my way through the door and nodding with a grunt to Ron when he lifts and turns his attention from his Bible to take me in, I move over to the corner, digging into my bag and grabbing out my phone before sitting down.

Bummed when after going into the messages and calls, I find that just like earlier, there are none.

It's not like I was expecting her to reach out when she got here. I mean, it would be ideal, but considering that other than talking about Jax and Avery we hadn't done much talking at all, much less about us, I knew to expect nothing.

I just hoped for different.

If she's here, where is she? And why haven't I seen her or even Avery anywhere?

Pulled from my questions, the locker room door swings back, earning a curse from Ron before he drags his body up and moves closer to where I'm parked in the corner.

"It's like Grand fucking Central in here tonight. Jesus. Can't a guy read in peace?" he complains and I offer up a tight smile same as I always do when every night he seems to repeat the same tired line.

"You're looking to find peace here?" I ask, but before I can hear his response, my attention is pulled away at the sound of the voices now filling our space.

One voice in particular.

"Tell the truth. What's the real reason you're here tonight? And don't even think about spouting that eye candy line again. We all know I'm the real eye candy."

"What did I tell you about that?" the voice of the girl that's done nothing but haunt my every waking moment for the last three months says and everything seems to stop.

Time. Space. Movement. All of it freezes like someone pressed the pause button on a tape until the voice of the guy she's with breaks it.

Fortune.

A champion that if he doesn't back the fuck up off Emery in the next two seconds is going to find himself laid out on the floor. His attention and how close he's standing to her when I finally take them both in driving my blood pressure through the roof.

"You weren't serious about that." He jokes, making her laugh and making me tighten the fist that my hand has flexed into.

"I was dead serious, Gavin, but to answer your question, I'm here for my sister."

"You two work together?"

"No, but since I've been coming to see you guys for years and this is basically her first event in years, I figured I'd lend my services."

Good answer, gorgeous. I commend her even though what I really want to be doing is stepping between them and having her focus all of that attention on me.

"Your sister seems capable of conducting an interview on her own. I mean, she interviewed me just fine, so try again, firecracker. What's the real reason?"

Oh, that's it. The time for Gavin to be digging for shit he'll just turn into a joke when we've moved onto the next city, is done. It's bad enough that he does it with every person stupid enough to talk to him around here. He's not pulling the same shit with Emery.

It's none of his business why she's here.

"Sorry, pretty boy. I'm not that easy. All you're getting is what I've already told you." She responds with a pat to his shoulder. Both of them turning to the left of the room and making their way over where I know he stored his gear. Completely oblivious to the face that they're not alone. At least until Gavin calls out.

"Any of you seen Ross and River around?"

I feel her eyes first, even though right before she looked up I managed to turn my attention to whatever passage Ron happened to be on in the good book. Peering across the room and seeing straight through me even though I'm still denying myself the connection that eye contact with her would provide. A sense of awareness, even with the eight or so feet between us, so strong that it's almost impossible not to lift my head up and respond to.

A sense of awareness that even with the nine years I spent married, I've never felt before.

"Out in the ring running over some of the spots for their match." Ron grunts and out of the corner of my eye, I see Gavin turn back to Emery, reaching out when she doesn't immediately respond and running his hand over her shoulder.

No fucking way. Over my god damned body he's allowed to touch her like that.

Jumping off the bench and crossing the floor just in time to hear Gavin whisper something about taking her out to the ring so she can get the interview, my fist flies and connects with his face.

"Brady!" I hear her cry, but the sheer amount of blood pumping through and rushing to my head has it coming out muffled. The only thing I can focus on in the moment, the way my hit has taken Fortune off guard and he's stumbling.

"What the fu—"

"Don't touch her! Don't you *ever* put your hands on her!"

"Brady, what the hell?" she cries out again and this time, I turn toward her, finally giving my eyes what they wanted so badly when I first heard her voice.

Not entirely sure what she's seeing staring back, but judging by the flicker of fear that filters through her eyes before she steps back, clearly not anything good.

Pulling back when feeling the hairs on the back of my neck stand on end, I shove an elbow into Gavin's side, knocking the breath clear out of him as he stumbles again, his hands landing across his midsection.

"What did I say? Stay the fuck away from her!" I hiss before looking back to Emery. This time, throwing all of the venom I've got from seeing them together her way. "And you! What the fuck are you thinking letting him get near you? Much less touch you? Do you have any fucking idea who he is? What he caused?"

Gavin is the reason Jackson went off the rails before meeting Avery. He's the guy that had no issue dipping his cock in someone else's dish and still shoots his mouth off with the guys bragging about it.

My brother and I aren't that close, but if the roles were reversed and it was him in this and not Emery's sister, I'd be ending the piece of shit. Not sitting around laughing with him.

What the hell is she thinking?

A pair of arms coming around my neck and squeezing has whatever response Emery had planned completely tuned out. My body being pulled back and away from her the only thing I can even register before I'm being flipped around and thrown back against the wall.

"Settle your shit, Raines." Ron growls before bringing his arm up and laying it heavy across my chest, mounting me in place as he turns his attention to the other two occupants. "Someone wanna tell me what the fuck this is about?"

When no one answers, Ron turns his attention back to me and loosening the hold but not releasing it, he eyes me the same way I can feel the other two sets of eyes in the room doing. Wanting answers and going straight to the guy that attacked someone in order to get them.

"I don't know what the fuck she said in order to get you to bring her in here," I spill out as I attempt to settle and get some air filtering back through my lungs. "But she lied. She's not a reporter."

This seems enough for Ron because just as quickly as he'd spun around for answers, he's now doing it again, only this time to Emery.

"He's right. I'm technically not the reporter. My sister is. We interviewed you earlier, remember? Girl with the wavy hair and the blazer?"

"I remember, but that doesn't explain what you're doing in here. This place is off limits."

"That's m-my fault." Gavin spits out. "She couldn't find River and Ross in the press room and I saw them head back here so I brought her with me."

"Even though you know that if it gets back to Smith, he'll blow a fucking gasket?"

"Emery..." I interrupt Ron, no longer caring why she's here. Only knowing that I need to get her the fuck away from Gavin. "He's the guy Melinda used to fuck with Jax!"

"I know, Brady."

She what?

The second I catch the movement of feet across the floor, I'm on it. Pushing my weight into Ron's, I attempt to knock him back and away. If Gavin wants to make a move on me, I want it free and clear. There's no way in hell I'm letting this douchebag do to me what he did to Jax. If he wants to go, we'll go, and I'll make him pay for the shit storm he caused that almost cost CPW one of the best damn guys it's ever had.

It's overdue anyway.

"Let me go, Ron!"

"No." he barks before shooting his other hand out in front of him and making Gavin pause mid step. "And don't you think about taking another step either. I think I've figured out what the hell is going on here. If you two boneheads would slow your rolls, I think I also have a way to solve it. No need for pretty faces to be getting pulverized for free."

Stepping back toward Emery, his arm brushing against hers completely blocking out everything Ron just said and making me see red again, I work my arm around until I'm gripping his and shoving him back.

With my breathing labored and my head about to explode from the rush of rage spilling over at seeing them so close, I step forward, cracking my knuckles before planting my feet and readying my hand into another fist.

"Gav, you and me are gonna have some words in the hall. Give these two a chance to talk." Ron calls out, stepping around me and doing his best to use his body as a shield. Moving again only when Gavin has stepped away from Emery and started for the door, pausing before following the piece of shit out.

"Take a breath, Brady. You're scaring the girl."

"Well, I don't even need to see the show now. I got one for free back here."

Pulling my attention away from the door, I finally do what Ron had been trying to get me to do since he pulled me away. Take a breath and stand down.

It's just you and Emery now. I repeat to myself as I allow my breath to even out and my body to relax. Though something tells me with the anger I see resting just on the surface in her eyes, calm is going to be the last thing that we end up having here.

"Em..."

"No, Brady. Don't Em me, alright? What the hell was that?"

"He was touching you!" I snap. "What the fuck did you think would happen?"

"Nothing!"

Nothing? Really?

She expected me to see another man touch her and nothing to come of it? Did she slip and hit her head before making her way in here? Doesn't she remember the way I reacted the last time she brought another man into this?

"Like hell I'm gonna stand by and do nothing when some asshole puts his hands on you."

Son of a bitch. I can't keep fighting this.

I'm pissed. Filled with all of this crap I can't get control of and no place to put it. Relaxing while she's standing there biting her damn lip like that and looking all fucking innocent when she's anything but, is pointless.

I need to just give in and embrace this shit. Let it run its course. No matter how it plays out in the end.

"You gave up the right to care who puts their hands on me three months ago, Brady! Or did you forget that in your pissing contest?"

Like fuck I could forget.

"I haven't forgotten a damn thing about you," I snarl, trembling from the force of the bitterness boiling over as I give it back as good as she's giving. "Even when it was proven it would have made things a whole lot fucking easier if I had. Not one god damned thing, Emery."

Starting across the room, I reach her and pull her body flush to mine as a gasp escapes through her now parted lips. The same lips I spent the last hour imagined smirking at me when we saw each other again, but fall into a straight line instead.

My actions pissing her off and her not even attempting to hide it. The same way I'm not going to attempt to hide the way I feel about her anymore.

Gripping her face with my hands, I pull her toward me until our lips are crashing together, the anger between us quickly turning to passion as a rush of air ending in a soft moan escapes her and I take her deeper. My mouth feeding on hers, our lips devouring before our tongues slip free of their restraints, finding each other and doing the same.

"Like for instance," I break free of her kiss, breathing heavily into her ear. "The way you cry and beg for more when I touch you."

At the sound of her breath catching, I tighten my hold, lifting her and tossing her legs around me. Emery tightening their hold as I take her lips again, moving until, when she moans into my mouth, I'm pushing her back against the door.

"God, I've missed this," I breathlessly admit as I bring her lip into my mouth, grazing it with my teeth before sucking on it. "Wanted this for so damn long."

"Brady," she breathes and it's time for my breath to be the one catching.

She's either going to agree and tell me she's been wanting this as long as I have or the next words out of her mouth are going to shut me down. Moving against her, pressing my body even harder into hers, reading her for any sign that she wants me to stop, she mewls softly and I've got all the answer I need.

Aware of the door and the intrusion of guys that at any moment could attempt to come through it, I reach over and flip the lock before driving my body hard into hers again. Her grip tightening against my neck, as her nails dig in so deep I can feel them grazing the skin under my shirt.

My hand brushing its way over her thigh, slipping the fabric that is the black skirt she's wearing up higher as one of her hands falls from its place around my neck and she's doing the same to the other side. Pushing it as high up as it can go and giving me the access to her body that I crave.

My dick rock hard and ready for her. Even more than I'd been when she first started yelling at me from across the room. Craving her the way it has every damn day for the last ninety, wanting what only she can give me.

Ecstasy. Heaven. Pleasurable Surrender.

Tracing the lining of her panties, teasing her and having her arch into me when I slip one finger under the fabric to the heat waiting for me underneath, I slip a second finger through and release a growl moan mixture of my own when her lips brush against the skin of my neck as she bites down while digging her nails even deeper.

"Fuck, Em."

"Mmm, Brady. How observant of you." She purrs, making my dick twitch. "That's exactly what I want you to do."

Running my fingers over her lips, my body arching into hers and letting her feel how close to the edge just being this close to her is bringing me, I slip one finger into her warmth, pushing deeper when she tightens and contracts around me, coating me in her slick wetness.

"Tell me." I demand with a growl as I pull my finger back out and prepare the second for entrance.

"Tell you what?" she pants, wiggling her body against mine, the need to have my fingers buried deep inside of her again almost as bad as mine is to do it.

"Tell me I'm the only one."

Her answer comes in the form of a cry as I shove both fingers rough and deep back inside. The yes of pleasure that bursts from somewhere deep inside her like music to my ears.

She's as much mine as I am hers.

"Yes what, Emery?"

"You—you're the only one." She pants out as I continue to move my fingers in and out, her pussy gripping me tighter with each thrust.

"Brady…"

"Three months," I tell her as I thrust my fingers into her one final time before pulling out and slipping my hand between us, releasing the stranglehold my workout shorts have on my dick. Untightening the knot and relishing the freedom that comes when they fall to the floor. "Three long months I tortured myself with thoughts of moments like this. Every night, the sound of my name falling from your lips while I drove myself inside you, the only thing that could get me off."

"The only thing I *wanted* to get me off." I clarify as she uses her feet to pull me and the raging hard on I'm sporting deeper into her, my dick getting a tease of its own as it rubs against her dampness.

Just the thought of us touching this way after going so long without it enough to make me wanna unload.

"Brady, please."

Guiding my dick toward her slit at the sound of her plea and shoving her panties to the side, I run it up and down teasing her, making her quiver and begin to shake, her grip around me loosening as she begs me again.

"Please what, Em? Tell me what you need me to do."

"Take me."

Resisting the strong urge my dick has to do just that, I keep control and continue to push her. Needing to hear her tell me what she wants me to do to her almost as much as I need to give in and do it.

"I plan to, but first you're going to have to tell me how you want me to take you."

"Brady...shit. You know how."

"No, princess, I don't. Refresh my memory."

It's only when her lips find and crash down on mine and her hand begins its descent from my shoulders down over my chest and around my arm until she's gripping my cock that she does me one better.

Showing me.

Stroking me a few times before guiding me back, she moves her body in time with mine until the head of my dick is slipping inside, connecting with the flood of warmth there to greet me.

"Emery..." I start cursing when just like she'd done with my fingers, she squeezes every inch of me as I bury myself in her. "Fuck, this isn't going to last long if you keep—"

"Keep what?" she laughs softly as she tightens herself so strong around me I'm brushing against her walls.

"That...keep doing that." I choke out. "Shit, Em. I'm afraid to fucking move."

"Move, Brady..."

"Not unless you're moving with me."

The full impact of what those words mean floods me the second her body begins to move against mine, pulling me deeper into her. This isn't just us fucking because I'd lost my shit seeing her with Fortune and needed to release the tension, or even her anger at me because of it. It's more.

So much more.

I don't want to do anything period unless she's doing it with me.

Gripping her as tightly as I can, I give her what she wants by moving, slowly at first until she's answering my movements with ones of her own, picking up the pace until I'm driving hard into her, deeper with each thrust I make. The locker room filled with the sounds of what I know is our lovemaking.

Panting breaths, names and curses mixing together until they're one and the same. Both of us together as one, as we climb to the top, her nails digging in and leaving marks in my skin as we reach the precipice.

Words I've not yet spoken but have spent the last three months dying to tell her fall as we both go over the edge, making the rush of release that much sweeter.

"I love you, Emery."

Chapter Eighteen

Avery

"You, Avery. I wished for you. And it came true because just like I wanted you to be, you're here."

This is what I was afraid of coming here.

This moment.

Where Jax would say the words that gripped my heart and pulled it tightly from the bowels that have been the last three months of despair.

Say the words that mirrored every secret wish of mine since that day in my house when I'd come across the text message and hadn't had time to process it before reacting. Letting the loss of my mother and the shock of what I saw staring back at me turn me into some kind of monster.

Every damn day once I realized the change, once I truly accepted the way my actions that day had brought about my own emotional downfall, I wished to be with him. Standing the way we are now, one step away from complete and utter surrender and instead of fighting it, just giving in.

But as time went on and the time we did connect not turning out quite the way I imagined it going in my head; it became painfully apparent that's all it was. A wish. A simple dream that had to remain that way. Never coming to fruition.

Now though, where his eyes on me cause my heart to flutter, along with the aching need to surrender to him and what for one blissful week had been one of the most beautiful moments of my life, what I pushed away is now running free.

Hope is reigning supreme.

"Don't, Jackson."

"Don't what?"

"Don't do this. I can't...I can't do this with you."

"What do you mean you can't do this? What exactly do you think *this* is?"

He's pushing me. What I mean very clear, but him unable or unwilling to accept it.

And why should he? I'm not even sure I want to accept it and I'm the one standing here saying the words.

"You know exactly what this is. You telling me you wished for me. You have to know what saying something like that would do."

Bringing his arms across his chest, he shakes his head. "But that's just it, Ave. I don't know what it does to you because for the last three months, other than one random call you answered, you've done nothing but shut me out. So since we're both here, why don't you clue me in? Tell me what you feel."

"I don't," I pause, lowering my eyes away from the intensity I see staring back at me in his. "I don't even know where to begin, Jackson."

Flinching from the coolness in my voice or the use of his full name, I can't be sure, he takes a step back and it takes everything in me not to reach out to stop him. Take my words back and bring back the closeness I felt when he caught me.

"How about you start by calling me Jax." He demands and just like that, he's not the only one flinching from the impact. "Doesn't feel so good having it thrown back at you does it?"

"No," I agree sadly. "It doesn't. I'm sorry."

"Don't apologize to me, Avery. That's not what I want."

"Then what do you want, Jax?" I ask, appeasing his request by releasing the near stranglehold I have on his name.

"A conversation." He finally answers. "All I want is to talk to you."

Something so simple, yet at the same time because of who he is and what we are to each other, is also incredibly hard.

"What do you want to talk about?"

"Why don't we start with why you're here?"

Okay, that really is an easy question. One that I don't have to swallow down my emotional response to. Maybe I *can* do this.

"Interviews. Markus got a call requesting one of his best reporters to fill in for someone that at the last minute had to pull out."

"So you're here interviewing what? The entire CPW locker room or just a few of us?"

"Not all of you. Just the ones on the card tonight."

"On the card, huh?" he laughs and knowing how ridiculous it sounds, I join him, though the sound of my own laughter pales in comparison to the soft lift in his.

"Yeah. I've also got to write up a full report on the event itself, so I'm trying to get as many out of the way as I can so I don't have to hunt anyone down later."

"Makes sense."

When nothing follows those two words, I decide to continue talking. If a conversation is what he wants, it's what he's gonna get. Even if he's not an active participant in it.

"Yeah…So, I'm supposed to interview you too. As well as anyone else involved in the Middleweight Championship picture."

Nodding, he untangles his arms and motions to the door with a sigh. "I've had what feels like fifty interviews in there tonight. I'm pretty sure my ability to answer with more than a grunt or body tick is officially gone. It's the reason I'm out here. I needed a break."

"That bad, huh?"

"Yes—no. Wait. It's not that bad. I mean, it's a part of the job I can do blindfolded. After a while though, it just becomes monotonous. Same questions, same people, same everything. I want something different. So out here under the stars? That's my different."

For the first time since coming out here and literally stumbling across him, I can feel my face beginning to lift in a smile and it's not long after that the laugh escapes.

"So it happens to the subjects just like the reporters. Who knew?"

"How have you been?" he asks, effectively taking the lighter mood we'd established and driving it straight into the ground.

"I don't really think you want to know the answer to that, Jax."

"I asked, didn't I?" he picks up, not missing a beat. His point made as I nod before releasing a heavy hearted sigh.

This is hard for me. Wanting so much to be able to reach out and touch him, tell him what he wants to know without questioning every damn thing, but knowing that in the end I can't because he's no longer mine to do that with.

"It hasn't been easy. I've taken on a lot more responsibility, even more than I originally signed on for in order to keep my mind busy. Being sure to throw in the occasional day off so I don't crash and burn. Basically, I go through the motions. I'm not even sure from one day to the next if I'm even living anymore."

"I hear that."

"It's been the same for you?" I delicately ask, not wanting to intrude, but curious to know how if he's gotten everything he ever wanted he could be feeling the same way that I am.

"Yeah. Ever since I came back, I've basically been doing the same thing. I throw myself into my matches, putting on the best show I can for the people that put their money down to come see me, basically becoming a proper company bitch. I just don't really live any of it. It's all just more of the sameness I was talking about earlier."

I hate that for him. I hate that this is the way things have turned out. I would have thought walking away the way I had and having minimal contact in the interim would have given him the freedom to go back to doing what he loves. What he lives for.

Not this.

This is the opposite of what I wanted.

"It doesn't have to be that way forever, does it?" he asks so softly that I'm not sure if it's directed at me or towards the universe in general.

"What do you mean?"

"Avery, I miss you. I told you that the night we spoke on the phone. I wake up every damn day and turn over, waiting for the moment when my arms will brush against your skin as my fingers make contact, only to find the bed empty and my heart aching because it's wondering where its beat is."

Brutal honesty. Words my mom if she were here would say were being spoken straight from his heart to mine. Ones that make the ever present hole where my heart used to be only ache more.

"I don't want it to be that way forever, Ave. It hurts too much. I want my beat back. I want *you* back."

Feeling the tears beginning to build, overcome by it, I reach out for the wall. Something tangible that I can hold onto in order to get control again. Anything that will stop the volcano that is seconds away from erupting inside me. The natural disaster that hits like a tidal wave as the first tear slips out and a sob releases garbled and messy from my throat.

Before I can react to the scraping sound of his boots against the ground, his arms are around me and I'm being pulled flush and tight against him. The tears falling more freely the second we make contact, the string holding my control together snapping apart completely as the final wall around my heart crumbles.

"I'm sorry, Ave. So damn sorry. I didn't mean...I didn't think."

"Don't, Jax." I somehow manage to speak through my tears.

"Don't what, sweetheart?"

Sweetheart.

A sweet pet name he'd given me that before he'd done it the first time, I never would have been taken in by. Never being one of the girls that needed those types of things. But a name that now, having heard it from others and gone so long without it from him has another wave of tears welling up and spilling over from the fullness that it brings to my heart.

He's the only person in the world I ever want calling me that.

"Apologize for what you said. Never do that. Not when everything you said is exactly what I've wanted to tell you every day for the past twelve weeks. Everything I feel."

Slipping his hand under my chin and lifting me up toward him, the effect of my truth on full display in his eyes, he run his fingers in delicate strokes over my cheeks before moving down and repeating the same action along my jawline. Almost as though with each touch he's committing me to memory, just the way he did when we made love for the first time.

It feeling now just like it did then.

Like Heaven.

Lowering his face down and closer to mine, each passing second making my pulse quicken and race in anticipation, his lips find mine. His kiss a soft caress, stealing my breath and setting my body ablaze in quick succession. Giving into the feelings that despite everything that's happened, I couldn't outrun or distance myself from. I answer his kiss, starting of gentle, almost timid until a vibration in his chest, what results in a moan escaping from somewhere deep inside him has me deepening it.

Needing more. Needing him.

Everything he's got to give.

"Jesus, Ave. I missed this." He admits before crashing his lips down onto mine again. A call that just as I'm about to answer in kind and completely give myself over to, is interrupted by the sound of the door clicking open.

Effectively taking the spell we'd be under and breaking it and us apart with a start.

Quickly collecting ourselves, we turn toward the interruption almost in tandem as a redhead with what I can only describe as the body of a Greek style goddess steps out, letting the door close behind her. A dangerous yet all knowing smile playing on her lips when she takes the two of us in.

It's only after she glances from me to Jackson and I turn and see the ashen expression that now covers his face that I realize exactly who this person is. When she speaks, her words only solidifying it.

"Jackson, baby! There you are! I've been looking everywhere for you."

Just like three months ago when I'd seen the text on his phone, it's happening again now. My entire body freezing, my breath seeming lodged in my throat. The familiar pang of my insecurities rising making me look away.

Anywhere but at the two of them.

The man I love beyond all reason and the woman that no matter what we just shared, he actually belongs to.

Stepping between them, needing to get as far away from the awkwardness as possible and hide the shattering that's only seconds away from being on full display for all to see, I mumble a quick apology and head for the door.

The sight of her arm coming out and slipping through his as she steps into him enough to break my heart all over again.

Pulling on the handle, I yank the door as far back as it can go, turning back before heading back in and seeing the look of utter devastation written all over Jackson's face.

That look, the same one he'd worn the day he dropped me off at the airport all that's needed for me to repeat the same words that I'd spoken then.

Making us really come full circle.

"Goodbye, Jackson."

Turning and racing through the door, running as quickly as my legs can carry me down the hall and further away from them, I don't stop until after turning a corner, I'm met with a secluded and dark hallway.

The perfect place to break.

Again.

My last thought as my body falls to the floor being the advice I've heard countless times before but until now, never believed in.

When it's over, it's really over.

Chapter Nineteen

Emery

"I love you, Emery."

With as much time as I spent wishing for those words from him, in all of the different places and ways he could have said it, this wasn't one of them.

Being buried balls deep in a woman who you've effectively got pressed against the locker room door while you collectively fuck her brains out, not exactly the best time for heartfelt declarations.

Probably not the best idea to declare your love when you're married to someone else either. Not that Brady's marriage had been an issue when he'd stalked across the room and took me the way a starving man takes water in the desert.

This was a mistake.

A humongous mistake.

What the hell was I thinking?

Am I really that hard pressed for a scrap of Brady's attention that I'm willing to let myself be taken and used in a locker room of all places?

Just what the fuck has gotten into me? When did I become this girl? Better yet, what happened to the girl that wasn't going to sleep with anyone until she was sure it was the person she was going to be with for the rest of her life?

Oh, come on! When were you ever that girl?

Right. I forgot. I've never been that girl. I'm pretty sure being that way skipped over me entirely and went straight to Avery.

I need to say something. Shift my body one way or the other to signal for Brady to release me from my place against the door. Something that won't come out as awkward sounding as every other thing floating around in my head right now.

This never should have happened.

Even if those words he whispered as he came were the ones I've spent the last three months dying to hear and even if he was the only one I ever wanted to hear them from.

It doesn't change anything because all the issues that were present that day in my kitchen, back when life just seemed so incredibly easy and perfect, are still there.

There's still another woman out there that's walking around wearing his name.

What deep down inside, even with all of the time apart, should only be for me.

At least that's the pretty picture I paint myself when it comes to him. Every word he uttered after Ron walked out with Gavin only feeding into it, making what came next, while so incredibly wrong, right at the same time.

I wanted Brady that way. I still want him.

I want to do it again.

Which, given who he is and who he actually belongs to, makes me the worst kind of slut.

Brushing his nose against the side of my neck, he murmurs something I can't quite make out before trailing that same line with his lips, nuzzling into me while releasing a contented moan.

A sound that given how quiet the room has been apart from the sound of our labored breathing as we got ourselves under control, almost sounds foreign. Like it shouldn't be there at all after what we just did.

Finally building up the strength to move, I shift and just like I'd been hoping, he situates my panties before sliding me down until my feet are firmly planted on the floor.

"Emery, that was..."

"Wrong." I blurt out and not wanting to risk another repeat of earlier even though my body seems to have other ideas, I lower my attention to my skirt, making sure it's pulled back down and situated the way it was before things had gotten out of hand. Doing my best at the same time to ignore the huff of breath Brady releases on receipt of what I said.

"I was going to say perfect, but apparently we didn't just experience the same thing."

I can hear the hurt in his voice, my belief wounding him, but refusing to give into it, I keep my attention focused on righting my clothing and getting control of my hair, bringing my hand up and running through it. Being met with the dampness from the sweat that's accumulated from our moment of weakness.

"Emery, would you look at me?" When I don't even attempt to move my head in one direction or another, focusing instead of picking a piece of lint off the skirt that my eyes had honed in on, he tries again, this time pleading. "Please look at me?"

Don't give in, Em. You know that when you do, you're going to fall victim to the Brady Raines man trap again.

"I need to go." I say instead, immediately pulling my gaze off my skirt and looking around the room. Anywhere but at him where he wants it to be.

It's not a lie. I need to get out of here. Before I look up, see those blue eyes of his and fall under his spell again, this time bent over the damn bench where I'd caught him sitting earlier while he slams into me from behind.

Whoa. I really do need to create some distance if my thoughts are this far off the reservation.

Attempting to turn around, I make out the lock on the door and reach out to flip it but before I can even get my hands around it, he's spinning me back around with enough force that I'm shaken up enough to actually meet his eyes.

Fuck. I'm screwed.

"You need to tell me where you went just now, because not five minutes ago you were as into this as I am, and now it feels like we're back in your kitchen and I've lost you all over again."

Is that what's happening here?

I mean, I can tell I'm pulling away based on the realization that hit me the second he told me how he felt, but I didn't think I reached that level yet. If anything, right now all I feel is awkward.

Have I got this all wrong?

No. I argue with myself and shaking my head. *Even if he meant what he said and he does love me, it doesn't change the fact that he's still married.*

"Em, please talk to me. I need to know what you're thinking. What you shaking your head like that means."

How the hell am I supposed to explain it to him when I don't even understand it myself?

"This was a mistake, Brady." I swallow hard. "You don't have to pretend to make me feel better. What you said, what we did, it's okay. We just took things too far."

This time using the release of his hand to my advantage, I do turn toward the door, flipping the lock and even managing to get the knob on the door to turn before he's again spinning me around.

Only instead of just holding me in place, he's pressing me back against it and his lips, they're on mine, fast and hard. His kiss anything but, easing up on the pressure and running over mine slowly. Tenderly. Not the kiss of a man overridden with need like before, but a man possessed by only one thing.

The feelings he has for the woman he's kissing.

"Brady..."

"Why do you think what happened was a mistake?"

"Which reason do you want first? There's a lot of them."

There it is again. His eyes softening and lowering before he seems to think better of it and meets mine head on. I hurt him with what I just said.

"Bullshit."

"It's not bullshit."

"Then let me have it. Every fucking reason you have for why what we did being wrong. I wanna hear them so I can prove every one of them wrong."

How can he flip gears like that? Go from being hurt to standing there looking all smug when the truth is, he should be the one calling what we did wrong given the truth. He's married for Christ sakes. Did he somehow dump his brain when he shot his load?

I can't be the only one that sees just how badly we screwed everything up.

"We just fucked against the locker room door, Brady. Which considering how quick Ron was to call Gavin on how much shit you'd all be in if Smith knew I was in here makes this a pretty huge mistake."

"Well, princess. Since I don't exactly plan on going to Smith and telling him, and with the beating I laid on Fortune, I doubt he will either, I'm pretty sure your secret is safe."

"You fucked me bare. How you gonna talk your way around that one, rich boy?"

The truth is, the first time we were together in the water, with as fast and frenzied as that had been, we'd been unsafe then too and again after the hockey game when we'd gone back to my place.

Every single time the two of us were together, our brains leaving the building.

Yeah, maybe this was the best choice to run with after all. This has *big mistake* written all over it. I'd gotten lucky so far in that I didn't end up knocked up, but how many chances do you really get at that before you finally end up with a bun in the oven?

This is so much worse than I thought when I said it.

"I don't need to talk myself around it. I've only been with two people in the last nine years, Em, and one of them I hadn't so much as looked at that way in months. I was on the road too much and when I did end up home, fighting sort of won out over getting my dick wet. Which only leaves you."

"It's still...it's not right." I stammer out and damnit if the stupid smug look he's sporting doesn't grow bigger.

Asshole.

"Everything about us is right, but fine. We should have been smarter about things."

Conceding should make me happy even if it is only a partial one, but considering the next reason on my list, it does the opposite.

"Any other reasons I need to disprove?"

"You already mentioned the other one, but since I get the feeling you shot off your brain when you came, I guess I'll spell it out. You're still married, Brady."

"Em," he says, his expression hardening but not stammering for words or tripping up the way I expect him to. "About that..."

Before I can press for more, there's a banging from the other side of the door. The vibration of it shaking the both of us and shattering whatever it was that he was about to tell me.

Great. Perfect fucking timing.

"Right." I say. Putting my hands out and shoving him away. "Looks like that's my cue."

Turning and twisting the knob, I push it open, smiling awkwardly at the group of men standing on the other side. The lot of them all locked on me in surprise when they realize it's not one of their own on the other side.

Stepping through, I wait until they all start making their way in, pushing in and around Brady and blocking his ability to get to me before finally looking over and meeting his eyes.

"Thanks for the interview, Raines. It was real enlightening." I cover myself when what I really want to say when I see the dejected look in his eyes is what I really feel.

That what he said before wasn't one sided. That I love him too.

But most of all, even though I'd given him reason after reason for it being the opposite, what we shared...it wasn't a mistake.

Things that no matter much I wish I could, I can never say. Not now. Not ever.

I really need to find Avery.

It's time to go.

Chapter Twenty

Avery

"Hey."

Hearing the voice but already having had my fill for the night and choosing to ignore it, I bury my face deeper into my legs and attempt to block it and the rest of the building out altogether.

What gets increasingly harder to do when the person behind the voice doesn't get the memo that I want to be left alone and tries again.

"Girl on the floor that I know can hear me but is choosing to ignore me?"

Completely unable to ignore him now that I know he's onto me, I finally look up from my crumpled position on the floor. Smoothing down my hair, knowing I must look like one hell of a hot mess, I pause when I meet the pair of eyes behind the voice, recognizing him immediately.

Matthias Kemper.

Otherwise known as the current CPW Middleweight Champion.

"Hey." I greet him with a half-hearted wave. "Are you the one they sent to kick me out of here?"

Raising an eyebrow, probably trying to figure out who let the crazy chick in, he shakes his head before leaning his body up against the wall and sliding to the ground.

"You do something worth getting kicked out for?"

Pointing to my face, like all the answers he's after are going to be found there, he nods in what I can only assume is sympathy for the girl with the raccoon eyes.

"Who did that to you?" he asks softly, pointing to my face.

"Who did what to me?"

Leaning over, he reaches forward and before I can react, tucks a stray tendril of my hair behind my ear before moving back against the wall again like it was the most natural thing in the world to touch a stranger's hair.

"I was trying to ask that delicately given you're a lady and all, but fuck it. I want you to tell me what dumbass piece of shit made you cry like that."

Okay the hair thing was weird, but this? Why in the world would Matthias want to know who made me cry?

"No one. I did it to myself."

"You're gonna have to excuse my language again, but like fucking hell you did that to yourself."

"You got experience making girls cry or something?" I ask, intrigued by how easily he can spot my lie.

"No, but I've been around my fair share of assholes that get enjoyment out of it, so I can spot it a mile away. Just like I know that you're covering now because you're trying to protect *your* asshole."

I've got to hand it to him. He's good.

"You might be right about that."

"If I promise not to hurt him, will you tell me who it is?"

Shaking my head, he curses and something about the way he doesn't even try to hide it has me laughing for the first time since I got here tonight.

"That's better. I like that sound. The smile's not so bad either."

If I didn't know any better, I'd think he was flirting, but considering he hasn't so much as smiled once since he came upon me in the hall, something tells me that for Matthias, flirting is the last thing on his mind.

"Thanks. I aim to please." I flippantly respond and the strangest thing happens. It's small, barely there really, but his lip quirks up.

What do you know? The guy smiles after all.

"You want something to drink? I need a drink. I could wrestle something up for ya." He jokes, motioning down the hall toward the soda machine a few feet away. "You look like you could use a drink."

He has no idea how right he is. The only thing wrong being the choice of beverage. Not exactly thirsty, but not missing him say that he was, I nod and watch as he hops easily to his feet and heads off down the hall toward the machine. Returning a few minutes later with two bottles of water and a can of ginger ale. Handing both over before lowering himself back down.

"What's the ginger ale for?"

"Once upon a time, when my mom was having one of those *assholes making her cry* days, she would ask for ginger ale to settle her stomach. Don't know if it's a chick thing or not, but figured it couldn't hurt."

Who is this guy? No, seriously.

The one sitting here offering me ginger ale and the one he is when he's in the ring, they're like night and day. Two different people. Fictitious or not, I would have figured aspects would carry over. So far, I see nothing.

"So you gonna tell me what happened or am I gonna have to beat it out of you?" Nudging me in the shoulder with his arm, his lip twitches again before he winks.

Maybe I was wrong about the flirting. That or he's one hell of an entertainer. Being caught up in his actions and the way he doesn't mince words, it's doing wonders for keeping my mind off the pain.

Matthias is a lifesaver.

"It's a long story. I'm pretty sure you've got better things to do with your time."

"Maybe, but since I'm here and clearly, you're here, how about we talk and just be here together?"

Can it really be that simple? Start from the beginning and tell a virtual stranger our whole sordid story? Can we really just be here together?

Well, it certainly beats being nowhere, which is exactly where you were when you sat down.

"Shit, you know what I just realized?"

"What?"

"I never told you my name." Smacking a hand off his head, he holds it out in front of him, the twitchy smile I'm starting to become familiar with lifting more when I take it, until wonder of all wonders, he's full on smiling at me. "I'm Matthias."

"I know. Nice to meet you."

"Nice to meet you, I'm...." he repeats motioning with his hands for me to continue. "Don't tell me your name is actually 'girl on the floor that I know can hear me but is choosing to ignore me', because fuck, that's a mouthful and not the kind I like."

Unable to hold back the laugh that bubbles up, I let it out and the smile returns.

"Yep. I was right before. That's a wicked sound."

Willing my cheeks not to flush, still unsure whether he's flirting or not but my face running with a will all its own, I put us back on topic.

"The name is actually Avery."

"Avery. Hmm, that's different. I like it." He announces before nudging me with his elbow again. "So, Avery. How did you end up backstage at a wrestling show with makeup running down your face?"

"I was—"

"Before you say another word, I just want you to know that you can tell me who did it. I promise I won't hurt him...much."

"Do you wanna know why I'm here or not?" I ask sternly. A tone I can't hold onto to save my life once he responds with a pout.

"Sorry, go ahead. I'm done trying to get a name out of you."

"I don't believe you."

Pounding a hand against his chest, he throws his body back hard against the wall, slumping over and resting a hand over his heart when I laugh.

"You wound me, Avery." Sitting back up, he frowns. "Seriously. How can you not believe this face?"

"Okay, okay. You got me. I believe you."

"Good. Now spill."

"I got involved with someone and it turned out badly. You already figured out he's someone that works here. Anyway, I ran into him outside and everything seemed so right and then it all just went wrong. Again. When we were together, he was free, but from what I just caught outside, it looks like he's back together with his ex-girlfriend. She showed up when we were getting close and well..." I pause motioning up and down the hall. "You know the rest."

"I know that I said I wouldn't hound you about this anymore, but I can't sit here listening to this and not know who it is. I swear on any part of my life that's actually worth something that I won't do shit to him, but I want you to tell me who it is."

Meeting his eyes, the roughness I'd seen before is gone and in its place, genuine curiosity and what I believe is honesty. He means it.

"Jackson—"

"Merrick." He finishes. "I should have known."

He should have known?

"You're her."

"I'm who?"

"You're the one."

"I don't understand what you mean."

"The one he bailed on the company for. The girl from Canada that he took time off to go see, and the one that he bailed on hitting the bars with us to run off and talk to a few months back."

Unbelievable.

"What do you mean *bailed on the company* for?"

Shifting his body closer to mine, he leans in, his eyes studying me, searching for something, but for the life of me I have no idea what. All I do know is, what had been a pretty comfortable existence up until this point was quickly turning into the opposite.

"You don't know?"

"I guess not since I asked."

"Avery, I don't know how much you remember, but when Jax and Brady took off out of town, they signed a contract that said if they weren't in Oregon after the two days, they'd be terminated. One of the boys got wind of Smith talking about it and it spread around pretty quick, which is how I know about it."

"Okay, but what does that have to do with me?"

"The show in Oregon got screwed, so Smith put all our asses on flights to Vegas. Shit, you really don't know about any of this?"

I haven't talked to Jax since our failed attempt over the phone, so of course I don't know any of this. I'd been too caught up in my own pain to even ask.

"I don't. So why don't you fill in the blanks?"

"He didn't go to Vegas. He never showed. The next day, Smith called a meeting to go over the lineup for the show that night and filled us in."

That can't be possible. We drove to the airport together. Sure, we'd gone our separate ways after I left the car and his plea to stay with him behind, but there's no way he stayed in Toronto.

He couldn't have, could he?

"Where did he go?"

"Truth?"

"Obviously." I respond with an eye roll and he laughs. A sound with as raw as it sounds might just be a first for the guy too.

"Merrick and I aren't close. I guess you could say we run in different circles. He chills with the boys, I tend to go along but stay out of the way."

"You're the lone wolf."

"Something like that, yeah. Because of that, I can't tell you where he was or what he did back then. I just know he didn't do it here. He only just came back."

The more Matthias tells me, the emptier I feel.

"What do you mean he just got back?" I ask, needing the answer to this in order to try and piece together just what the hell had gone on back then. What Jax, even though he had the chance outside never said a word about and what even if he had, I probably still wouldn't have truly heard.

"Smith pulled him back in a few weeks ago."

A few weeks ago. The last time we'd spoken on the phone.

That can't be a coincidence.

"So the two of you reconnected tonight?" Matthias speaks up when after a few minutes of just sitting and attempting to process everything he said, I still haven't spoken a word.

"It was heading that way. It was like the last three months hadn't even happened. Like we picked right back up where we left off, not missing a beat. It was just that easy. At least it was until his girlfriend showed up."

"I don't know what to say." He admits and I just shrug. I get it. *What can he say?*

"That makes two of us. I'm sort of at a loss myself."

"No, wait. I do know what to say. I just don't think it's going to be anything you want to hear."

"Can't be any worse than what I've already had to endure tonight, so have at it."

"I don't know shit about relationships. The longest one being the one I'm currently in with my hand." He laughs, lifting his hand and shaking it. "But before you upchuck all over my boots, hear me out. I don't know much about them because I've never given a fuck about anything but wrestling before, but I have seen enough over the years to pick up a thing or two."

"Like?"

"Like for one, he's not with Melinda. I guarantee she wants him, but seeing as she's made it pretty clear she wants half the roster, that doesn't really mean much. He's not with anyone."

He's not with Melinda?

"And for two?" I ask, needing Matthias to distract me from the road my thoughts are taking and just how right they might be if everything he just told me is the truth.

Jackson meaning every word he's ever said. Every explanation he's given in the messages and letters he left me since. My mom's last words to Emery, the ones she told me about the day of the funeral being more than just words. A truth she had learned too late, but that she wanted me to hear in order to prevent history repeating itself.

I'm running in the wrong direction.

A realization that Matthias obviously picks on me realizing as he offers me a weak smile before leaning in and resting his forehead against mine, giving me his answer.

"If you want the rest, you're going to need to turn around."

Huh? Turn around?

"Why?"

"Because what I've picked up over the years, what I really think you need to hear, is standing right behind you."

Before I can even process what he's said, much less make sense of it, another voice joins the conversation.

"Avery…"

What Matthias knows, it's not a lesson or a bunch of facts. It's a person. One who despite the misunderstandings, the distance, the anger and confusion, with just one word becomes the only answer I want to hear.

The answer is Jax.

Jax

When I made the decision to become a wrestler and began training, one of the first moves I asked to learn was a sleeper hold, and not just the basic one. Every imaginable variation of it.

There was just something about it that called to me, especially after witnessing Roddy Piper do it on more than one occasion on television when I was barely even old enough to lace up my own boots, let alone someone of his calibers.

When I broke away from the training and headed out into my first independent promotion, I settled on the dragon sleeper and went about making it my own.

After slipping out of Melinda's grip and heading after Avery, coming across her down a vacant hallway with none other than the guy I'm supposed to be facing off against tonight in Matthias, I felt a lot like the opponents I used to put in the hold.

My airway was constricted, all of the blood draining away, leaving me lightheaded and seconds away from collapse. My heart, even though I knew it hadn't, sure as shit felt like it had stopped and when he leaned into her? I'm pretty sure I got an up close and personal look at just what she felt seeing Melinda slip her arm through mine.

He didn't need to get me in the ring and proceed to kick my ass for the fan's enjoyment. He'd managed to do that before we even walked through the curtain. The intimate way they look huddled together making me wish we were in the middle of a match so I could tap.

Hit the mat so fucking hard that there could be no mistaking my need to give in.

Give up.

It's only when she lifts her head away from his and turns in my direction, and I'm given the clear view of his face that I see what up until then had been alluding me.

The slight nod of his head and the miniscule lift to his lips before he shifts back and gets to his feet, proving that just like she'd misinterpreted things before, I had done the same here.

Matthias helping instead of hindering.

"Hear him out, alright? It's pretty obvious with the way you're both looking at each other that whatever it is, it's worth hearing." He tells her softly before squeezing her hand and making his way toward me, giving me more of the same.

"I see any more lines on her face later and they look as angry as the ones there now, I will end you. We clear?"

"Crystal." I whisper and with one final shove to my shoulder as he passes, he's gone and it's just the two of us.

Five steps.

That's all it would take to end this and bring the girl I love back into my arms. Steps I can't seem to take because just like I heard Matthias say, the angry lines of black running down her cheeks have left me paralyzed.

When am I going to stop being the cause? When do I finally get to have things go right and have those beautiful lips raised at me instead of crestfallen and quivering? When do things finally get to go right and I get to see her eyes dance the way they did on the boardwalk in Delaware?

If the way they seem to fly to the floor when I shift in order to take my first step is any kind of indicator, it's a *not yet* answer to all of the above.

"Jax..."

"Interview me." I blurt out. What seems to work as the second her head starts to lift in my direction, I notice her makeup has stopped running.

Maybe being a complete imbecile has its advantages after all.

"What?"

"You heard me."

"I did," she laughs softly. "I'm just not sure if you're being serious or not."

"It's no joke, sweetheart. You need to interview everyone here tonight. You didn't do me yet, so here I am. Hit me with your best shot." I say, motioning between us. "I'll even make it easy on you. I'll ask and answer the first question."

"Okay..." she answers hesitantly, her uncertainty at my motives mirroring my own.

I have no idea what I'm doing, but meaning what I told her outside earlier, needing to hear anything and everything she has to say because it's her doing it, I need to keep her talking. If answering nonsense questions I've probably already answered fifty times already tonight gets me that, so be it.

"Is Jackson Kennedy Merrick a complete idiot?" I ask into the air and answer just as quickly. "He's the worst kind of idiot."

Taking a step once I see the slight twitch of her lip as she fights against the smile I know is attempting to break through on her face, I keep it going.

"Is that the first time I've told someone my middle name?" I ask and answer. "Why yes it is, but if it gets the girl to smile, even if it is in pity, I'd admit it a million times over. Publicly even."

Where I think I'm going to have to keep this going, she switches gears and besides the smile, I'm gifted the sound of an actual laugh. One as natural as she'd been the day I saw her at the gas station.

"Does Jackson Kennedy Merrick realize he was named after two dead presidents?" She asks once her laughter has subsided and just like I didn't waste any time answering my own questions, I don't here either.

"Not at first, but I learned real quick when I got the crap kicked out of me for it when I was eight."

"No way. I don't believe it."

"Believe it, sweetheart. Apparently my parents didn't get the memo about crappiest name combos and I ended up paying the price for it."

I've managed to take one step toward her and even though I know things are still nowhere near right between us, she's at least more open to the idea of it than she had been when I first showed up. Do I dare take another step? Risk the relative calm we've found?

Of course I do. It's Avery.

Bringing my right foot out, I take another step, following it up with another, pausing when she finally shifts her attention to what I'm doing and again I'm hit by the makeup on her face.

"Why did you stop?"

"Stop what?"

"Walking."

"Your eyes."

"What about them?"

Do I tell her that I can't seem to move every time I catch sight of the jagged black lines running down over her cheeks because I can't stand the twist that takes place in my gut knowing I'm the cause? Can I even call attention to it at all?

"They're piercing."

Okay, not exactly a lie. They are that. But not at all what I should have said.

"Avery, shit. That's not what I meant to say."

"So what did you mean to say?"

Before I can answer, she's claiming the final two steps it would take to complete us, stopping at the exact moment her arm brushes against my own. The small action speaking volumes.

"I hate that I caused them to cry like that. Hate even more than I'm the reason your cheeks are stained."

"You know," she says, looking up. "Matthias didn't like it much either. Kept trying to get me to tell him who did it."

"Did you?" I ask even though I already know the answer.

Biting her lip, her eyes begin to slip again only this time I'm not letting them. Reaching out and touching her face, I silently plead with her to lift them back and when she doesn't, I slip my fingers under her chin like I've done in the past and lift them until they are.

"Please don't look away. I like the way it feels having your eyes on me."

"I told him, Jax."

With the way I've seen Matthias be with some of the women that work here, I'm not all surprised he threatened me. He might not say too much when he's here, but I think we've all gotten the memo on just how he feels about women being hurt by us.

Making me glad he's the one that found her. God only knows what would have happened if it had been anyone else.

"What are you doing here, Jax?"

"Answering a pretty reporters' questions?"

"By answering with another question? How thoughtful of you."

"Well, if she would give me an actual question I can answer, I wouldn't need to ask questions of my own."

Leaning back against the wall with a sigh, turning her attention back toward me, almost as if she's realizing her mistake, she hits me right where it hurts.

"Are you and Melinda back together?"

"No."

"Then what was that outside?"

"Melinda being Melinda. We're being put in a program together and just like she did with Gavin, she's doing with me now."

"Which is what exactly?"

"Pushing herself on me."

"Is it working?"

Just like the answer to her first question was easy, requiring no thought whatsoever other than how to do it without puking, this one is too. I'm going to make her see that all of that crap with Melinda, was all on Melinda and had nothing to do with what I actually felt.

"No, and for the record, it won't ever work."

"But you're working with her…"

"I work with a lot of women, Avery. I always have. It doesn't mean I feel the need to do anything with them. That honor goes to one woman only."

This, my admission, seems to halt her. Whatever it was she had planned after my answer obviously not coming. Giving me an opening to get some answers of my own.

"Has there been…are you seeing anyone?"

"Which one do you want me to answer?"

"Both." I respond, even though I couldn't even bring myself to finish asking the first. Not sure I really wanted to know if there had been anyone since things ended with us.

I know that Emery told me she wasn't in the right frame of mind to see anyone, much less date and that from what she could tell Avery was still tightly wrapped up in me, but that could have just as easily been bullshit.

"The answer is the same for both, Jax. No. I'm not seeing anyone and there hasn't been anyone else. There won't be."

"What do you mean won't?"

"Where did you go when you dropped me off the airport?" she asks instead. "When I got on the flight to Delaware, where did you go?"

"Nowhere." I admit and just as she's about to fire off what I'm sure is going to be another question related to that day, I give her everything she's after. "I changed my flight when I finally managed to make my way inside and instead of heading out to Vegas like Smith wanted, I took the next flight to Delaware."

"Oh my God!' She gasps. "It's true."

"What is?"

"Matthias, after he found me out here and we started talking, told me some things. I wasn't entirely sure I bought it, at least not until now. Everything he said was right."

I have no idea what Matty might have told her, but with the widened state of her eyes and the way her mouth sits open in the tiniest o shape, with her jaw about to drop any second, I damn sure wanna know.

"Did you sign a contract before you came to Toronto?" she fires off before I can even attempt to ask and I don't even bother with a verbal response, choosing to just nod instead.

"Jax..."

She knows. All of it. Every god damned bit of what happened after the blow up in the car, she somehow found out about from Matthias. I shouldn't care so much that she knows considering I didn't do a damn thing to hide it, but the look of absolute devastation on her face as she processes what he's told her and what I'm standing here not denying the way she probably assumed I would, all I do is care.

"Brady wanted to see your sister, I told you that. I also told you that I managed to work out a deal with Marie so that we could save it since it looked like we weren't going to be able to get the time off. I just never bothered telling you exactly what it was that I did."

"Then why don't you tell me now?"

"I thought Matthias already did that for me."

"Not all of it. Just pieces and like I told you, I didn't want to believe him."

"But you'll believe me?"

Her answer coming almost as quickly as all of mine, but not at all one I'm prepared to hear. The complete opposite of the one she's given me both spoken and unspoken over the last three months and opening a whole new can of worms in the process.

"Always, Jax."

Chapter Twenty-One

Brady

I'm a fucking bonehead.

No. I'm pretty sure I'm worse than a bonehead.

How is it that I manage to execute what might be the world's best plan of all time, get everything I ever wanted under the same roof and still manage to screw it up?

Oh, that's right. It happened because Jax was right the day I told him about the plan.

I suck at this.

Making love to her against the door—and yes it was love making despite the frenzied nature of it—and then admitting what I did, the first time I've uttered those words and felt the truth of them through every damn part of my body, it doesn't get better than that.

At least, that's how I felt until she blurted out her reasoning for what we shared being a mistake.

Why wasn't that the first damn thing out of my mouth when I finally got her alone?

When I texted her to put the entire plan in motion, things hadn't been settled yet, at least not on the divorce front, but since a whole lot had changed since then, why didn't I use the opportunity presented and admit that before thinking with my dick?

I'm not what she thinks. I'm not married anymore.

Sure, the ink is barely dry on the papers, but that doesn't matter. We've been separated and apart for so long, I was divorced long before I even met Emery. I just didn't realize it at the time.

The gigantic tidbit I'd left out completely and that now had her running.

Again.

"You two sort yourselves out?" Ron strolls over to me and asks.

Giving him the stink eye, I grunt out my reply and stalk my way over to where I'd thrown my duffel earlier. Yanking out my gear and without so much as a passing glance, shove my way past him straight for the showers.

"Nice talking to you too, Raines!" he calls out as I turn the corner and I just roll my eyes. The last thing I care about right now being what Taylor thinks, even if he is the reason I didn't go full homicidal and Emery and I were able to have the moment at all.

Flipping the nozzles on the shower and pushing in the button, I step straight into the spray as it pours and give in to the rush of emotion bubbling to the surface. Emotions I'd been holding onto since my declaration, but that with everything going on, I swallowed down.

What I can now, with the solitude I've got in here, finally let free.

The water from the shower mixing with the warmth of the flow freely running from my eyes. The only thing keeping me from a complete and utter meltdown being the knowledge that the girl I let slip through my fingers was still in the building and not completely lost.

As long as Avery was still here, no matter what way things played out if and when she ran into Jax, I had a chance to make this right. Even if I had to recreate what I'd done during my time with HFWA and take a stand inside the ring in order to do it.

You're not getting away from me that easy, Emery.

Looks like I'm going to have to execute part two of the plan after all, praying to god that in doing it, I don't end up making an even bigger mess of things.

Big gestures.

I've never been good with them, but if I want Emery, and with the way that even now, just thinking about her in the solitude of the shower has more than just my body reacting, I obviously do, I'm gonna have to get acquainted with them real quick.

It's time to put it all on the line. Bring phase two of my plan, the one strictly for me and my girl to fruition, even if it is different than what I originally wanted.

Making quick work of scrubbing myself down and rinsing off in record time, I head out, falling into place by Ron before leaning over into my duffel and grabbing the smoking gun inside.

What I knew I was going to end up having to use, but didn't exactly figure I'd have to use in the way I now have planned.

A brown manila envelope, similar in size and weight to the one I passed to Kelly in order to have her sign, but this time, holding the result I was after when I made my choice three months ago.

Bringing my heart and home back together again.

Emery

This place is fucking ridiculous.

Not only did I not manage to find my sister, even though I found the door she went out of to get air before, but I somehow also managed to wander around just enough to end up at the backstage curtain.

I really have no clue how they do this. This place is massive.
I miss home.

Shit. I miss more than home. I miss everything about home. The comfort that comes from working at the store, the way it felt coming home every day and just curling up on my sofa and unloading like every other human within a hundred foot radius. I miss my best friend. The cliffs. God, I even miss the piece of crap bowling alley right now, even though just thinking that reminds me of Brady.

Most of all though, standing here, knowing that if I just slipped my hand through the curtain I'd be able to see the show that's about to start and the crowd already packed in, I miss her.

I miss my mom.

This, what Avery and I are experiencing tonight, she would be all over it. Maybe even more excited than I'd been when I first entered the press room and came across Gavin Fortune.

An experience that she'll never get to be a part of because she's gone. And I'm here standing alone with my heart in tatters, god knows how far from the only other person on the planet that knows what it's like to be me, wishing I could be anywhere else.

"Fuck! There you are!"

Oh no. Not again.

The backstage curtain probably should have been the last damn place I landed if staying hidden from him is what I wanted.

Turning to face him, amazed with how easily shifting my body and managing to put one foot in front of the other actually is, I eye him and the envelope he's got the death grip on in his hands.

"What do you want, Brady?"

"Two things."

"Which are?"

"First, I'm gonna need you to move your cute little butt out of the way since I'm the next match." He smirks, motioning to the curtain and just how in the way I actually am.

Great.

Starting to back away from my place, Brady shoots his arm out and across before I can move too far and like a deer caught in headlights, my eyes meet his and just like in the locker room earlier, I can't look away.

Who am I kidding? I can never look away from Brady. I'd dare anyone to try, especially when he's leveling those intensity filled baby blues on you.

Women and men everywhere would be powerless.

Such is the power of a rich boy.

"And the second thing?"

Not so much as slipping in his grip on my wrist, his other hand comes out, handing over the manila envelope.

"What is this?"

"Take it and find out." He states, pushing it toward me and when after a few seconds, I take it, he smiles. "Thank you."

"You're welcome, but I don't understand what this even is, much less why you want me to take it."

"All will be revealed soon, Padawan." He jokes and despite the lameness of his Star Wars joke, I laugh.

"If you say so, Yoda."

"Don't open that until after I'm done in the ring, okay?" he shifts gears, as the trace of humor that was in his eyes vanishes in place of something more serious. Final. "It will all make sense—at least I hope it will—after I've said what I need to out there."

None of this makes any sense. He's been cryptic before, like the night he took me to the hockey game, but this is a whole new level.

"Brady, what are you doing?"

"You'll see, but for right now, I'm just going to ask you to trust me, alright? Every damn question you've got, all those doubts running rampant in your head, they're all gonna get answered in say, ten minutes. Can you hang in there with me just one more time?"

His question is even more ridiculous then the size of this place. Even with the way I took off, I'm still as drawn to him as ever. What we shared in the locker room meaning a hell of a lot more than a quick screw.

Of course I can wait him out.

"Okay…"

Hearing the sound of voices from down the hall, he turns at the same time as I do, but where I expect him to step away and put distance between us, he does the opposite. Stepping even closer until I can feel the warmth of his breath across my face. What turns into a full-fledged burn with what he does next.

His lips leaning down until they're pressing against the hardness of my forehead, a contented sigh escaping as he pulls away and rests his forehead in the place of where he kissed. A move so surprisingly tender, that I'm not sure what to say, much less do.

He's officially stolen my breath.

Slipping his hand into mine, he brings the other free one around and pulling away from the intimacy of the moment, tips my chin up until our eyes meet.

"Soon, Emery. I promise."

With another soft brush of his lips against my forehead and a tight squeeze of our hands, he separates himself from me, moving over to the middle of the curtain and situating himself the way I assume he does at every show. Stepping through it the second I hear the familiar beat of his music begin to hit.

Music that given the way he made me feel in less than five minutes together, I'm finally starting to see suits him to a tee.

Rock you like a hurricane indeed.

So caught up in the music that I don't even register when it stops. The sound of his opponent for the night clearing his throat to my right before stepping forward being what brings me out of my reverie and back into the present. What I can now hear is Brady's voice, loud and clear coming from what I think is the middle of the ring.

What I'm now jealous I'm not out there getting to witness because like every other time tonight, I have no idea where I'm even supposed to be, much less where I'm supposed to go.

A question it seems that the man talking seems to have the answer for when after honing in on every word he's saying, he says the strangest thing.

My name.

Chapter Twenty-Two

Avery

I'm tired.

Tired of letting fear of past mistakes dominate the present and ruining any chance I might have at a really great future. Tired of letting my insecurities win out over what is so blatantly obvious that even a guy that barely knows me can see it.

Tired of running period.

I love this man and even with the hurt I experienced when I saw him and Melinda together, I need to take a breath and hear him out.

See what's been there all along.

Jax.

When you find the one whose heart beats for yours; the person that makes your life brighter just being a part of it, but most of all, the one that when pushed away, doesn't take it sitting down and pushes back even harder, hold on to it.

Hold onto them and let them do what they're meant to.

Transform you.

Looks like my mom was right after all.

"When I brought up the idea of the contract, I really didn't see how it could all go so horribly wrong. At the time, all I could see was Brady being able to get to your sister and set things right and that I would have two days completely away from everything with you. It was crazy, sure, but at the time all that mattered to me was not having to ride the road for two days surviving on phone calls with the rest of the time spent wishing I was there. I could actually be there."

"But why would you risk everything for someone you barely knew a week?"

"Love doesn't exactly work on a timetable, Avery. It doesn't look at your appointment book and schedule itself in around things. It just happens and when it does, at least in my experience, you act on it. Even if you're acting on it after only a week. I'm pretty sure with the way it felt for me when I was with you, and how twisted I spent my time away from you, I knew it that first night."

"The hotel bar?"

"Yeah." He nods and where I expect to feel some sort of shock at hearing that he may have been in love with me right from the very start, I don't. There's nothing about what he said that surprises me at all.

Maybe because you felt it too.

"I fully intended on being in Oregon before Smith changed it to Vegas and I have to assume that if things had gone according to plan, Brady was the same way. We just needed those couple of days to secure what we both knew was happening to us. Lock it down no matter how crazy it seemed at the time with how fast it was all going down."

"You did it." I admit softly. "You got what you came for."

"Until I screwed up and lost it."

"It wasn't you, Jax. What happened that day, the way I reacted and how everything fell apart after, it's my fault."

"How do you figure?"

"Yes, you had a text from Melinda on your phone. A text that I saw you didn't respond to, but that for whatever reason, even without Emery calling about my mother, I didn't want to hear you out about because all I could see was that it was happening all over again."

"What was?"

"My father."

I can tell this is confusing him. Knowing what he does about what my father held back from me, it can't come as a shock that the two things might be related, but the way my mind seemed to lump them together, that's not at all clear.

"You know everything he kept from me, so I won't rehash it. What you don't know is that instead of taking time and coming to terms with that, I pushed it away in favor of focusing on what I gained. Which, when Emery called and told me our mom died, finally brought all of that stuff I pushed away, back again. All I could see was that text. Every time I closed my eyes or took a breath while we were rushing around and getting things ready for the flight, all I could see were those fourteen words and what they would mean."

"And what did they mean?"

"I was losing you too, but more than that, history was repeating itself. It stopped being you that I saw and instead, it was him. My dad. The years of lies he fed me and I stupidly believed. You not telling me about the text, it was him all over again."

"So it *was* my fault." He deduces and as easy as it would be to agree with him, it wouldn't be the truth so I immediately start shaking my head. Bringing my hand up and wiping at my eyes before the tears have a chance to fall.

Hearing him blame himself for any of this makes my heart hurt.

"No, Jax. It's not. If I had just given you a chance to explain, what happened later wouldn't have. I probably would have had the same issues where my dad is concerned, but it would have been issues we worked through together. The way we should have been, but what I didn't give you the chance to do."

"Avery, I—"

"I'm sorry." I blurt out cutting him off from whatever it is he's about to say next. "I'm sorry that instead of owning up to the real issue every time you sent me a text or called, I chose instead to keep it to myself. That for the last three months I thought I had to get through it alone. That even tonight, when I should have seen it for what it really was, I still chose to run from instead of face head on. It was never you, Jackson. It was me this entire time."

"Avery, I don't..." he pauses, shaking his head before bringing his eyes back to find mine. "You don't need to be sorry. Even though you don't want to admit it, I played a part in the way things turned out. Even tonight. I could have shoved her away sooner. Made it so you didn't even make it through the door. Stopped you from running. I didn't. I stood there the same way I stood by as it happened last time. I messed up. We both did."

I feel a but coming.

"But as long as we always end up right back here when we do, what we did to get there doesn't matter. It doesn't win."

It doesn't win because love does. Love *always* wins.

"So, what you're saying is, when we screw up, we're going to end up right back here? This hallway, surrounded by these people?" I joke, motioning around us and smiling when I notice that unlike some of my others, this joke didn't fail as his entire face is lifting. His smile so big it reaches right where I wanted it to.

His eyes.

"Well, maybe not here. As cool as MSG is, with as often as I'll probably screw up, I don't think I can afford it."

"Even though you're a shoo-in for the Middleweight Championship?"

"Even then." He laughs lightheartedly. "What I was trying to say though, is that as long as we end up standing together, talking this openly with nothing to fear, we'll get through anything."

Parting my lips, more than a little ready to tell him I agree, he places a finger to them halting me.

"As for the other thing you said. You were never alone, Ave. I was always with you, even when you didn't want me to be. The same way that you were with me. Right here." He traces an X over his heart, affectively making my eyes swell up again. "Even when I'm not physically there, I'm with you. I'll always be with you."

I know that now. I knew it then. I just wouldn't allow my heart to hear it. Forgoing my own mother's words in favor of turning into the carbon copy of the man that stole me from her and started this mess to begin with.

"If you let me, Ave, I swear you'll never have to go through anything alone again."

Fully prepared to respond to tell him I'd like nothing more than to spend the rest of my life with him, even knowing how heavy a proclamation it would be, his own words from before stop me.

"You were at the funeral, weren't you?"

"I was."

"And after?"

"I stayed in Delaware until you went home. Kept an eye on you and Emery since I promised Brady that I would."

"And Toronto?"

"I stayed at a piece of shit motel a few blocks from your place, but ended up walking the beach overlooking your place most nights."

He meant what he said before. I was never alone. For weeks he made sure I wasn't. Physically *and* emotionally. He was always watching over me. The same way my mom promised she would.

They were working together all this time.

"How deep did this go, Jax? How many people knew what you were doing?"

This question changes him. Jackson blushing a lot more telling than the amount of names I'm sure he's going to drop when he does speak again. He never gave up. Even when the voicemails stopped coming. He was just giving me what he promised in his last message.

Time.

"A few. Not a lot. Just the people that could be there for you when I couldn't be."

"Who are the few?"

"Markus and your assistant. Brady. Emery of course and umm..." he pauses, blushing what looks like an even deeper shade than he previously had. "Your mom."

My mom?

"I don't understand."

"The day of the funeral, I called Emery. She wasn't gonna give me the information I was after, but something I said, well, it must have gotten through because she ended up telling me where you were burying her and where the service would be. I stuck around after you all went back to Emery's place."

He talked to my mom.

"Emery kept saying she was doing things for me because it was what your mom would have wanted, so I figured that meant we were on good terms. So when everyone else left, I asked her for help."

"And?"

"And what?" he looks at me quizzically.

"Did she help?"

"She did." He admits, studying me for a second or two before stepping forward and bringing his hand over my face again. Pausing at my lips and letting his eyes linger. "She made it possible for me to do this again."

Lowering his face down, his forehead leaning ever so softly against mine, he slips his hand away right before his lips capture mine. Taking the look I'd seen outside earlier and giving me the only answer I'm ever going to need in the intimate touch.

Forgiveness.

The feeling of being complete. Put back together. Set right. But more than all of those things, giving me something more.

His love.

Chapter Twenty-Three

Brady

What I'm about to do has the ability to sever every tie I have with Smith, his wife Marie, and every single person I work with here at CPW. Guys that I've worked with inside of the ring, ridden the road with before Jax, and even spent time with on the outside. Don't even get me started on the reach outside of CPW. What I'm about to do could blackball me from every promotion, big or small, for the rest of my time in wrestling.

I know this. I know the tremendous risk I'm taking and what I'm about to piss down the drain. I also know that the sliver of doubt one experiences right before they do something that could potentially be the biggest mistake of their lives, isn't there.

I honestly could care less.

What happens after I'm out of the center of this ring and what Emery does with the information sitting in her hands and the spot I'm about to put her in, is the only thing garnering my focus.

A lot of which is because of the quick call I made before I went off in search of her. What a guy from Canada gave me that I don't think even working for him for the rest of my life would be able to repay.

*****

Pulling my phone out and ignoring the questioning eye of Ron when I pull up the name in my contact list and press call, I wait with baited breath as the rings go in, praying as I do that when he does pick up, he's got the answer I'm after.

"Well, isn't this a surprise." He chuckles. "How goes it, Superstar?"

"I'm about to do something stupid."

"Why doesn't that surprise me?"

"Ha-ha. I mean it, Bryan. I'm about to go out for my match and use the time Smith is giving me on the mic to take a pretty big fucking leap. Something that I'm pretty sure once I've done it is going to get me fired."

"Shit." He curses under his breath. "Why?"

"A girl. One that's a large part of the reason I ended up in HFWA in the first place. One that if I don't step out of the box and do something big for, I think I'm going to lose forever."

"The girl from the show?"

"No. Well, yeah, kind of. Look, it's complicated."

"So why are you calling me? Is this one of those things where you need me to be your conscience or something, because man, ask Kemper. I suck at that."

His friendship with Matthias aside, I'm gonna clear up this misconception really quick. This call isn't about being talked out of something. It's about talking myself into something.

It's about doing what's right for me.

"If I said I wanted to come back to HFWA, what would you say?"

"Well," he sighs. "I'd tell you that I think you're a fucking idiot given how much CPW can give you, but after I was done that, I'd tell you that you're welcome back here anytime. What does that have to do with what you're about to do, though?"

"I never should have left."

"That bad being back, huh?"

"Yes—no." I fumble over my words. "It's not bad being back, it's just not where I belong."

"And you're saying Harbour Front is?"

"Yeah."

"Then do whatever you gotta do, brother. I didn't even want you to leave when that old asshole showed up and demanded to talk to Reese. I haven't felt right about it since. You've got a place here. You always will."

That's all I need to hear. Just like I hoped, Bryan came through.

Making this the first damn thing to go right for me since I put this entire plan in motion weeks ago. Leaving me with only one thing left to do.

Get the girl.

✳✳✳✳✳

"When Smith called me in for this Superstar Showcase, I have to admit, I wasn't stoked. I mean, sure. I was honored to be considered one of the best, but I just didn't see what it was about me that made me showcase worthy. I still don't. My idea of what should be showcased, well, it's changed over the last few months."

Okay Brady, you've gotten over the hump. Time to take it the rest of the way home.

"The best beating I ever had, wasn't one that took place in the middle of the ring for your enjoyment. It came in the form of a wakeup call. One that came right when I needed it, by the very last person you'd probably ever expect it from. One of you. Someone that just like all of you did when word dropped that CPW would be rolling through, slapped down their money without question in order to be a part of history."

"For me," I pause, inhaling deep. "That's who should be in the middle of the ring right now. The people that nobody gets to see because you're only shown one side of things. The 'Superstars' the promoters want you to see. The truth is, the real superstars are the ones standing on the sidelines cheering us and expecting nothing in return. Loving us from afar because we spend more time riding the road than we do with them. The ones that despite how many time we screw up, and god, let me tell ya'll a little secret—we screw up hard—still stick by our side. Seeing things in us that we're too damn stupid or blind to see in ourselves."

God, I'm so damn revved up over what I'm doing, the bridges I'm burning and the chanting of my name that's starting to make its way from one part of the arena to the other that I'm shaking. A slight tremble beginning in my hands, causing the mic to slip until it gains momentum and works its way straight down through my legs. Any second the rush of what's happening about to hit and knock me off my feet altogether.

I might go down physically, but given what I'm about to wrap this up with, there's nowhere for me to go but up.

Please God, let this work.

"So before my opponent for the night comes out and proceeds to kick my ass around all four corners of the ring for your enjoyment, I want to showcase my superstar. The little spitfire standing just on the other side of that curtain who is probably gearing up to lay a bigger beating on me than the one I'll take in a few minutes because of what I'm out here doing," I laugh, one that as it filters over the space around me, I see I'm not alone in. The crowd joining in with me.

Standing in the middle of what has always been my home, a place of reverence and telling the truth. Selling it better than any of the other bullshit lines I'd been given before. It's life altering.

"Emery, baby. Open the envelope now."

Dropping the mic to the ground, I move from my place at the center of the ring over to the corner, but not before catching wind of the applause I'm being given, the sound of it growing louder with each second that passes, along with the chant of Emery's name that follows. My words having more of an impact than I expected.

One that has the curtain opening and the stunned but beautiful face of the woman I love stepping through it instead of my opponent. The envelope, even from my position in the ring, secure in her hand, underneath what I can just make out is the white of what I hope are the papers that were slipped inside of it.

Lifting my arms in the air as the chants of her name, I work them into doing it even louder. What I can see when she gets close enough for me to make out her features, embarrasses the hell out of her, but that when she finally makes her way around to my side of the ring and begins to climb the ring steps, also has her smiling so brightly, it sets fire to her entire face.

Plopping myself down on the middle rope, lowering it enough for her to slip through, she pauses when she's through, looking down to the envelope before lifting her eyes straight to mine. The words she mouths next not exactly the love declaration I was after, but definitely ones that prove my earlier ones right.

You're so dead, rich boy.

She's committed to making me pay. Committed to me period.

The little spitfire from that Podunk town in Delaware.

She's all mine.

Answering the call from the crowd, I move toward her as Cameron's music hits. Pulling her to me and crashing me lips down onto hers. Giving her everything in the moment that I can with the answers she's still clutching tightly in her hands.

All of me.

Getting the biggest and best payoff of all when as the cheers roll out around us, she kisses me back.

My heart back home where it belongs.

Emery

Finally backstage after what felt like hours instead of the twenty minutes it actually was, I waste no time spinning him around and getting to the bottom of just what the hell he was thinking doing what he did.

Breaking kayfabe.

By definition, what is considered by some the very life blood of wrestling. A term they use to describe everything that's not based in reality. Basically, it's what is scripted beforehand.

If you need an example, one that you'll probably understand best—wrestling fan or not—look no further than WWE. Guys like The Undertaker, or say, even less prominent guys like Dean Ambrose. One definitely not a dead man and the other, as far as I know, definitely not a lunatic once he steps out of the ring and is at home with his girlfriend.

Sure, in an age of social media, kayfabe has been dead for a while, but for a lot of places, CPW being one of them, they still take it seriously.

So damn serious in fact, I know the second Brady heads to the locker room, not only is he going to end up being ripped apart by the guys he works with, he's also going to end up meeting what I'm sure is going to be Radley Smith's bad side.

Only when I force him to stop, I don't see concern looking back. I don't see worry or fear at all. All I see is the man I saw the day we dived off the cliff together. His eyes filled with wonder and amazement. Excitement even. He looks more alive in the moment, especially after having his ass handed to him out there, then I think he ever has.

"That felt...amazing!" he yells before grabbing me by the shoulders and pulling me flush to him. The sweat from his chest transferring over and dampening my shirt. What when he finally releases his hold on me, I see has turned my white shirt almost sheer.

A fact that after he hungrily presses his lips to mine again, completely oblivious to any and all movement around us, he finally takes note of and pulls me out of view over.

"We need to go to the locker room." He says, looking from me to my shirt. "I can grab you one of my sweatshirts or something. I'm sorry, Em. I didn't even think."

Not a half bad idea, but one that after what just happened out there is gonna be the last thing that happens.

"Not yet, rich boy. We're not going anywhere until you tell me what the hell that was out there."

"You mean, besides the obvious?"

"Brady, what you said. It was...everything." I admit, continuing despite my need to stop once I see his smile. "But I don't think Smith is going to see it that way."

"I don't care what way he sees it. I did it. It's done. It's not like I can rewind it and start over. And even if I could, I wouldn't. I'd do it all the same way."

"Why?"

"Because I love you, Emery. Between you calling what happened between us wrong and us getting interrupted before I could lay waste to your last reason, I had to do something."

"Okay, but did you really have to go out and do it in the ring?"

Groaning at my question, he takes a step back and after pacing back and forth in front of me a few times, he finally stops. The light in his eyes significantly dimmer than before.

"You stressing on what I did so much…did I screw up? I mean, I figured I might have, but I didn't really think about it, ya know? I just…I needed you to hear me and figured this was the best way to make that happen."

"No. Like I told you before, what you said, what you did, it was everything to me. I'm just worried about the impact it's going to have on you."

"You're worried about me." He repeats, not in question but statement, almost as though it surprises him that I'd worry.

"Of course I am! You just went out to the ring and committed career suicide! How the hell did you expect me to react?"

"I love you." He blurts, pulling me to him again.

"I love you too." I whisper against my place in his chest. "Even if you are bat shit crazy."

Chuckling when he catches what I've said, I hone in on the vibration I feel against my face as his chest contracts and shakes. How good it feels hearing it but how much better it is feeling it. The hard beat of his heart adding to it like the perfect crescendo.

"There's so much I need to tell you. So much I want to say, Em. Answers to questions I know you have that I want to give. I just…after what you just said, I have no idea where to start."

Welcome to my world, pal.

"Start at the beginning then. Where did you go after you left my house?"

"Home." He answers easily. "To Mississippi. I went straight to my old man."

"Why did you go there first?"

"After I left your place, I went to the airport. I knew when I got there that I made a mistake leaving you, but considering everything I had going on at the time, what he was threatening me with, what he wanted me to do with Kelly and everything I stood to lose, I knew I couldn't go back. Not until I made shit right."

"Made things right for who?"

"Me." He again answers automatically. "I knew I wanted to be with you, but I couldn't do it the way I already had. I couldn't go back the same man I was in your kitchen. You deserved better than that."

"So you went home to your parents instead."

"Yeah, but there was this moment before I went inside that I almost turned right back around."

"What happened?"

"Jax called and told me about your mom."

The pain of that day, while not as brutal as it had been the day it happened, still hurts to think about, much less talk about the way Brady is now. The way it felt getting that message and rushing home and finding her gone, well, I don't think I'll ever get over it.

"I had a decision to make. A split second one. Go back to you the same man that walked away or do what I went there to do and come back to you better."

"What exactly was it that you went there to do?"

"As much as I love wrestling, I was doing it for all the wrong reasons toward the end. Somewhere along the way, I stopped doing it for me and I was just going through all of it for him. Riding the Raines name for all it was worth. I stepped on people that were honestly, a lot better than me. Taking their spot and then pissing it away all because I could. I can't even remember the last time someone called me Brady for Christ's sakes. It's always just Raines or Bill's kid. After he called your house and you asked me to leave, it was like a light bulb went off. One that had been flickering and trying to get my attention for years, but that I just kept ignoring until finally, I couldn't anymore."

"What did you do, Brady?"

"I renounced his name, the money, and everything that came with it. I gave it all up. Including CPW. I didn't want anything to do with him or what his name afforded me anymore. I was determined that if I was gonna make it in this business, I'd do it as myself. Brady."

"And this?" I ask when he finishes, slipping my hand from around his body until I'm pressing the divorce papers and envelope against his chest. "What about this?"

"That was me doing what I should have done years ago." He answers, matter of fact. "It was me doing what was right for me, while at the same time keeping the promise I made you in the letter I wrote. I was determined that when we did see each other again, I would be the man you deserved. Which meant, being free of every noose I had wrapped around my neck."

"The date on the papers was weeks ago, Brady. If you wanted to be free to be with me the way you're saying, why didn't you reach out when it went through?"

"Honestly? I wasn't where I needed to be. Hell, even now, I'm not sure I'm where I want to be in terms of deserving you, especially after my stunt out there. I still had some work to do. Still *have* some work to do."

"So basically you're a work in progress?"

"Yeah, I guess I am." He shrugs before laughing softly. "But at least I'm a free one."

"Brady Raines, lost puppy. Free to a good home."

"You're wrong." He tells me, shaking his head. "I'm not lost anymore. I found my home. That is, if a certain spitfire that lives there is in the market for a broke ass, partially housebroken but willing to be trained dog that's always going to be in heat whenever she's around him."

His obvious joke, not nearly as funny as I'm sure he wanted it to be with just how telling it really is given everything he's admitted.

He was wrong in his letter.

Brady didn't need to be better for me. He was already the best. He only needed to be better for himself. The same way that now, officially having to face life on my own, without the crutch of my mom, my sister and Mike behind me, I've got to do the same.

It's time for me to be better and show Brady that what he asked for in his letter and what my mom wanted for me, he's gotten.

Me.

I didn't give up on him and the second my words fall, I know in my heart that I never will. When it comes to us, what is lost is always going to be found because just like my mom said...love always wins.

"Welcome home, Brady."

Chapter Twenty-Four

Jax

"Jax, my man! That was one hell of a match!"

"Looks like Kemper's got some serious competition for the belt after what went down out there. Who lit the fire up under your ass?"

I'd give anything to turn around and tell Ortiz the reason I went out there and put on the show I did, but I can't. Avery and I reconnecting again, how good it feels, I need it to stay just mine for a little while longer.

"Yeah, Merrick." Matthias smirks, joining the conversation as he makes his way back out from the showers. "Tell them how you got your groove back."

"Don't tell me!" Cameron calls from across the room. "Melinda gave you a pre-match workout, right?"

All the guy is doing is mentioning her and I can feel the bile growing. With everything these guys have bared witness to when it comes to me and her, I can't believe that would even be a thing. Much less something they actually put a voice to.

"Like hell it was. Melinda was too busy gluing herself to River. Where the fuck you been?" Matty speaks up again, nodding when I mouth a silent thank you for the save. "Besides, we all know the reason the match was so good was because of me."

I've been working with Matthias since I got to CPW, him already working for Smith when I was brought in, and I can count on my hand the amount of times he's sat back like this and talked.

Twice, counting this one.

I'm not sure what's possessing him to do it now, but I'm definitely not going to ask him to stop. If he wants to take all the credit for the match we just put on out there, the holy shit chants damn near blowing the roof off the place, he can have at it. I owe him a lot more than that after what he did for me tonight.

"You heard the man. Kemper is God." I announce, turning to Matty and bowing before turning my attention back to my bag. About to stuff my gear inside when the shiny glint of white inside catches my eye.

Slipping my hand in and pulling it out, Kemper leans over and taking in the box now resting in my hand, his eyes widen before his jaw drops.

"Is that what I—"

"Yeah."

"You and Avery?"

Not sure how I feel about saying it out loud considering the fact that not even six hours before, I wasn't even sure she was going to show, I nod slowly.

"Shit. You really do love her, huh?"

"Yeah, man. I do. She's it."

Seeming to ponder what I've said, I turn my attention back to my bag, slipping the box gently back in, making sure to situate it in between some of my clothes before grabbing my phone out and tossing the rest of my gear inside, zipping it up.

"You're gonna end up leaving again, aren't you?" He asks and all I can offer up is a shrug in response.

Having already walked away once and not entirely feeling it since I've been back, I know I could easily do it again. I'm just not sure if I'm going to. It's something that with as serious as I am about the girl waiting for me on the other side of the locker room door, I don't want to make any rash decisions about. Not until I talk to her first.

She was more than willing to be with me before when I wrestled, so I know she wouldn't hesitate to do it again, especially with how she handled Melinda's run in during my match before. We could make this work. I just don't want to jump the gun and twist it all up before it really gets off the ground.

"I don't know, man."

"Well, whatever you end up deciding, don't take her away completely. After the way Bry went on about her the last time we talked, I'm pretty sure you'll have him camped out on your front lawn."

Say what?

"Okay, you lost me. Who is Bryan and how does he know my girlfriend?"

My girlfriend. God that sounds fucking amazing.

"Michaelchuk. You know who I'm talking about. My buddy from TO. The one that started his own promotion?"

Harbour Front Wrestling Alliance. *Right.*

The fact that Matthias is sitting here and actually talking to me must be messing with my brain. The amount of words we've spoken to one another tonight definitely a record.

"How do you know it's the same person?"

"I don't talk a lot, Merrick, but I do pay attention. You bail ass out of here months ago for a girl in Canada. Bryan calls me up, talking to me about Raines and mentions a woman reporter named Avery. I find an Avery crying on the floor of our show and after bugging the living hell out of her, out pops your name. Doesn't take a rocket scientist to put it all together."

I guess given all of that, he's got a point.

"Well, tell your buddy Avery's all mine. He's gonna have to camp out on someone else's lawn."

"You put that ring on her finger and something tells me you'll be telling him yourself." Matthias laughs, turning his attention away and digging around in his own bag.

Free from the conversation, but not from the ring that even though it's been sitting in my bag for weeks, I somehow managed to put out of my mind, it hits me.

I want to put that ring on her finger. I wanted to put it on her finger even before I found and bought it. If I had it in Toronto with me, I have a feeling with how I was feeling at the time, just how clear she was to me, I would have gotten down on one knee and asked her then.

That's how serious I am about her. About what I feel and the person I am when I'm with her. How she can take what for months was so damn empty and in the span of a few minutes fill it to capacity again. Be the reason I walked out there tonight and stole the damn show. The first time in months that I could actually feel myself come alive under those lights, when for so long I was just going through the motions.

It's all her. All Avery.

But can I do it? *Should I do it?* With as quickly as everything imploded the last time we seemed to cross over into something more, do I really want to risk it happening again?

Damnit.

Why did I have to pull the damn box out of my bag and worse, let someone else see it?

Now my head is swimming with questions and not nearly enough answers. One answer though, coming through louder and clearer than all the others.

When you know, you just know.

My mother's advice when I first started dating. What she offered after telling me all about how she met and fell in love with my father.

Advice that now, with all of the questions swimming around inside my head, I want to take, but that fear has me holding back on.

There's only one way to settle this. If I want to know what the right thing to do is, I'm going to have to go to the one person who can give it to me.

My mom.

*****

"Mom…"

"Jax? Is that you?" she asks, her voice going from clear to distant as I barely make out her calling to my father. "George! I think there's something wrong with the damn phone again. I can barely hear a thing."

Shit. My nerves have got my mom thinking the phone's messed up. *Great.*

Swallowing down my nervousness over the reason I'm calling, I take a deep breath and try again. This time, my own voice bouncing back at me with as loud as I sound.

"God," I groan loudly. "Could this get any worse?"

"Well, seeing as I can hear you now, I figure the worst has passed." My mom laughs, her attention officially back on the conversation. "Now why don't you tell me why you're calling? Aren't you supposed to be wrestling tonight?"

"Yeah, I am, or well, I did. We just finished."

"And how did it go?"

I don't know why they bother asking me this. It's not like I've got a say in how everything is going to play out. I'm just there to do my part.

"I lost, but Ma, that's not exactly what I'm calling to talk about."

"Well, don't keep an old woman waiting, Jackson. If you're not calling to brag about your loss tonight, what else could there be?"

Brag about my loss. That one was actually pretty good.

"I need to ask you a question."

"Well, shoot."

"How long were you and dad together before he proposed?"

I already know the answer to this. I swear with as many times as they told us the story of how they met and just how quickly they ended up shacked up together and married with a baby on the way, I can recite it from memory. But considering what it leads into, I think I'm going to need to hear it just one more time.

"Jax, why are you asking me this?"

"No reason." I lie and of course, she sees right through it.

"Try again."

"Can you just tell me please? I'll explain it all after, I promise."

"About two months." She answers. "Your turn."

"Why did you say yes?"

"Jackson Kennedy Merrick." She sighs heavily. "Would you just tell me what all these questions are about? Did something happen? Are you okay? You don't sound like yourself."

Of course I don't sound like myself. Considering the last time I brought up marriage with her I was a blink away from asking Melinda to marry me, I'm definitely not myself.

Jackson Merrick doesn't go on dates, much less get serious about a girl.

I'm pretty sure my mom was ready for the call from the monastery more than she was this one.

"Yes, something happened. No, I'm not going to tell you about it. Not until after you answer my questions."

"I said yes to your father because from the moment I met him, I knew he was it."

"How? How did you know he was it? Was it something he did specifically or was it a combination of things?"

Where I expect her to either complain about the lack of information I'm giving her about what's going on or worse, question my sanity again, she does the opposite. Proving why she's my mother by figuring it all out on her own.

"You've found her, haven't you?"

"Found who, Mom?" I play dumb and when she scoffs like she knows better, I know I've been caught.

"You really need me to spell it out for you? Her, Jackson. The one. The yin to your yang. The blue to your sky."

The blue to my sky.

Well, shit. All things considered, I'd say that one is pretty damn accurate.

"Yes, okay? I found her. Now can we please get back on topic?"

"I can't tell you how I knew, Jax. I just did. What I might have seen in your father, you might see differently with your girl. That's what makes it so unique. Your love is personalized only for you."

"Way to make her sound like a novelty gift, Mom."

"Hey! I'll have you know that some of those novelty gifts are rare treasures. Just the way I suspect with the way you're jumping on your dear old mom now, your girl is too. Now, you wanna tell me what all these questions are about?"

"I did something a couple of months ago."

"Okay…" she trails off, probably waiting for the other shoe to drop. "A good something or a bad something?"

"Do you remember when I bought the house?"

"Against our wishes? Of course I do. How could I forget?"

Ignoring the sarcastic undertone, I give her the rest. "That wasn't the only thing I bought."

"Now you're just pausing on purpose to build suspense. Spit it out, Jackson."

"I bought a ring, alright? I stopped in at this little store on the way into Laguna and I found this ring with a blue sapphire in the middle. It was—*is* perfect."

"And you're calling now because you need to know if it's wrong to want to use that ring so soon?" she guesses. "Does that about sum it up?"

"Yeah. I met her a few months ago. We were together for a little over a week before Melinda...no. Before I screwed it up. We've only just reconnected again, but all I can think about is what you used to tell me when I was a kid."

"That when you know, you just know?"

That's the one.

There's a whole other list of tidbits she's given me over the years that are relevant here too, but that one more than all of the others. Seeing Avery tonight, knowing that Brady's plan worked and both of us were still feeling what we did then, it's making it all come back around again.

Only this time, there's this feeling deep down in my gut, more than just the one in my heart that tells me it's right.

Where Melinda was wrong, Avery isn't.

She's it.

She's my one.

"Yeah."

"Then what the hell are you on the phone with me for? If you're sure this girl is your one then your place is with her. Not on the phone debating whether or not the timing is right with your mother."

"You mean, you're not gonna try and talk me out of it?"

When I was with Melinda all they did was tell me to slow down. Take things at a snail's pace. It was easy to see why. I mean, she wasn't exactly the nicest person in the world to them or me with everything that ended up happening, so to just call her up now and drop a bomb like this on her, I'm expecting resistance. A whole lot of it.

But there just isn't.

"I'll tell you a secret. Your grandfather, back when I first told him about your father, tried everything to get me to slow down, short of tying me to the bedpost. That's how certain he was that what I had with your father was nothing more than puppy love at its finest. Now almost forty years and three grown kids later, I never miss an opportunity to rub it in his face." She says with a laugh. "Love doesn't have a timetable, Jackson. As long as the love you feel for her is returned to you, then who the hell cares how it came about or how long it took to realize it?"

This right here is why I called. The one woman in the entire world that not even knowing a thing about Avery, is still telling me to go for it. Trusting me to do what she always taught me to do.

Follow my heart.

Something I fully plan on doing the second I pull myself out of this call.

"Thanks, Mom. I needed that."

"Anytime, sweetheart. Just promise me something would you?"

"Sure."

"Promise you'll bring her home to Mom."

Avery

"As cute as you're being, what with the straight face you've been trying to maintain since we got off the plane and the cryptic little hints you give me that aren't really hints at all, I think you should probably just save yourself the aggravation and tell me where we're going."

Truth is, he doesn't need to tell me. I just want to see if bugging him enough will make him do it. Needing to find out just how much it will take to make my man crack. Which, considering how long we've actually been on the road—entering hour number three now—looks like it will be a lot longer than I thought when I took on the mission.

"Nice try, sweetheart, but just like the other fifty times you've tried, this one is a fail too. Looks like you're gonna have to just do what I told you before we even got on the plane and trust me."

Damn him and that grin of his.

The one that even now, when he's not even really aiming at me still has my heart melting. A grin that if I had given into all of the doubts and crazy thoughts I was having over the last three months, I wouldn't get to witness now.

Thank god for wakeup calls.

"Trust isn't the problem, Jax. Not being sure where we're going and who we might see is. Have you forgotten that you ignored my request to go back to the hotel and change before you swept me away on this little expedition of yours?"

Slipping one hand off the wheel and bringing it down between us, he rests it on my leg and squeezes as his laughter fills the car.

"I didn't forget, but since when do you care about being in the same clothes?"

"Since you could be bringing me to meet your family and I spent the night surrounded by sweaty men."

Glancing over, he smiles before squeezing my leg again. "I swear to you, we're not going to meet my family. Not yet. I just got you back. The last thing I want to do is take you to the one place guaranteed to send you running again."

"Very funny." I say, sticking my tongue out. Resisting the urge to jump from my seat in exaltation when the sound of his laughter fills the tiny space again.

As easy as it is to joke with him now, it was just last night when the threat of it had been very real. A threat that if it hadn't been for Matthias seeing what I just wouldn't allow myself to and Jax being there to capitalize on it, forcing me to talk when the image of him and Melinda that was burned in my brain had me wanting to do anything but, would have come to fruition.

"We're almost there." he says, interrupting my thoughts and bringing my attention back to our surroundings. What I can now make out is a whole lot of beach property.

What could he possibly have to show me here? The last I knew, he'd been content to live his life out of a bag like a nomad. What could possibly be waiting on the beach?

Keeping my eyes trained on everything passing us by as he takes two turns in quick succession, even more questions filter their way through my mind.

"Who lives here?" I ask as he slows the car to a crawl before turning into a driveway and shifting it into park.

"All of those questions rumbling around will be answered soon, reporter lady. Just stay put for a sec."

Slipping off his seatbelt, he exits the car, but where I expect him to make a beeline to the door, he jogs around the back and around to my side, knocking on the window and smiling down at me when I turn and meet his gaze.

Unlocking the door, I push it open and slipping my hand into his outstretched one, allow him to pull me up and toward the door of the house I still know nothing about.

"Before we go in, there's something you should probably know."

"Okay."

"It's not finished."

"What's not finished?" I ask and slipping his free hand into his pocket, he pulls out a key and turning toward me, holds it out between us.

"Unlock the door and find out."

Okay, him not telling me much after whisking me away overnight, maintaining the game the entire drive here has been nerve-racking, but easy enough to deal with. Now though? Standing outside of some random house? What are we about to walk into?

"Jackson, what's going on?"

"Well, that didn't take long." He chuckles under his breath.

"What didn't?"

"You calling me Jackson and sounding a hell of a lot like my mom did last night when I called her."

Pulling my hand from his and taking a step toward the door with a heavy sigh, I slip the key in the lock, bringing it back out when I hear the click and handing the key to him before turning back to open the door.

"Wait!" He calls out and before I can even turn to acknowledge why he's telling me to stop, his arms are around me and he's hoisting me off the ground. Making quick work of the knob and pushing the door open, he carries me through, kicking the door shut behind him. Placing me down after a quick kiss to my forehead and a grin that only seems to grow in size the more we stand in place.

Looking around, I see a family room to the left of us and a dining area that connects just off from it, a slim wall separating the two. The décor of the place what catches my eye next. The entire place painted and styled in various different shades of blue.

"Welcome home, Avery." He whispers against my ear and when I turn into him, lifting my head and meeting his eyes, he smiles.

"What do you mean welcome home?"

"Do you remember when I told you what I've been doing for the last three months? Specifically what I was doing after you caught me in Toronto and I came home?"

Of course I remember. He bought a place, started giving lessons at the surf shop and then went back to working for CPW.

Oh, right. This is his place.

"So this is the place you bought?"

"Mhmm." He murmurs. "This is home."

"It's beautiful."

"It is now." He says, turning to me with a soft smile. One that based on the compliment he's giving and the way he looks as he's doing it, has my cheeks heating into a full on blush. "Do you want a tour?"

Slipping my hand into his, he walks us through the family room before making his way around to the kitchen. One that considering my vantage point when we first walked in is actually a lot larger than I first thought. Moving out of the room after he's motioned around it with his free hand, he pauses once we get to the short staircase leading to the second floor.

"Are you ready to see the best part?"

Ready as I'll ever be.

"Sure."

Making quick work of the stairs, he moves to the left once we've reached the top and making our way in, I notice the bed first. A king sized bed sitting directly in the middle of the room. The covering matching the downstairs to a tee, everything from the blankets to the pillowcases all a darkened blue.

"I guess I know what your favorite color is now."

"Yeah." He chuckles. "I guess you do."

Moving across the room to the dark oak dresser that rests near the window, I let my eyes fall to the picture frames on top. Six in total. One's of a younger him, alone and standing beside two similar looking girls that I just know without ever having seen them are his sisters, all the way down to the frames at the end.

Pictures of us. Three of them. One of them a picture I wasn't even aware he'd taken.

It's of me, but where the other two have us both together, this one is me alone. Eyes closed with the most serene looking smile on my face.

"When did you take this?"

"Your place. The morning that..." his voice trails off and I'm thankful. He doesn't have to say anything more. This was taken before we made our way downstairs for breakfast. Before Emery's call and the fight that took place after.

"I look happy."

"You were. And I was happy because that look on your face, I put it there."

"Why did you take it?"

"Honestly," he says, pausing as he moves across the room to stand behind me. "When I told you in the car that day that I woke up thinking I could do this for the rest of my life and never need anything else, I meant it. This was my way of capturing that thought. Even if last night never happened and we were still apart, I wanted that memory of you with me forever."

"Oh Jax," I sigh. "I'm so sorry."

"For what?"

"For staying away for so long. For taking that beautiful thought you had and ruining it."

"What did we say last night, Ave? As long as we end up standing together, it doesn't matter what happened to get us there. It's forgiven. *You're* forgiven. Besides, you're here now, which means more of those moments."

How easily he can forgive me—love me—after everything we've been through, is astounding. Everything about him is. I wish I'd seen and known then what I do now. That I'd done what my mother told me to do the day we spoke on the phone and actually listened to his heart when it was speaking to mine. If I had, I would have been able to see what's been there along.

The most beautiful soul in the world.

The one that even at my most undeserving, I'm positive was made just for me.

"This room," I whisper softly. "Is perfect. You're perfect."

"For you." He says, planting the softest kiss on my nose and silencing any argument I might want to give. "I'm perfect for you."

Yes, Jackson Merrick. Yes you are.

"So, you ready to see the best part?"

"You mean this isn't it?"

"Nope."

"Is this where you take me out back and show me the killer view I bet you have of the beach?"

"Nope." He repeats. "This is where I take you to the other room and show you the real reason this was the place I chose."

"There's another room?"

I don't get it. Why would he need a second bedroom?

"Yeah." Finding my hand and locking our fingers together, he leans down, placing a kiss to my forehead before moving toward the door. Picking up speed the more he walks until he stops cold in front of another door.

"Open it." He says, motioning to the handle with his head. "But what I said earlier about the place not being finished, this is why. So remember that when you go in."

"Okay..."

Doing what he said, I twist the knob on the door and push it open, letting the door fall all the way back before stepping through it with Jax closely on my heels.

A room with walls bathed in the softest yellow I've ever seen, but partially split as just across from us, there is another set of walls and a door. A space small in comparison to the room as a whole, but as I move toward it and again turn the knob and step through, takes my breath away when I realize just how large it really is.

And what it is.

"What do you think?" he whispers, jolting me. So caught up in the room I'm now standing in, I hadn't even heard him come close.

Along one side of the wall are bookshelves—three of them—large and filled to the brim with books and in the centre, a wooden desk with a laptop perched on top, the lid up, but the screen black, the plastic covering that came with it still adorning the screen. What with the small window directly behind it and the sunlight pouring through it, makes it shine.

"It's amazing." I admit. "But why?"

"I wanted you to have a place. A place to write, read...and well, decompress after work."

Catching his arm as it comes out around me, aimed at the other side of the room, I pull my gaze away from the desk and settle in on the other piece of furniture filling the room.

A sectional sofa along the far wall, the shorter end coming to a stop close to where we're standing.

I can't believe this.

Even though he knows my place is in Toronto, when he bought his own he thought enough about me, especially given we weren't even together, to make a place for me to be when I'm here.

Proving he never gave up.

Proving his love.

"You didn't have to do this."

"Yeah, sweetheart. I did." He says before turning and making his way back out of the space, motioning with his hand for me to follow.

"Why?" I ask when I make my way out into the main room. "And when you're done answering that, maybe you can also tell me what your plan is for the rest of the room?"

"Before I answer that, do you think you could answer a question for me?"

"Anything."

"How do you feel about being in Toronto? Do you still hate it as much as you did when I was there, or have things changed over the last few months?"

My feelings on Toronto aren't a secret. As handy as it's always been living in such a huge city, the only real time I was ever happy there was when I was at home and sitting on my veranda. Where it was just me, the moon, and the stars. What for the last three months has been even more important because of the connection that it gives me to my mom.

"I still feel the same. I think I always will. Toronto was my dad's thing, not mine. Why?"

"This place, Avery. I didn't just buy it because it was close to the beach and was the only thing like it in my price range."

"So why did you?"

"For us. I wanted a home, sweetheart. And now that you're standing here and looking at me like that, I have it. This space, it isn't just a place anymore. It's a home. Our home."

Our home.

Jax bought this house, furnished the hell out of it, not because he wanted to put down roots in California or just have a place to lay his head on one of the rare days he had off.

He bought this place so we could make it a home.

"I...I don't know what to s-say." I say, the surprise at what I'm hearing making me stumble over my words. What little of them I've got.

"Say you'll move in with me, Avery. That you'll let this—let me, be your safe place to fall. Tell me this can be our home."

The yes is on the tip of my tongue, but so is the question of why this room isn't finished. A question that's eating at me despite the fact that it won't change my answer.

"Why is this part of the room unfinished?"

Stepping into me, he rests his hand over my stomach before leaning his forehead against mine with a soft smile.

"Because I couldn't finish it without you. Which, now that you're here, I hope means that we can. I want us to finish it. Make it complete."

Even if I didn't already pick up on what he meant, the subtle brushing of his fingers against my abdomen would be enough. What Jax wants for this room is a baby.

A family.

His welcome home when we got here all too clear now. The only thing missing, being my answer. One I'm more than happy to give.

"Yes."

Chapter Twenty-Five
One Month Later...

Emery

"Are you sure you want to do this?"

This isn't the first time he's asked this. Just like my response isn't changing at all from the one I've given him the last thirty times he's asked. My decision being as final as the day I made it about a week before I even landed in New York and in his sights again.

If I really focused on it, the choice would have been made right after she passed, but I'd been so caught up in making sure I didn't lose anything that connected me to her and the life we had together that I held onto it. Holding on to the pain at the same time.

"Yes, Brady. For the hundredth time, I'm positive."

"We don't have to make any rash decisions. I mean, I know my going across the border and working with Bryan and Reese is gonna put a serious cramp in the *us* time that you being there with me would provide, but babe..."

I know what he's going to say. This is my home. The place I grew up and spent the first twenty-five years of my life making memories in. The one place in the world that held the best of Rebecca Davis. The parts I didn't want to let go of for fear of letting go of her.

He's said all of it before and he's kept on saying it since I told him what I wanted to do.

It doesn't change the fact that it's what's best for everyone, though.

My mom included.

"She'd want me to do what makes me happy, Brady. And just in case you need a reminder, you are what makes me happy." I tell him, planting a quick kiss to his lips. "I want to be where you are, and considering this place is the only thing keeping me here, what with Mike moving out of state to go to back to school, well, I've got to do it."

"But you don't." he continues to argue. "You don't have to do anything. You can keep the house and still be with me. I mean, you're bound to get sick of living out of seedy motels pretty quick."

Silly man. He actually thinks I care about where I end up staying.

"I'm coming with you, Brady. Unless of course, you're the one having second thoughts."

Silencing that pretty quick he grabs me and pulls me into him, wrapping his arms around me tightly before pressing his lips down on mine possessively.

"Like fuck I'm having second thoughts. I just don't want you making a mistake you'll end up regretting and hating me for later."

There's a lot of things I regret about my life.

Not stopping to smell the roses more, instead taking everything on my shoulders and working so much I knew the inside of the store backwards and forwards. Sometimes even better than I did the very house we're standing in.

Not talking to Mike sooner and preventing the weeks where I thought for sure I'd lost him.

Not putting my brain to good use and searching for Avery before my mom finally called the private investigator and bringing her home sooner so she could have more time with us than she had.

All things that when you think about it, I have no reason to feel bad about, but still things I wish I could go back and change, because maybe in doing so, I could have carved out a much different ending.

One of my biggest regrets, besides not spending more time with my mom near the end, being that I let Brady go. Even if it had been to better himself and carve out a better chance for us. I regret not fighting to make him stay.

"You're doing it again. What did I tell you about that?" He gently interrupts and just like every other time he's caught me thinking something he believes I shouldn't be, I give myself away by blushing.

"Don't know what you're talking about."

"Sure you don't. Is this where you try and tell me that you weren't standing here wallowing in the past again?"

Okay, okay. So I've done that a lot over the last few weeks. But considering how quickly everything's happened since he handed me the envelope with his divorce papers and called me out to the ring, can you really blame me?

"What happened wasn't your fault, Em. Everything that happened, it was going to go down whether you were there or not. You being there just smacked it into me sooner. When you think about it, you're my lifesaver."

"The candy or the big orange thing lifeguards throw in the water to save drowning people?"

"That's a preserver, but since it does save lives, whatever. You're the candy. Because just like every other time I've been around you, all I want to do is suck on your sweetness."

Bringing my hand up between us and laughing when he wiggles his eyebrow I smack his chest.

"You're a pervert, you know that? Is that all you ever think about?"

"Maybe. Didn't seem like you minded last night."

Right. Last night.

After spending the better part of the last three weeks getting things situated in Toronto, we'd swung by my sisters and one look at the view from her back porch had Brady sold. Even with the warm and cozy allure of the bed waiting for us back inside, we'd spent the night making love under the stars. That is, after we ended up doing it a couple of times in the water.

The man holding onto me for dear life now, more insatiable than I thought.

"When have I ever minded?"

"That, future Mrs. Raines, is a very good point."

Future Mrs., what now?

"Brady…"

Pressing his lips to mine again, affectively silencing me, I'm captured like always by the smile he's sporting when he finally pulls away.

"We can talk about that later. Right now, though, we need to get back to the issue at hand. An issue that doesn't even have to be one at all with what I'm trying to tell you."

"After what you did with the money you made from the showcase, along with everything I put down with what I saved from work, we're debt free. I'm debt free. My mom, she would have wanted me to move on from here. This is the right move, Brady. It's time to let another family experience what I did here."

"So you really want to do this? Put the place on the market and move to Toronto?"

"Toronto, Delaware, Australia, hell, Afghanistan. I don't care where it is. I'll go, as long as it's you I'm going with." I tell him. "Now, you wanna explain what you just called me?"

"You mean, when I called you what you're going to be?"

Well. I guess that answers that.

"You're that sure of yourself, huh?"

"Of course." He smirks. "Who can resist a one-time rich boy, turned broke as fuck wrestler with nothing to offer but a cheap as shit motel and all the love in the world?"

Who can resist indeed.

Releasing his hold before I have the chance to respond to his question, this time more than a little ready to tell him what my thoughts are, he's dropping to his knees on the floor, realizing his mistake when I laugh and righting himself before pulling something from his pocket and bringing it out in front of him.

Holy crap.

"This isn't what you think." He grins when he looks up and sees what I'm sure is a mixture of absolute fear and shock all over my face. "When I do that, it will be much better."

Not really seeing how it could get much better with the way he's situated on the floor along with the look of absolute adoration that's flowing from his eyes, I continue to stand in stunned silence.

It's only when he unclenches his hand, laying it flat out that his words become much clearer.

A plastic ring, the kind I'm always trying for with the gumball machines at work is sitting in the middle of his outstretched palm. Dark blue in color, with a painted pink heart in the middle. The furthest thing you can get from a diamond solitaire, but perfect in its simplicity and relevancy to us and our relationship.

"I know it's not exactly the ring you should be wearing, but since I was sort of limited in what I could do and I saw you eyeing these when we were at the store, I improvised."

"You should improvise more often." I joke softly before reaching out and attempting to grab the ring.

"I'll remember you said that the next time I find myself on my knees in front of you." He teases and rolling my eyes, he takes my hand in his, and just like that night in New York in front of thousands of fans, he speaks from his heart.

"I knew in the bowling alley that you were different. Your energy that day, the urgency I saw in your eyes when you really put your all into beating me in order to get me cliff diving, it did something I hadn't been able to do for myself in months. Years even. I was finally able to breathe again, Em. You and your crazy ideas changed me. Changed everything. And even though it was a bit of a ride to get here, and I've got three months of time I still need to make up for, I wouldn't change a second of it. My only wish being that the next three months, three years, or even thirty, are more of the same. I want your brand of crazy. What I'm trying to say here is, I don't want to move forward in my life unless you're moving with me."

"Brady..."

I know he said this wasn't what it looked like and he's not down on one knee proposing marriage right now, but with everything he's just said, it's hard to think of anything else it could be. The answer, no matter what the question, always going to be a yes.

"I love you, Emery Davis." He says, picking up the ring and sliding it down over my finger. "And this ring is my promise to you. A promise to always keep breathing no matter what crazy curve balls are thrown in my path. My promise to love you even more tomorrow than I do today, and most of all, it's my promise that when the time is right for both of us; to find you wherever you are and do this again. Put a real ring on what I've known in my heart to be true from the moment I met you four months ago."

"What's that?"

"Wherever you are is home, Emery. You're home. One that now that I'm here, I'm never leaving again."

Avery

This isn't scary at all.

It's been planned for weeks, Jax having set it up practically the second I said yes to living with him in California and making sure to remind me of every damn chance he got.

What at first I thought was his own excitement over bringing me home to meet his parents but that after ending up on the phone with his mother last week when he was on the road for a show, I quickly learned was all her.

It was Brenda Merrick that couldn't wait to meet the woman that had made her son so happy. Even pulling her husband George into the conversation when I picked up the phone and she realized this was her shot at talking to the mystery girl that Jax purposely hadn't told them anything about.

"Are you sure I look okay?" I ask him for the tenth time since we left the house and got in the car. "You don't think I'm overdressed?"

It's been a really long time since I've had to worry about how I'm dressed, even longer since I had to worry about it because I was meeting someone's parents. Especially the parents of the man that even though he hasn't asked yet, I just know I'm going to spend the rest of my life with.

The black pantsuit with the navy blue blouse, even though I feel comfortable in it and I know I look great, making me feel like I'm going to a business meeting instead of a get together with his parents.

"You look fantastic, and besides, what you're wearing is my fault since I insisted on picking you up from work so I could beat traffic."

Another change over the last four weeks. My job.

One that even after talking to Jax about wanting to stay working for Markus when he offered me a position with one of the papers he owns in California, had still been met with resistance.

"Says the guy dressed in jeans and a ratty t-shirt."

"Don't mock the shirt, sweetheart. It's my good luck charm."

"Yeah." I scoff. "A good luck charm that's one tug away from ripping off you completely."

"And that's a problem, how? I thought you enjoyed when I walked around shirtless."

"At home. I love it when you walk around shirtless at home. Which, if you've forgotten, is the place we just left because we're about to have dinner with your parents."

"Oh, you mean the parents that saw my naked ass for three years straight?" he laughs, pulling his attention off the road long enough to blow me a kiss turning back.

"I'm never gonna win this argument, am I?"

"Nope. Never. Sorry, sweetheart."

"Right." I pout. "I'm sure you're real sorry."

"Ave, you look amazing. My mom, who hasn't stopped going on about you since you two talked, is going to love you. She already does. So you want to tell me what this is really about?"

When Jax said I was the only thing that was clear to him, I thought it was just sweet words. But after being together for an entire month, under the same roof no less, I've found out it's way more than that.

He can see me so clearly that I can't hide anything from him. He sees it all. Even what I've been doing everything in my power not to focus on.

"I'm scared." I admit and in the time it takes me to blink, his hand is pulling off the wheel and wrapping itself around mine. The strength behind his touch doing what it's done since we got back together and settling me.

"Do you remember when we went to Toronto to pack your things and I went out for a few hours?"

"Of course. What about it?"

"I was out on the beach."

"So you never went anywhere?"

"No, I did. I just told you. I went to the beach."

"Semantics, Jax, but fine. Why did you go to the beach?"

"To talk to your mother."

Telling him how often I spoke to her from the back porch is proving to be one of the smartest things I've ever done.

"I told her I was taking you to California and I would keep the promise I made and take care of you. Be there for you. But, more than all of that, I told her I was taking you home."

"You told her you were bringing me to meet your parents?"

"Of course. My mom, after the show in New York, said something that no matter what happened after, I couldn't let go of and well, I wanted to talk to your mom about it."

"What did she say?"

"She made me promise I'd bring you home to her."

"I don't get it. What does that have to do with my mom?"

"Her exact words were…bring her home to Mom. Maybe I read too much into it, but I got the feeling that when she said that, it wasn't her saying it. That it was your mom."

I've never been one of those people that believes in things she can't see. Love aside. What I feel with Jax, the love I just know I have for him, I can't see it, but I do believe with every fiber of my being that it's there and it's real. Anything else though, higher powers and signs and what not, I mean, without factual information backing it up, I've just never been much of a believer.

Until my mom.

Her claim to Emery that the love I wanted in my life was in the blue and the amount of times that color actually played a part in everything that came after she passed, it's hard not to believe.

What Jax pulled from what his mom said, it's like another one of those signs.

"I don't think you read too much into it, Jax. It sounds like something she'd do."

Presenting me with the gift of Brenda Merrick the same way she did with her son. Giving me love in as many ways and forms as she can.

Yeah, that's definitely my mom alright.

"Thank you for sharing that with me."

"Did it help with the fear?"

"Yeah, it did. I mean, I'm still nervous, but not as scared as before."

"Good." He says before pointing out the windshield. "Because we're here."

*****

"Oh, Jackson! She's absolutely enchanting!" Brenda says after opening the door and ushering us in. Handing our jackets over to her husband George before taking my hand and pulling me into an embrace.

After being warned by Jax that his mom was a hugger, I'm still unprepared for the tightness of the embrace when it happens. What is familiar though, and what has me melting into her arms like someone who has known her for years instead of mere minutes is the scent she's wearing.

Lilac.

She really is here with me.

Thanks, Mom.

"I told you she was beautiful. What more do you want?"

"Ignore her, Jax. She's just trying to get a rise out of you." An unfamiliar voice calls out from somewhere behind Jax and when he turns, I'm able to see is one of the women from the pictures on his dresser.

His sister.

"Hey." She steps forward, hand extended. "I'm Denise."

"Nice to meet you. I'm—"

"Avery." she answers for me, releasing my hand and much the way her mother did before her, brings me into a deep hug.

"I'm glad to finally meet you. With as much as he's gushed about you lately, I feel as though I already know you."

"Deni..." Jax interrupts and Denise just laughs.

"Don't worry. I won't embarrass you too much."

This place. I've only been here for a few minutes and I can already see the way it must have been for Jax growing up. How filled with love it is. The way they all seem to want to hug me showing me, but the easy banter back and forth between Jax and his sister solidifying it.

"Can we at least wait until after dinner to scare her off?" Jax pleads, his body brushing against mine as he moves closer. His hand much the way that he did in the car finding mine and covering it. "I was hoping to be able to show her the place before you spook her."

"Sure thing, but all those things you swore me to secrecy about when we were kids, they're all coming out once the table is clear." Denise winks and when Brenda and George start laughing, I join in, which after a groan, I see has Jax pouting.

"There's still a few minutes until dinner, so go ahead. Take her on a tour." Brenda says, patting us both on the arm before turning and heading into the other room.

Leaving us alone with Denise, who after a quick grin at her brother, one I've seen in Emery's eyes before when she's up to no good, slips her arm through mine and pulls me away from Jax's side.

"Quick! Lean in and smile." She says when we're far enough away that Jax can't hear.

"Why?"

"Because I want him to think I'm embarrassing him."

"When you're actually going to do what?"

"Tell you that I'm really glad you're here. Thank you for the smile he was wearing as the two of you made your way up the path, since I know you're the reason it's there. It's the first time in a very long time that I've seen him like this. So thank you for making my brother happy."

She's got it all wrong. Maybe I do make Jax happy, but he does that and more for me.

I'm really the one that should be thanking them. All of them. For being a part of the reason he's the man he is. For sharing him with me. But most of all, for giving me back what I thought I'd lost.

Love and Acceptance.

"You don't need to thank me for that. It's all him. I'm sure you already know this, but he's kind of impossible not to love."

"And that's why you're the one."

"I don't follow."

"You make the impossible possible, Avery."

"Deni, are you going to hoard her all day?" Jax interrupts and flashing him the smarmiest grin I've ever seen, she lets me go.

"I was thinking about it, but since I can already see your panties starting to bunch from here, I'll save the rest for later. She's gotten enough for now." She responds with a wink before turning and heading up the stairs, leaving us alone.

"What did she tell you?"

"Not much, honestly."

"Avery…"

"Jackson…" I copy him and pull him close when he groans again. "She thanked me for making you smile. That's all I swear."

"Really?"

"Yes."

"Thank God." He sighs with relief, eyeing me skeptically when I laugh. "What's the laugh about?"

"Honestly? At first, it was just a laugh of happiness, but with the way you're reacting, how relieved I can tell you are, it's more a laugh of wonder."

"Wonder?"

"Yeah. With as relieved as you are, it's got me wondering just how much she has on you. Is it wrong that I'm actually looking forward to dinner being done so I can find out?"

"Very, very wrong." He admonishes before reaching out and pulling me to him. "But I forgive you."

Brushing his face against mine and breathing me in, he leans in close and after meeting my eyes, brings his lips down on mine softly.

"You've got me. Every damn part."

"I'm yours." I finish for him and seeing the smile it brings, take it one step further. "And you're mine. You captured me."

Running his hands in gentle strokes over my cheek, he exhales deeply before moving over to where his jacket is hung on the hooks in the corner, digging around in the pocket and pulling something about before making his way over and dropping down to knee.

"I was going to wait and do this outside since my mom has like the perfect backdrop out there, but after what you just said and the way it felt hearing it, I can't wait that long." he pauses, holding his hand open and producing a small white box, pulling the lid back and slipping the ring resting inside out and holding it up in front of us.

"I know that the last month has been erratic with the move, and this is probably the worst time to be asking you, but I want the rest of our lives together to start now. I don't care that it started as a case of mistaken identity and we've spent more time apart than together. All I know is that you're mine, I'm yours, and when we're together, everything is clear. You're still the only thing that is. You always will be."

"Avery Davis," he looks up with a smile. "Will you marry me?"

Looking from Jackson to the ring, the blue sapphire in the middle glistening and the light blue diamonds on the sides sparkling, I'm reminded of Emery's words at our mother's funeral. Words that have never been more relevant than they are now.

"Make Avery see that the love she so desperately wants in her life is already there. It's always been there. It's just buried in the blue."

The ring he's holding taking those words, one's he's never even heard, and turning them physical. Turning them into a tangible piece of her that when I say yes, I'm going to carry with me forever.

The same way I will Jax.

Lowering myself to one knee and getting on his level, he reaches out and wipes a stray tear away from my eye at the exact moment that I give him the answer he's waited more than long enough to hear.

"Yes."

Epilogue
One Year Later...

Brady

"Remind me again how we got talked into this?"

I'm not a moron. Well, not a total one anyway, and I didn't sleep my way through the last year of my life. I do know how we ended up here. I'm also well aware of the part I played in it, starting the ball rolling when I promised myself to Emery almost a year ago to the day.

I just can't believe it's actually happening, or that my speed demon brother who is currently standing across from me attempting to right his tie, actually waited this long.

He must really love Avery if he was willing to slow down for a whole three hundred and sixty-five days. I would have expected the two of them to end up in front of some justice of the peace with how fast Jackson seemed to move when it came to his girl.

"You're telling me you didn't see this coming when Emery popped the question?"

That's another thing.

Not a damn thing that happened with us followed any traditional order. Sure, I'd gotten off the sweet but simple promise before starting over in HFWA, but where I figured I'd wait a while and pop the question when Emery was least expecting it, she beat me to the punch.

Bringing about this whole double wedding.

Welcome to 2015 people. Men don't have to get down on their knees anymore. Women can do it too.

Shit. That didn't come out the way I wanted it to.

"No. As alike as Avery and Em are, I really didn't see Em being the one to go for something like this. If anything, I was expecting my ass to land in Vegas."

"Right. Because that's what every girl wants when she gets married. To do it standing in front of some drunk Elvis." Jackson announces with an eye roll.

"Roll your eyes all you want, but you don't know Emery."

"But I do know her sister and I was also there when Emery suggested this." He motions around the room. "She may have needed to be talked into it because she had ideas of something more private, but at the end of the day, this is exactly what she deserves. Emery too."

I can't exactly argue with that. Knowing everything I do about how the two of them came to be, it makes sense that things happen this way.

"So when are we gonna talk about the elephant in the room?" Jax asks, turning to me after finally getting his tie right.

"What do you mean?"

"This isn't exactly your first rodeo. How are you handling it? Any regrets saying yes?"

"No way. It sucks that I wasn't the one to do it because I had this whole big plan in my head about how I wanted to spring it on her, but marrying Emery is a no brainer."

"And?"

"And, Dr. Phil, I'm handling it fine. At least I will be once we actually get this show on the road."

"You're that damn eager to make her a Raines, huh?" Jackson laughs, taking a step back from the mirror and heading over closer to mine. Immediately reaching out and doing my tie, when for like the hundredth time, it all falls apart.

My skills limited to wrestling obviously.

"I'm eager to make her mine."

"Thought you already did that a year ago?"

"Yeah, but when we walk out of here today, the rest of the world will know it."

Despite the fact that I've got nothing to worry about with Emery, especially with the way things have gone with us over the last year and everything she's put up with even when she didn't have to, I still can't help the rise of jealousy that imagining her around other men gets out of me.

The beating I laid on Fortune the last time I ever got physical with it, but definitely not the last time I felt the familiar rise of my blood where she's concerned. I have a feeling that with as amazing as she is, that's never going to go away.

Putting the finishing touches on my tie, he steps back and with as long as I've known him, the size of the smile he's sporting when he does, takes me completely by surprise.

Years I watched Jax walk around with what seemed like the world's biggest cloud over his head. Before Melinda entered his life, especially during, and then after. I was starting to think with the shit hand he seemed to constantly be dealt, the cloud was gonna follow his ass around forever.

It's nice being shown different.

If there's anyone in the world deserving of everything he's ever wanted, it's him.

Which is hilarious considering how we started.

"Remember when we got pulled into CPW and how much we hated each other?" I ask, curious to see just how much he can remember from back then.

"I try not to."

"Yeah. I was a pretty big asshole back then, huh?"

"Nah, man. I'm pretty sure that award went to me. Don't you remember the first thing I said to you?"

"Enjoy your stay at the bottom. I'll shoot you a wave from the top." We answer in unison, the both of us laughing our asses off at just how juvenile the entire thing is now.

"Yeah, and then I was the one that got pushed."

"Makes sense now why Cameron thought I was the fucking Anti-Christ." He admits and all I can do is laugh. Cameron would have thought Jax was the devil regardless. His head firmly planted in the fantasy.

"If it helps, with me bailing out and heading across the border, I'm pretty sure I'm the devil now."

"It doesn't. You know I'd much rather have you there then where you are. Even if I do understand why you did it."

"How much longer you think you got before you end up off the road indefinitely?"

"That is the million dollar question. Also one I don't have an answer to. Right now, things are working. Smith has me on a limited schedule. Me and Matthias are tearing the house down for the Middleweight belt, and Avery, well, she's right there for all of it."

He's leaving something out. The one thing I know beyond a shadow of a doubt he doesn't want to talk about, but that's as much of an elephant in the room as my prior marriage is.

"And Melinda?"

"Still Melinda and still none of my concern, but when it comes to the performance, its working as well as it did the last time. Smith is happy."

"What about your wife to be?"

"Considering how often we talk when I'm on the road, it's safe to say Avery is fine. Happy even. It's all good, man. What happened is in the past."

Looking down at the watch on my arm and catching the time, I'm about to fill him in on what else is about to become a thing of the past—our girls last names—when a knock beats me to the punch.

"You expecting anyone?" I ask as he turns toward the door.

"Nope. You?"

"I could fill you in on a few fantasies I had about Emery showing up, but other than that, no."

"Yeah, smart move keeping those to yourself." Moving toward the door, he pulls it back just far enough to stick his head through as the sound of voices from the other side begins to filter in.

Familiar voices.

Ones that considering the way I'd left things over a year ago, I definitely wasn't expecting to hear again anytime soon. Least of all today.

Pulling his head back and turning toward me, his raises his brow in question and I nod.

Even if it turns out to be a mistake, I've gotta do it.

"I'm gonna head out there and give you guys some time to talk." Jax says and again I just nod in response. The sight of my parents walking into the room doing what I'm sure they were hoping for and stripping me of my voice completely.

Passing by my father, Jax heads out, making sure to close the door behind him and the part of me that's eager to get this over with screams at me to go after him. To not waste another second with whatever this is and focus instead on making this the perfect day for the damn near perfect girl that's going to be my wife.

"What do you want?" I demand, turning my back on them and focusing on the mirror instead. Thankful that from where they're standing, I can't see them. "Better yet, what you are doing here?"

"Cameron called us, Brady." My mom says first, stepping forward. "There was nowhere else we needed to be after that."

"I might believe that about you, but what's his excuse?"

"He's here for the same reason, son. I know you don't believe that, but a lot has changed for all of us over the last year."

"And that involves me how?" I snap, finally turning around to face her. Wanting to look her in the eye when she tries to plead my old man's case for him. Again, standing by his side when it's the very last place she should be.

"He knows what he did is wrong."

"I'll believe that when he says it, Mom. Coming from you it's just more of the same."

"She's telling the truth." My old man finally speaks up. "The reason I'm here, everything that's happened right on down the line to me knowing that what I did to you was wrong. It's all true."

"And what if it's too late, huh? What if I don't want you here? Did you even think of any of that before you hopped on the plane?"

I need to chill out. Not let them get to me. Today of all days, I need to just take a step back from this. Nothing is going to ruin it, least of all my parents.

"Is it too late?"

Where I expect that question from my mom, she's not the one asking it. Looking away from her, my eyes land on the man standing behind her and what she said when they first came in, it's there, laid out free for all to see.

The cold angry look I spent the majority of my life used to him wearing, stripped away, and in its place the look of a man that's lost everything that matters.

Maybe walking away changed him after all.

"I don't know, Dad. You tell me. Are you here to ride me about my decision to go to HFWA? Tell me I'm making a big mistake marrying Emery?"

"No. What you do with your life is your choice."

"But let me guess. You don't agree?"

"What I think one way or the other doesn't matter. Are you happy with the choices you've made?"

"Extremely." I answer without even thinking and saying it makes me realize just how damn true it is. I'm the happiest I've been in years and in a few minutes, when I stand at the front of the church and my spitfire joins me, it's only going to get better.

"Then that's all that matters."

Since when?

"What is this? I mean, really. Since when does my happiness matter to you?"

"It always mattered, Brady. I just had a shit way of showing it."

"No kidding."

"I'm not here looking for your forgiveness. I don't deserve it after all the shit I pulled with you over the years. But for your mother if nothing else, I'd really like to stay and be a part of your special day. What you had with Kelly, I knew the day you took that walk down the aisle that it wasn't going to last. I knew she wasn't the one, but just like I bungled everything else up, I did it there too. This time...well, this time I'd like to stand in the church and watch you get it right."

Watch me get it right.

He has no clue just how true those words are.

"So what do you say, Brady? Can we put our bullshit aside for today so that your mother and I can watch you get married?"

Looking between them, seeing the glistening just waiting to fall in the corners of my mother's eyes, knowing how much it would mean to her to be here for this and hating myself for not thinking enough about her feelings in all of this to invite her, I don't even hesitate in my answer.

"Okay, but there's something I need you to do for me."

"Name it."

Turning to my mom, I step forward and bending down, whisper my request in her ear. Which judging by the smile that seems to appear and encompass her entire face, is one she's more than happy to fulfill.

"I'd be honored."

Jax

"You did what?"

Leave it to Brady to go at the last minute and change things. I mean, it's a solid idea and one I think Emery will go for the same way that Avery agreed with my idea of having my mother walk her down the aisle, but still.

I'm all for stealing the show, but does he really have to do it at our wedding too?

"You heard me, Jacky boy. Now wipe the scowl off your face before you start scaring people."

I'm about to tell him where he can stick his scowling comment, but the sound of the organ starting up stops me cold.

The opening bars of Mendelssohn's Wedding March beginning to play pulling my eyes away from Brady altogether and toward the door as it opens. My dad standing on one side, Brady's on the other, their faces betraying nothing as Avery and my mom step through first, quickly followed by Emery and Brady's mom.

Searching my girl's face for any sign of the ache I know she has to be feeling knowing her father despite everything he'd done isn't here to walk her down the aisle and finding nothing, I look over to Brady and find him doing the same.

Both of our girls as they begin the walk up the aisle with our mother's displaying the only emotion that the both of us wanted them to.

Happiness.

Both women dressed in matching gowns with their hair, both back to their natural shade of brown, only adding to the inability to tell them apart. Their identical hazel eyes the closer they get, shimmering.

The subtle hint in their veils being the only thing setting them apart. Emery's being made of pure white, while Avery's having the faintest line of blue woven into the band at the top of her head. Embracing her mother's words even more and incorporating it into the day flawlessly.

"Holy shit." Brady curses when pausing at the bottom of the circular stairs, Emery smiles before raising her hand and blowing him a kiss as the man who had gotten himself ordained just to be able to preside over the ceremony steps forward.

The one man that when I told him I was getting married, after telling me for the first time in years that he was proud of me, proceeded to threaten to cut off my balls if I ever told anyone he'd said it.

No one better to marry us then the man that hates love, Radley Smith.

"We are gathered here today in front of friends and family to join together in the act of holy matrimony, Brady Michael Raines with Emery Rose Davis, and Jackson Kennedy Merrick with Avery Marie Davis. An honorable and solemn estate not to be entered into unadvisedly or lightly." He pauses, looking down at the paper in front of him and ripping it in half. "Who in the blue hell writes this shit?"

Looking from me and over to Brady when I shrug, Emery snickers before Avery steps forward and taking Smith's hand in hers, whispers something to him that has him smiling before moving back and taking my mom's hand in hers again.

"As per the young ladies wishes, I'm just gonna do this the Radley Smith way. We're here to join these two couples together in what despite my hard stance on it, I hope is true love. But if any of you out there get the bright idea to tell anyone I said that, I will find you and make you regret it."

"Smith!" Brady hisses and when the old man looks over, he brings his arm up across his neck in an attempt to stop him.

Though with the way Avery and Emery seem to be enjoying the show, I'm half tempted to let him keep going.

Seeing the girls this happy exactly what this day is supposed to be about.

"Right, sorry." Clearing his throat and stepping forward again, he continues. "Who gives these women to these men?"

"We do." Our girls speak in unison, causing not only me and Brady to laugh but our friends and family too, at least until Emery speaks again. "I mean, obviously."

"What my beautiful daughter in-law means is, we do." Brady's mom interjects before both women let the girl's hands go and they come up the stairs to stand beside us. Smith clearing his throat before moving over until he's dead center with us.

"If anyone can show just cause why these four people should not be lawfully joined together, let them speak now or forever hold their piece. And just in case there's one of you assholes out there so much as thinking about it, my earlier threat still stands."

"Who hired you again? Brady jokes and looking away, I just shake my head.

"That would be me. Hush it Raines or I'll object. Smith is doing great." Avery beams at the old man before slipping her fingers through mine and squeezing gently.

"Well, in that case, carry on."

Thank you. I mouth when she finally turns her attention away from Smith and I'm met head on with the same glowing smile she'd just given him. The smile that right from the first time I'd seen it, had made me fall.

When no one so much as coughs to signal their displeasure at what's about to take place, Smith turns to Brady and all traces of earlier humor are gone as he makes good on his place here and does what's best for business.

"Brady, do you take Emery to be your lawfully wedded wife? Will you love, honor, comfort and cherish her from this day forward, forsaking all others, keeping only unto her for as long as you both shall live?"

"You're damn right I do." Brady announces. "She's stuck with me forever."

Smith, smirking at Brady turns toward me and repeats what he said before but just as he announced earlier, doing it as only he can.

"Jacky boy, do you take Avery to be your lawfully wedded wife? Will you love, honor, comfort and cherish her from this day forward, forsaking all others, keeping only unto her for as long as you both shall live?"

"I do." I tell him, the words I've spent the better part of a year dying to say, falling easily and without reservation. There being nothing in the world I want more in my life than to spend the rest of it with the woman beside me now.

"Alright ladies, your turn." Smith turns and eyeballs them. "But before I ask you the same thing, I just gotta check. Are you sure these two boneheads are the ones you want?"

Oh God.

"Back off, old man." Brady answers for them, making Smith flash an even bigger shit eating grin.

"Alright, ladies. Kind of the same deal as the other two. Do you take these two clowns in holy matrimony? Promise to love, honor, comfort and cherish them from this day forward as long as you both shall live or they drive you bat shit crazy?"

"We do." Both women answer simultaneously, earning another round of laughs from the crowd of people sitting in the pews and making Brady throw both fists in the air.

"Yes!" he exclaims. "Finally."

"Settle your shit, boy. You ain't married yet." Smith admonishes. "I could forget the line when the time comes."

"Like you forgot proper wedding etiquette?" Brady snaps, and before I can reach out and hit him, Emery does it for me, elbowing him in the side.

"Hush it, Raines or I'm gonna pull Kemper out of the crowd and marry him instead."

"Like fuck."

"Now who's forgetting proper wedding day etiquette, rich boy?"

"Are you sure you two aren't married already?" Smith interjects, causing both me and Avery to laugh. All seriousness flying out the window so long ago there's no sense even trying to get it back.

Thank god we're only doing this once.

"We would be if you'd just get on with already."

"Fair enough." He agrees, turning his attention back to the congregation. "Since both couples explicitly told me that they wanted to forgo their own vows in favor of the ones I had to spend weeks memorizing, it's time for the rings. Raines, get yours ready and repeat after me."

Motioning to Logan, who is sitting in the front row, legs swinging back and forth, paying no attention at all to the nonsense going on around him, I call out and he runs forward. First handing the gold band to Brady, before turning toward me and doing the same with the white gold and blue band I had made for Avery.

"With this ring, I marry you and bind my life to yours. It is a symbol of my eternal love, my everlasting friendship, and the promise of all my tomorrows."

Repeating Smith's words back, Brady slips the ring down onto Emery's finger before Smith turns his attention to Emery and asks her to do the same with the ring Logan stands in front of her holding out on a white gold pillow.

Slipping the ring down onto his finger and smiling brighter than I think I've ever seen her, she wastes no time repeating Smith's words back.

"With this ring, I marry you and bind my life to yours. It is a symbol of my eternal love, my everlasting friendship, and the promise of all my tomorrows."

"Your turn, sweetheart." Smith says, turning to Avery and the strangest thing happens when he does. It's there and gone in a second, but the old codger actually swipes at his eyes when Avery picks the band she had made for me off Logan's outstretched pillow.

I'll be damned. The man actually feels something after all.

Whatever Avery told him when she whispered to him earlier, obviously doing the same thing she'd done with me a year and a half ago.

Capturing him.

"Repeat after me. With this ring, I pledge my love and faithfulness to you. For today, tomorrow and always."

Stepping to me, she repeats his words to me and after slipping the ring down over my fingers swipes at her eyes before leaning in and saying the words that really make her mine. "I want the rest of our lives together to start now."

Shifting his eyes to me and raising them in question, I just smile as Smith asks me to repeat the same declaration to Avery. My eyes misting when they see the tears falling from hers as I say the words and slip the ring slowly down over her finger.

Affectively making her mine in every sense of the word.

The way we've been meant to be from the start.

"I'm yours." I whisper before Smith again commands the attention of the room and gives Brady exactly what he's been after from the moment we stepped into the church.

"Brady and Emery, Jackson and Avery, I now pronounce you husband and wife. Guys, you can now officially kiss your brides."

Brady and I stepping forward and working in tandem, we slip the veils back and as Brady moves in and kisses his bride, I just take mine in. From her relaxed posture, to the smile on her face and glow to her cheeks right up to the dance that takes place in her eyes as she looks back doing the same with me.

Placing both of my hands on her face, I press my lips first to her forehead, moving down to her cheeks and over until just like my buddy before me, I seal this day and my feelings for her in a soft kiss to her lips.

Smith picking up again the second I pull away and bringing things to a close the same way he started them. A way Brady and I know all too well.

His way.

"What God and the Almighty Radley Smith has joined together, may no man ever put asunder. If they do, they'll be in for a world of hurt. You can believe that."

Clearing his throat when Brady growls under his breath, he steps down and grips us both hard around the shoulders and as loud and as gravelly as ever, officially announces us.

"Ladies and gents, I give you Mr. and Mrs. Brady Raines and Mr. and Mrs. Jackson Merrick."

And with those seventeen words, Smith erases the fourteen that came before it, solidifying the words I'd spoken to Avery the night I proposed a year ago.

Our lives, hers and mine and Brady and Emery's, they start now.

The End

Emery's Swan Song

When I lost my mother almost two years ago, she left a letter behind. A letter filled with words I truly believe she wanted me to take to heart and carry with me long after she was gone.

Words that despite the two that mark the ending of this particular story, really aren't what they appear to be.

This isn't the end for me and Brady or even for Jackson and Avery.

It's the beginning.

The start of something more.

Rebecca Davis did say it best after all.

When is a goodbye ever really a goodbye? When does the story of our lives truly end?

The answer to those questions is...it never ends.

Our stories remain long after our bodies fail because they're not driven by cause and effect, action and reaction. They continue on, never ending, because love never dies.

Love always wins.

And even though it was hard more times than it was easy and our road to being found again had to start with us getting well and truly lost, even at times frustratingly so, I wouldn't change a second of it. Because it was real and it was ours.

What was once lost has been found and just like she said, this isn't goodbye or even the end. Those are final; and love, well love is infinite.

Brady, Jackson, Avery and myself, we're living proof.

XOXOXO – Emery Raines

Shades of Blue/Into the Blue Playlist

Shades of Blue by Nick Lachey
Stitches by Shawn Mendes
All I've Ever Wanted by Brian Melo
Take Me As I Am by Tonic
Black and Blue by CFO$
Kiss Me by Ed Sheeran
No Pressure by Justin Bieber & Big Sean
I'm a Mess by Ed Sheeran
Tomorrow by Olly Murs
The Search is Over by Survivor
Open Arms by Journey
Rock You Like A Hurricane by The Scorpions
When I See You Smile by Bad English
When The Stars Go Blue by Tyler Hilton & Bethany Joy Lenz
Everything You Want by Vertical Horizon
Never Stop (The Wedding Version) by Safetysuit
Bleed For Me by Saliva
When You Look Me In The Eyes by Jonas Brothers
One Call Away by Charlie Puth
I'll Show You by Justin Bieber
Love You Goodbye by One Direction
Fool With Dreams by Framing Hanley
Lost In You by Three Days Grace
Paperweight by Joshua Radin and Schuyler Fisk
The Promise by Framing Hanley
Without You by Three Days Grace

Acknowledgements

It takes a village.

That's been true in the past with my other books and it most definitely is with these as well. This book, and the one that started these characters journey in **Shades of Blue**, wouldn't exist if it wasn't for some very important people. So here's where I pull a Brady and thank the real people that deserve it.

My mini Winchesters.

Goes without saying. There is no greater acknowledgement I can give than the one to you four. Thank you for inspiring me, pushing me and teaching me while I'm attempting to do the same with you. There is no me (at least not one worth knowing) without you. I love you. All of you. Forever and for always. You can believe that ;)

Cheryl

Let's face it. This story wouldn't have existed without you. What it was and then what it became (which in my estimation, is something even better than before), it all centers on you. Your support, your love and your undying adoration for all things wrestling and the written word. So, sweetheart, these are for you. Mordiase forever.

My beta-readers.

You're invaluable and none of my books would exist without you and your advice, expertise and support. You're a gigantic piece of that village I mentioned before and for as long as I'm doing this, you always will be. Thank you.

Wrestling.

I'm pretty sure this one should go in every book I write based on the fact that wrestling saved my life more times than I can count and even these days, still has the ability to do so.

Without this sport (yes, it's a sport), I'm not entirely sure I'd be the person standing here today. So thank you. Whether it's the Indies, the WWE, TNA or ROH, you all impacted my life, and for that and everything else you do in the world apart from the sport, thank you.

Tim

Sometimes, people enter your life and during their time there, they leave beautiful indelible marks on the person you are. You are one of those people for me and are a big part of the reason this story and the one that will follow it exist. So thank you for being that person. For leaving a mark that no matter where either of us goes in life, will never be erased.

Joey

"But every Bonnie got a Clyde with her. Every woman needs somebody that's gonna ride with her." Thank you for being my Clyde. For being everything really. There's no better ball busting, ass kicking guard dog than you. You and me, it's an always and forever thing. Love you like madness.

Reader, Bloggers & Reviewers

Now in a sense, I saved the best part of this village for last, because quite honestly, without all of you there is no me. There is no author at all. You play such a huge part in our lives—in my life, and I thank each and every one of you. Whether you like something I've written, hate it or are indifferent one way or the other; for taking the chance, you'll have my unwavering love and thanks forever. We appreciate everything you are, everything you've done and will continue to do in the future. Much love for all your faces.

About the Author

Melyssa is a mother of four from Toronto, Ontario, Canada.

She's currently working on Luke Grayson's story from *Remembering Sunday*, **Ready When You Are** and the third book in the *Black & Blue* series, **Heroine.**

When she's not writing, you can find her buried under the covers with her portable DVD player, watching marathons of Supernatural and Veronica Mars. When those aren't available, she can be found curled up in a corner with her e-reader and a plethora of books, falling in love with characters written so well she deems them her book boyfriends and girlfriends.

If you want to find her, check Facebook or Twitter (@WinchesterBooks) as she may just have an addiction to both. If those don't work you can always keep up with her progress on her personal site.

Other Works by Melyssa Winchester

Count On Me Series
Count On Me
Hear Me Now
Take Me With You
All My Heart
Here & Now (w/Joey Winchester)
Unbroken
What Lies Beneath

Love United Series
Holding On To Heaven
No Surrender
Wanted
Stairway to Heaven
A Light in the Dark
My Heaven (Alternate ending to Holding On To Heaven)

Before The Light Series
Hold On To Me (Michael's Story)
Absence of Light (Ryan's Story)

Standalone Titles
The Space in Between
Remembering Sunday

Black & Blue Series
Shades of Blue
Into the Blue

Coming Soon

Heroine (Black & Blue #3)
Ready When You Are (Luke Grayson's story)
Infinity (Standalone – Second Chance Adult Romance)